cover design
wckright kaufer

THE MODERN LIBRARY
OF THE WORLD'S BEST BOOKS

SANCTUARY

The publishers will be pleased to send, upon request, an illustrated folder setting forth the purpose and scope of THE MODERN LIBRARY, *and listing each volume in the series. Every reader of books will find titles he has been looking for, handsomely printed, in unabridged editions, and at an unusually low price.*

Sanctuary

BY WILLIAM FAULKNER

WITH A NEW INTRODUCTION BY THE AUTHOR

THE
MODERN LIBRARY
NEW YORK

COPYRIGHT, 1931, RENEWED 1958, BY WILLIAM FAULKNER

INTRODUCTION COPYRIGHT, RENEWED 1932,
BY THE MODERN LIBRARY, INC.
COPYRIGHT, 1959, BY WILLIAM FAULKNER

Random House IS THE PUBLISHER OF

THE MODERN LIBRARY

BENNETT A. CERF · DONALD S. KLOPFER · ROBERT K. HAAS

Manufactured in the United States of America

By H. Wolff

INTRODUCTION

THIS BOOK WAS WRITTEN THREE YEARS AGO. To me it is a cheap idea, because it was deliberately conceived to make money. I had been writing books for about five years, which got published and not bought. But that was all right. I was young then and hard-bellied. I had never lived among nor known people who wrote novels and stories and I suppose I did not know that people got money for them. I was not very much annoyed when publishers refused the mss. now and then. Because I was hard-gutted then. I could do a lot of things that could earn what little money I needed, thanks to my father's unfailing kindness which supplied me with bread at need despite the outrage to his principles at having been of a bum progenitive.

Then I began to get a little soft. I could still paint houses and do carpenter work, but I got soft. I began to think about making money by writing. I began to be concerned when magazine editors turned down short stories, con cerned enough to tell them that they would buy these stories later anyway, and hence why not now. Meanwhile, with one novel completed and consistently refused for two years, I had just written my guts into *The Sound and the Fury* though I was not aware until the book was published that I had done so, because I had done it for pleasure. I believed then that I would never be published again. I had stopped thinking of myself in publishing terms.

But when the third mss., *Sartoris,* was taken by a publisher and (he having refused *The Sound and the Fury*) it was taken by still another publisher, who warned me at the time that it would not sell, I began to think of myself again as a printed object. I began to think of books in terms of possible money. I decided I might just as well make some of it myself. I took a little time out, and speculated what a person in Mississippi would believe to be current trends, chose what I thought was the right answer and invented the most horrific tale I could imagine and wrote it in about three weeks and sent it to Smith, who had done *The Sound and the Fury* and who wrote me immediately, "Good God, I can't publish this. We'd both be in jail." So I told Faulkner, "You're damned. You'll have to work now and then for the rest of your life." That was in the summer of 1929.

I got a job in the power plant, on the night shift, from 6 P.M. to 6 A.M., as a coal passer. I shoveled coal from the bunker into a wheelbarrow and wheeled it in and dumped it where the fireman could put it into the boiler. About 11 o'clock the people would be going to bed, and so it did not take so much steam. Then we could rest, the fireman and I. He would sit in a chair and doze. I had invented a table out of a wheelbarrow in the coal bunker, just beyond a wall from where a dynamo ran. It made a deep, constant humming noise. There was no more work to do until about 4 A.M., when we would have to clean the fires and get up steam again. On these nights, between 12 and 4, I wrote *As I Lay Dying* in six weeks, without changing a word. I sent it to Smith and wrote him that by it I would stand or fall.

I think I had forgotten about *Sanctuary*, just as you might forget about anything made for an immediate purpose, which did not come off. *As I Lay Dying* was published and I didn't remember the mss. of *Sanctuary* until Smith sent me the galleys. Then I saw that it was so terrible that there were but two things to do: tear it up or rewrite it. I thought again, "It might sell; maybe 10,000 of them will buy it." So I tore the galleys down and rewrote the book. It had been already set up once, so I had to pay for the privilege of rewriting it, trying to make out of it something which would not shame *The Sound and the Fury* and *As I Lay Dying* too much and I made a fair job and I hope you will buy it and tell your friends and I hope they will buy it too.

WILLIAM FAULKNER.

New York, 1932.

FROM BEYOND THE SCREEN OF BUSHES WHICH surrounded the spring, Popeye watched the man drinking. A faint path led from the road to the spring. Popeye watched the man—a tall, thin man, hatless, in worn gray flannel trousers and carrying a tweed coat over his arm— emerge from the path and kneel to drink from the spring.

The spring welled up at the root of a beech tree and flowed away upon a bottom of whorled and waved sand. It was surrounded by a thick growth of cane and brier, of cypress and gum in which broken sunlight lay sourceless. Somewhere, hidden and secret yet nearby, a bird sang three notes and ceased.

In the spring the drinking man leaned his face to the broken and myriad reflection of his own drinking. When he rose up he saw among them the shattered reflection of Popeye's straw hat, though he had heard no sound.

He saw, facing him across the spring, a man of under size, his hands in his coat pockets, a cigarette slanted from his chin. His suit was black, with a tight, high-waisted coat. His trousers were rolled once and caked with mud above mud-caked shoes. His face had a queer, bloodless color, as though seen by electric light; against the sunny silence, in his slanted straw hat and his slightly akimbo arms, he had that vicious depthless quality of stamped tin.

Behind him the bird sang again, three bars in monotonous repetition: a sound meaningless and profound out of a suspirant and peaceful following silence which seemed to isolate the spot, and out of which a moment later came the sound of an automobile passing along a road and dying away.

The drinking man knelt beside the spring. "You've got a pistol in that pocket, I suppose," he said.

Across the spring Popeye appeared to contemplate him with two knobs of soft black rubber. "I'm asking you," Popeye said. "What's that in your pocket?"

The other man's coat was still across his arm. He lifted his other hand toward the coat, out of one pocket of which protruded a crushed felt hat, from the other a book. "Which pocket?" he said.

2

"Dont show me," Popeye said. "Tell me."

The other man stopped his hand. "It's a book."

"What book?" Popeye said.

"Just a book. The kind that people read. Some people do."

"Do you read books?" Popeye said.

The other man's hand was frozen above the coat. Across the spring they looked at one another. The cigarette wreathed its faint plume across Popeye's face, one side of his face squinted against the smoke like a mask carved into two simultaneous expressions.

From his hip pocket Popeye took a soiled handkerchief and spread it upon his heels. Then he squatted, facing the man across the spring. That was about four oclock on an afternoon in May. They squatted so, facing one another across the spring, for two hours. Now and then the bird sang back in the swamp, as though it were worked by a clock; twice more invisible automobiles passed along the highroad and died away. Again the bird sang.

"And of course you dont know the name of it," the man across the spring said. "I dont suppose you'd know a bird at all, without it was singing in a cage in a hotel lounge, or cost four dollars on a plate." Popeye said nothing. He squatted in his tight black suit, his right-hand

3

coat pocket sagging compactly against his flank, twisting and pinching cigarettes in his little, doll-like hands, spitting into the spring. His skin had a dead, dark pallor. His nose was faintly aquiline, and he had no chin at all. His face just went away, like the face of a wax doll set too near a hot fire and forgotten. Across his vest ran a platinum chain like a spider web. "Look here," the other man said. "My name is Horace Benbow. I'm a lawyer in Kinston. I used to live in Jefferson yonder; I'm on my way there now. Anybody in this county can tell you I am harmless. If it's whiskey, I dont care how much you all make or sell or buy. I just stopped here for a drink of water. All I want to do is get to town, to Jefferson."

Popeye's eyes looked like rubber knobs, like they'd give to the touch and then recover with the whorled smudge of the thumb on them.

"I want to reach Jefferson before dark," Benbow said. "You cant keep me here like this."

Without removing the cigarette Popeye spat past it into the spring.

"You cant stop me like this," Benbow said. "Suppose I break and run."

Popeye put his eyes on Benbow, like rubber. "Do you want to run?"

"No," Benbow said.

Popeye removed his eyes. "Well, dont, then."

4

Benbow heard the bird again, trying to recall the local name for it. On the invisible highroad another car passed, died away. Between them and the sound of it the sun was almost gone. From his trousers pocket Popeye took a dollar watch and looked at it and put it back in his pocket, loose like a coin.

Where the path from the spring joined the sandy byroad a tree had been recently felled, blocking the road. They climbed over the tree and went on, the highroad now behind them. In the sand were two shallow parallel depressions, but no mark of hoof. Where the branch from the spring seeped across it Benbow saw the prints of automobile tires. Ahead of him Popeye walked, his tight suit and stiff hat all angles, like a modernistic lampstand.

The sand ceased. The road rose, curving, out of the jungle. It was almost dark. Popeye looked briefly over his shoulder. "Step out, Jack," he said.

"Why didn't we cut straight across up the hill?" Benbow said.

"Through all them trees?" Popeye said. His hat jerked in a dull, vicious gleam in the twilight as he looked down the hill where the jungle already lay like a lake of ink. "Jesus Christ."

It was almost dark. Popeye's gait had slowed. He walked now beside Benbow, and Benbow

5

could see the continuous jerking of the hat from side to side as Popeye looked about with a sort of vicious cringing. The hat just reached Benbow's chin.

Then something, a shadow shaped with speed, stooped at them and on, leaving a rush of air upon their very faces, on a soundless feathering of taut wings, and Benbow felt Popeye's whole body spring against him and his hand clawing at his coat. "It's just an owl," Benbow said. "It's nothing but an owl." Then he said: "They call that Carolina wren a fishingbird. That's what it is. What I couldn't think of back there," with Popeye crouching against him, clawing at his pocket and hissing through his teeth like a cat. He smells black, Benbow thought; he smells like that black stuff that ran out of Bovary's mouth and down upon her bridal veil when they raised her head.

A moment later, above a black, jagged mass of trees, the house lifted its stark square bulk against the failing sky.

The house was a gutted ruin rising gaunt and stark out of a grove of unpruned cedar trees. It was a landmark, known as the Old Frenchman place, built before the Civil War; a plantation house set in the middle of a tract of land; of cotton fields and gardens and lawns long since

6

gone back to jungle, which the people of the neighborhood had been pulling down piecemeal for firewood for fifty years or digging with secret and sporadic optimism for the gold which the builder was reputed to have buried somewhere about the place when Grant came through the county on his Vicksburg campaign.

Three men were sitting in chairs on one end of the porch. In the depths of the open hall a faint light showed. The hall went straight back through the house. Popeye mounted the steps, the three men looking at him and his companion. "Here's the professor," he said, without stopping. He entered the house, the hall. He went on and crossed the back porch and turned and entered the room where the light was. It was the kitchen. A woman stood at the stove. She wore a faded calico dress. About her naked ankles a worn pair of man's brogans, unlaced, flapped when she moved. She looked back at Popeye, then to the stove again, where a pan of meat hissed.

Popeye stood in the door. His hat was slanted across his face. He took a cigarette from his pocket, without producing the pack, and pinched and fretted it and put it into his mouth and snapped a match on his thumbnail. "There's a bird out front," he said.

The woman did not look around. She turned

7

the meat. "Why tell me?" she said. "I dont serve Lee's customers."

"It's a professor," Popeye said.

The woman turned, an iron fork suspended in her hand. Behind the stove, in shadow, was a wooden box. "A what?"

"Professor," Popeye said. "He's got a book with him."

"What's he doing here?"

"I dont know. I never thought to ask. Maybe to read the book."

"He came here?"

"I found him at the spring."

"Was he trying to find this house?"

"I dont know," Popeye said. "I never thought to ask." The woman was still looking at him. "I'll send him on to Jefferson on the truck," Popeye said. "He said he wants to go there."

"Why tell me about it?" the woman said.

"You cook. He'll want to eat."

"Yes," the woman said. She turned back to the stove. "I cook. I cook for crimps and spungs and feebs. Yes. I cook."

In the door Popeye watched her, the cigarette curling across his face. His hands were in his pockets. "You can quit. I'll take you back to Memphis Sunday. You can go to hustling again." He watched her back. "You're getting tat here. Laying off in the country. I wont tell them on Manuel Street."

The woman turned, the fork in her hand. "You bastard," she said.

"Sure," Popeye said. "I wont tell them that Ruby Lamar is down in the country, wearing a pair of Lee Goodwin's throwed-away shoes, chopping her own firewood. No. I'll tell them Lee Goodwin is big rich."

"You bastard," the woman said. "You bastard."

"Sure," Popeye said. Then he turned his head. There was a shuffling sound across the porch, then a man entered. He was stooped, in overalls. He was barefoot; it was his bare feet which they had heard. He had a sunburned thatch of hair, matted and foul. He had pale furious eyes, a short soft beard like dirty gold in color.

"I be dawg if he aint a case, now," he said.

"What do you want?" the woman said. The man in overalls didn't answer. In passing, he looked at Popeye with a glance at once secret and alert, as though he were ready to laugh at a joke, waiting for the time to laugh. He crossed the kitchen with a shambling, bear-like gait, and still with that air of alert and gleeful secrecy, though in plain sight of them, he removed a

9

loose board in the floor and took out a gallon jug. Popeye watched him, his forefingers in his vest, the cigarette (he had smoked it down without once touching it with his hand) curling across his face. His expression was savage, perhaps baleful; contemplative, watching the man in overalls recross the floor with a kind of alert diffidence, the jug clumsily concealed below his flank; he was watching Popeye, with that expression alert and ready for mirth, until he left the room. Again they heard his bare feet on the porch.

"Sure," Popeye said. "I wont tell them on Manuel street that Ruby Lamar is cooking for a dummy and a feeb too."

"You bastard," the woman said. "You bastard."

II

WHEN THE WOMAN ENTERED THE DINING-
room, carrying a platter of meat, Popeye and
the man who had fetched the jug from the
kitchen and the stranger were already at a table
made by nailing three rough planks to two tres·
tles. Coming into the light of the lamp which sat
on the table, her face was sullen, not old; her
eyes were cold. Watching her, Benbow did not
see her look once at him as she set the platter on
the table and stood for a moment with that
veiled look with which women make a final sur-
vey of a table, and went and stooped above an
open packing case in a corner of the room and
took from it another plate and knife and fork,
which she brought to the table and set before
Benbow with a kind of abrupt yet unhurried
finality, her sleeve brushing his shoulder.

As she was doing that, Goodwin entered. He
wore muddy overalls. He had a lean, weathered

face, the jaws covered by a black stubble; his hair was gray at the temples. He was leading by the arm an old man with a long white beard stained about the mouth. Benbow watched Goodwin seat the old man in a chair, where he sat obediently with that tentative and abject eagerness of a man who has but one pleasure left and whom the world can reach only through one sense, for he was both blind and deaf: a short man with a bald skull and a round, full-fleshed, rosy face in which his cataracted eyes looked like two clots of phlegm. Benbow watched him take a filthy rag from his pocket and regurgitate into the rag an almost colorless wad of what had once been chewing tobacco, and fold the rag up and put it into his pocket. The woman served his plate from the dish. The others were already eating, silently and steadily, but the old man sat there, his head bent over his plate, his beard working faintly. He fumbled at the plate with a diffident, shaking hand and found a small piece of meat and began to suck at it until the woman returned and rapped his knuckles. He put the meat back on the plate then and Benbow watched her cut up the food on the plate, meat, bread and all, and then pour sorghum over it. Then Benbow quit looking. When the meal was over, Goodwin led the old man out again. Benbow watched the two of them pass out the door and heard them go up the hall.

The men returned to the porch. The woman cleared the table and carried the dishes to the kitchen. She set them on the table and she went to the box behind the stove and she stood over it for a time. Then she returned and put her own supper on a plate and sat down to the table and ate and lit a cigarette from the lamp and washed the dishes and put them away. Then she went back up the hall. She did not go out onto the porch. She stood just inside the door, listening to them talking, listening to the stranger talking and to the thick, soft sound of the jug as they passed it among themselves. "That fool," the woman said. "What does he want. . . ." She listened to the stranger's voice; a quick, faintly outlandish voice, the voice of a man given to much talk and not much else. "Not to drinking, anyway," the woman said, quiet inside the door. "He better get on to where he's going, where his women folks can take care of him."

She listened to him. "From my window I could see the grape arbor, and in the winter I could see the hammock too. But in the winter it was just the hammock. That's why we know nature is a she; because of that conspiracy between female flesh and female season. So each spring I could watch the reaffirmation of the old

ferment hiding the hammock; the green-snared
promise of unease. What blossoms grapes have,
this is. It's not much: a wild and waxlike bleeding less of bloom than leaf, hiding and hiding
the hammock, until along in late May, in the
twilight, her—Little Belle's—voice would be
like the murmur of the wild grape itself. She
never would say, 'Horace, this is Louis or Paul
or Whoever' but 'It's just Horace.' Just, you
see; in a little white dress in the twilight, the
two of them all demure and quite alert and a
little impatient. And I couldn't have felt any
more foreign to her flesh if I had begot it myself.

"So this morning—no; that was four days
ago; it was Thursday she got home from school
and this is Tuesday—I said, 'Honey, if you
found him on the train, he probably belongs
to the railroad company. You cant take him
from the railroad company; that's against the
law, like the insulators on the poles.'

" 'He's as good as you are. He goes to Tu-
lane.'

" 'But on a train, honey,' I said.

" 'I've found them in worse places than on
the train.'

" 'I know,' I said. 'So have I. But you dont
bring them home, you know. You just step over
14

them and go on. You dont soil your slippers, you know.'

"We were in the living-room then; it was just before dinner; just the two of us in the house then. Belle had gone down town.

" 'What business it is of yours who comes to see me? You're not my father. You're just— just—'

" 'What?' I said. 'Just what?'

" 'Tell Mother, then! Tell her. That's what you're going to do. Tell her!'

" 'But on the train, honey,' I said. 'If he'd walked into your room in a hotel, I'd just kill him. But on the train, I'm disgusted. Let's send him along and start all over again.'

" 'You're a fine one to talk about finding things on the train! You're a fine one! Shrimp! Shrimp!' "

"He's crazy," the woman said, motionless inside the door. The stranger's voice went on, tumbling over itself, rapid and diffuse.

"Then she was saying 'No! No!' and me holding her and she clinging to me. 'I didn't mean that! Horace! Horace!' And I was smelling the slain flowers, the delicate dead flowers and tears, and then I saw her face in the mirror. There was a mirror behind her and another behind me, and she was watching herself in the

15

one behind me, forgetting about the other one in which I could see her face, see her watching the back of my head with pure dissimulation. That's why nature is 'she' and Progress is 'he'; nature made the grape arbor, but Progress invented the mirror."

"He's crazy," the woman said inside the door, listening.

"But that wasn't quite it. I thought that maybe the spring, or maybe being forty-three years old, had upset me. I thought that maybe I would be all right if I just had a hill to lie on for a while— It was that country. Flat and rich and foul, so that the very winds seem to engender money out of it. Like you wouldn't be surprised to find that you could turn in the leaves off the trees, into the banks for cash. That Delta. Five thousand square miles, without any hill save the bumps of dirt the Indians made to stand on when the River overflowed.

"So I thought it was just a hill I wanted; it wasn't Little Belle that set me off. Do you know what it was?"

"He is," the woman said inside the door. "Lee ought not to let—"

Benbow had not waited for any answer. "It was a rag with rouge on it. I knew I would find it before I went into Belle's room. And there it was, stuffed behind the mirror: a handkerchief where she had wiped off the surplus paint when she dressed and stuck it behind the mantel. I put it into the clothes-bag and took my hat and walked out. I had got a lift on a truck before I found that I had no money with me. That was part of it too, you see; I couldn't cash a check. I couldn't get off the truck and go back to town and get some money. I couldn't do that. So I have been walking and bumming rides ever since. I slept one night in a sawdust pile at a mill, one night at a negro cabin, one night in a freight car on a siding. I just wanted a hill to lie on, you see. Then I would be all right. When you marry your own wife, you start off from scratch . . . maybe scratching. When you marry somebody else's wife, you start off maybe ten years behind, from somebody else's scratch and scratching. I just wanted a hill to lie on for a while."

"The fool," the woman said. "The poor fool." She stood inside the door. Popeye came through the hall from the back. He passed her without a word and went onto the porch.

"Come on," he said. "Let's get it loaded." She heard the three of them go away. She stood there. Then she heard the stranger get unsteadily out of his chair and cross the porch. Then she saw him, in faint silhouette against the sky, the lesser darkness: a thin man in shapeless clothes; a head of thinning and ill-kempt hair; and quite drunk. "They dont make him eat right," the woman said.

She was motionless, leaning lightly against the wall, he facing her. "Do you like living like this?" he said. "Why do you do it? You are young yet; you could go back to the cities and better yourself without lifting more than an eyelid." She didn't move, leaning lightly against the wall, her arms folded. "The poor, scared fool," she said.

"You see," he said, "I lack courage: that was left out of me. The machinery is all here, but it wont run." His hand fumbled across her cheek. "You are young yet." She didn't move, feeling his hand upon her face, touching her flesh as though he were trying to learn the shape and position of her bones and the texture of the flesh. "You have your whole life before you, practically. How old are you? You're not past thirty yet." His voice was not loud, almost a whisper.

When she spoke she did not lower her voice at all. She had not moved, her arms still folded across her breast. "Why did you leave your wife?" she said.

"Because she ate shrimp," he said. "I couldn't — You see, it was Friday, and I thought how at noon I'd go to the station and get the box of shrimp off the train and walk home with it,

18

counting a hundred steps and changing hands with it, and it—"

"Did you do that every day?" the woman said.

"No. Just Friday. But I have done it for ten years, since we were married. And I still dont like to smell shrimp. But I wouldn't mind the carrying it home so much. I could stand that. It's because the package drips. All the way home it drips and drips, until after a while I follow myself to the station and stand aside and watch Horace Benbow take that box off the train and start home with it, changing hands every hundred steps, and I following him, thinking Here lies Horace Benbow in a fading series of small stinking spots on a Mississippi sidewalk."

"Oh," the woman said. She breathed quietly, her arms folded. She moved; he gave back and followed her down the hall. They entered the kitchen where a lamp burned. "You'll have to excuse the way I look," the woman said. She went to the box behind the stove and drew it out and stood above it, her hands hidden in the front of her garment. Benbow stood in the middle of the room. "I have to keep him in the box so the rats cant get to him," she said.

"What?" Benbow said. What is it?" He approached, where he could see into the box. It contained a sleeping child, not a year old. He looked down at the pinched face quietly.

"Oh," he said. "You have a son." They looked down at the pinched, sleeping face of the child. There came a noise outside; feet came onto the back porch. The woman shoved the box back into the corner with her knee as Goodwin entered.

"All right," Goodwin said. "Tommy'll show you the way to the truck." He went away, on into the house.

Benbow looked at the woman. Her hands were still wrapped into her dress. "Thank you for the supper," he said. "Some day, maybe . . ." He looked at her; she was watching him, her face not sullen so much, as cold, still. "Maybe I can do something for you in Jefferson. Send you something you need . . ."

She removed her hands from the fold of the dress in a turning, flicking motion; jerked them hidden again. "With all this dishwater and washing . . . You might send me an orange stick," she said.

Walking in single file, Tommy and Benbow descended the hill from the house, following the abandoned road. Benbow looked back. The gaunt ruin of the house rose against the sky, above the massed and matted cedars, lightless, desolate, and profound. The road was an eroded scar too deep to be a road and too straight to

20

be a ditch, gutted by winter freshets and choked with fern and rotted leaves and branches. Following Tommy, Benbow walked in a faint path where feet had worn the rotting vegetation down to the clay. Overhead an arching hedgerow of trees thinned against the sky.

The descent increased, curving. "It was about here that we saw the owl," Benbow said.

Ahead of him Tommy guffawed. "It skeered him too, I'll be bound," he said.

"Yes," Benbow said. He followed Tommy's vague shape, trying to walk carefully, to talk carefully, with that tedious concern of drunkenness.

"I be a dog if he aint the skeeriest durn *white* man I ever see," Tommy said. "Here he was comin up the path to the porch and that ere dog come out from under the house and went up and sniffed his heels, like ere a dog will, and I be dog if he didn't flinch off like it was a moccasin and him barefoot, and whupped out that little artermatic pistol and shot it dead as a door-nail. I be durn if he didn't."

"Whose dog was it?" Horace said.

"Hit was mine," Tommy said. He chortled. "A old dog that wouldn't hurt a flea if hit could."

The road descended and flattened; Benbow's feet whispered into sand, walking carefully.

21

Against the pale sand he could now see Tommy, moving at a shuffling shamble like a mule walks in sand, without seeming effort, his bare feet hissing, flicking the sand back in faint spouting gusts from each inward flick of his toes.

The bulky shadow of the felled tree blobbed across the road. Tommy climbed over it and Benbow followed, still carefully, gingerly, hauling himself through a mass of foliage not yet withered, smelling still green. "Some more of—" Tommy said. He turned. "Can you make it?"

"I'm all right," Horace said. He got his balance again. Tommy went on.

"Some more of Popeye's doins," Tommy said. " 'Twarn't no use, blocking this road like that. Just fixed it so we'd have to walk a mile to the trucks. I told him folks been coming out here to buy from Lee for four years now, and aint nobody bothered Lee yet. Besides gettin that car of hisn outen here again, big as it is. But 'twarn't no stoppin him. I be dog if he aint skeered of his own shadow."

"I'd be scared of it too," Benbow said. "If his shadow was mine."

Tommy guffawed, in undertone. The road was now a black tunnel floored with the impalpable defunctive glare of the sand. "It was about here that the path turned off to the spring,"

Benbow thought, trying to discern where the path notched into the jungle wall. They went on.

"Who drives the truck?" Benbow said. "Some more Memphis fellows?"

"Sho," Tommy said. "Hit's Popeye's truck."

"Why cant those Memphis folks stay in Memphis and let you all make your liquor in peace?"

"That's where the money is," Tommy said. "Aint no money in these here piddlin little quarts and half-a-gallons. Lee just does that for a-commodation, to pick up a extry dollar or two. It's in making a run and getting shut of it quick, where the money is."

"Oh," Benbow said. "Well, I think I'd rather starve than have that man around me."

Tommy guffawed. "Popeye's all right. He's just a little curious." He walked on, shapeless against the hushed glare of the road, the sandy road. "I be dog if he aint a case, now. Aint he?"

"Yes," Benbow said. "He's all of that."

The truck was waiting where the road, clay again, began to mount toward the gravel highway. Two men sat on the fender, smoking cigarettes; overhead the trees thinned against the stars of more than midnight.

"You took your time," one of the men said. "Didn't you? I aimed to be halfway to town by now. I got a woman waiting for me."

"Sure," the other man said. "Waiting on her back." The first man cursed him.

"We come as fast as we could," Tommy said. "Whyn't you fellows hang out a lantern? If me and him had a been the Law, we'd had you, sho."

"Ah, go climb a tree, you mat-faced bastard," the first man said. They snapped their cigarettes away and got into the truck. Tommy guffawed, in undertone. Benbow turned and extended his hand.

"Goodbye," he said. "And much obliged, Mister——"

"My name's Tawmmy," the other said. His limp, calloused hand fumbled into Benbow's and pumped it solemnly once and fumbled away. He stood there, a squat, shapeless figure against the faint glare of the road, while Benbow lifted his foot for the step. He stumbled, catching himself.

"Watch yourself, Doc," a voice from the cab of the truck said. Benbow got in. The second man was laying a shotgun along the back of the seat. The truck got into motion and ground terrifically up the gutted slope and into the gravelled highroad and turned toward Jefferson and Memphis.

III

On the next afternoon Benbow was at his sister's home. It was in the country, four miles from Jefferson; the home of her husband's people. She was a widow, with a boy ten years old, living in a big house with her son and the great aunt of her husband: a woman of ninety, who lived in a wheel chair, who was known as Miss Jenny. She and Benbow were at the window, watching his sister and a young man walking in the garden. His sister had been a widow for ten years.

"Why hasn't she ever married again?" Benbow said.

"I ask you," Miss Jenny said. "A young woman needs a man."

"But not that one," Benbow said. He looked at the two people. The man wore flannels and a blue coat; a broad, plumpish young man with a swaggering air, vaguely collegiate. "She seems to like children. Maybe because she has one of her own now. Which one is that? Is that the same one she had last fall?"

"Gowan Stevens," Miss Jenny said. "You ought to remember Gowan."

"Yes," Benbow said. "I do now. I remember last October." At that time he had passed through Jefferson on his way home, and he had stopped overnight at his sister's. Through the same window he and Miss Jenny had watched the same two people walking in the same garden, where at that time the late, bright, dusty-odored flowers of October bloomed. At that time Stevens wore brown, and at that time he was new to Horace.

"He's only been coming out since he got home from Virginia last spring," Miss Jenny said. "The one then was that Jones boy; Herschell. Yes. Herschell."

"Ah," Benbow said. "An F.F.V., or just an unfortunate sojourner there?"

"At the school, the University. He went there. You don't remember him because he was still in diapers when you left Jefferson."

"Dont let Belle hear you say that," Benbow said. He watched the two people. They approached the house and disappeared beyond it. A moment later they came up the stairs and into

26

the room. Stevens came in, with his sleek head, his plump, assured face. Miss Jenny gave him her hand and he bent fatly and kissed it.

"Getting younger and prettier every day," he said. "I was just telling Narcissa that if you'd just get up out of that chair and be my girl, she wouldn't have a chance."

"I'm going to tomorrow," Miss Jenny said. "Narcissa—"

Narcissa was a big woman, with dark hair, a broad, stupid, serene face. She was in her customary white dress. "Horace, this is Gowan Stevens," she said. "My brother, Gowan."

"How do you do, sir," Stevens said. He gave Benbow's hand a quick, hard, high, close grip. At that moment the boy, Benbow Sartoris, Benbow's nephew, came in. "I've heard of you," Stevens said.

"Gowan went to Virginia," the boy said.

"Ah," Benbow said. "I've heard of it."

"Thanks," Stevens said. "But everybody cant go to Harvard."

"Thank you," Benbow said. "It was Oxford."

"Horace is always telling folks he went to Oxford so they'll think he means the state university, and he can tell them different," Miss Jenny said.

"Gowan goes to Oxford a lot," the boy said. "He's got a jelly there. He takes her to the dances. Dont you, Gowan?"

"Right, bud," Stevens said. "A red-headed one."

"Hush, Bory," Narcissa said. She looked at her brother. "How are Belle and Little Belle?" She almost said something else, then she ceased. Yet she looked at her brother, her gaze grave and intent.

"If you keep on expecting him to run off from Belle, he will do it," Miss Jenny said. "He'll do it someday. But Narcissa wouldn't be satisfied, even then," she said. "Some women wont want a man to marry a certain woman. But all the women will be mad if he ups and leaves her."

"You hush, now," Narcissa said.

"Yes, sir," Miss Jenny said. "Horace has been bucking at the halter for some time now. But you better not run against it too hard, Horace; it might not be fastened at the other end."

Across the hall a small bell rang. Stevens and Benbow both moved toward the handle of Miss Jenny's chair. "Will you forbear, sir?" Benbow said. "Since I seem to be the guest."

"Why, Horace," Miss Jenny said. "Narcissa, will you send up to the chest in the attic and get

28

the duelling pistols?" She turned to the boy. "And you go on ahead and tell them to strike up the music, and to have two roses ready."

"Strike up what music?" the boy said.

"There are roses on the table," Narcissa said. "Gowan sent them. Come on to supper."

Through the window Benbow and Miss Jenny watched the two people, Narcissa still in white, Stevens in flannels and a blue coat, walking in the garden. "The Virginia gentleman one, who told us at supper that night about how they had taught him to drink like a gentleman. Put a beetle in alcohol, and you have a scarab; put a Mississippian in alcohol, and you have a gentleman—"

"Gowan Stevens," Miss Jenny said. They watched the two people disappear beyond the house. It was some time before he heard the two people come down the hall. When they entered, it was the boy instead of Stevens.

"He wouldn't stay," Narcissa said. "He's going to Oxford. There is to be a dance at the University Friday night. He has an engagement with a young lady."

"He should find ample field for gentlemanly drinking there," Horace said. "Gentlemanly anything else. I suppose that's why he is going down ahead of time."

29

"Taking an old girl to a dance," the boy said. "He's going to Starkville Saturday, to the base ball game. He said he'd take me, but you wont let me go."

IV

TOWNSPEOPLE TAKING AFTER-SUPPER drives through the college grounds or an oblivious and bemused faculty-member or a candidate for a master's degree on his way to the library would see Temple, a snatched coat under her arm and her long legs blonde with running, in speeding silhouette against the lighted windows of the Coop, as the women's dormitory was known, vanishing into the shadow beside the library wall, and perhaps a final squatting swirl of knickers or whatnot as she sprang into the car waiting there with engine running on that particular night. The cars belonged to town boys. Students in the University were not permitted to keep cars, and the men—hatless, in knickers and bright pull-overs—looked down upon the town boys who wore hats cupped rigidly upon pomaded heads, and coats a little too tight and trousers a little too full, with superiority and rage.

31

This was on week nights. On alternate Saturday evenings, at the Letter Club dances, or on the occasion of the three formal yearly balls, the town boys, lounging in attitudes of belligerent casualness, with their identical hats and upturned collars, watched her enter the gymnasium upon black collegiate arms and vanish in a swirling glitter upon a glittering swirl of music, with her high delicate head and her bold painted mouth and soft chin, her eyes blankly right and left looking, cool, predatory and discreet.

Later, the music wailing beyond the glass, they would watch her through the windows as she passed in swift rotation from one pair of black sleeves to the next, her waist shaped slender and urgent in the interval, her feet filling the rhythmic gap with music. Stooping they would drink from flasks and light cigarettes, then erect again, motionless against the light, the upturned collars, the hatted heads, would be like a row of hatted and muffled busts cut from black tin and nailed to the window-sills.

There would always be three or four of them there when the band played Home, Sweet Home, lounging near the exit, their faces cold, bellicose, a little drawn with sleeplessness, watching the couples emerge in a wan aftermath of motion and noise. Three of them watched

Temple and Gowan Stevens come out, into the chill presage of spring dawn. Her face was quite pale, dusted over with recent powder, her hair in spent red curls. Her eyes, all pupil now, rested upon them for a blank moment. Then she lifted her hand in a wan gesture, whether at them or not, none could have said. They did not respond, no flicker in their cold eyes. They watched Gowan slip his arm into hers, and the fleet revelation of flank and thigh as she got into his car. It was a long, low roadster, with a jacklight.

"Who's that son bitch?" one said.

"My father's a judge," the second said in a bitter, lilting falsetto.

"Hell. Let's go to town."

They went on. Once they yelled at a car, but it did not stop. On the bridge across the railroad cutting they stopped and drank from a bottle. The last made to fling it over the railing. The second caught his arm.

"Let me have it," he said. He broke the bottle carefully and spread the fragments across the road. They watched him.

"You're not good enough to go to a college dance," the first said. "You poor bastard."

"My father's a judge," the other said, propping the jagged shards upright in the road.

"Here comes a car," the third said.

It had three headlights. They leaned against the railing, slanting their hats against the light, and watched Temple and Gowan pass. Temple's head was low and close. The car moved slowly.

"You poor bastard," the first said.

"Am I?" the second said. He took something from his pocket and flipped it out, whipping the sheer, faintly scented web across their faces. "Am I?"

"That's what you say."

"Doc got that step-in in Memphis," the third said. "Off a damn whore."

"You're a lying bastard," Doc said.

They watched the fan of light, the diminishing ruby taillamp, come to a stop at the Coop. The lights went off. After a while the car door slammed. The lights came on; the car moved away. It approached again. They leaned against the rail in a row, their hats slanted against the glare. The broken glass glinted in random sparks. The car drew up and stopped opposite them.

"You gentlemen going to town?" Gowan said, opening the door. They leaned against the rail, then the first said "Much obliged" gruffly and they got in, the two others in the rumble seat, the first beside Gowan.

34

"Pull over this way," he said. "Somebody broke a bottle there."

"Thanks," Gowan said. The car moved on. "You gentlemen going to Starkville tomorrow to the game?"

The ones in the rumble seat said nothing.

"I dont know," the first said. "I dont reckon so."

"I'm a stranger here," Gowan said. "I ran out of liquor tonight, and I've got a date early in the morning. Can you gentlemen tell me where I could get a quart?"

"It's mighty late," the first said. He turned to the others. "You know anybody he can find this time of night, Doc?"

"Luke might," the third said.

"Where does he live?" Gowan said.

"Go on," the first said. "I'll show you." They crossed the square and drove out of town about a half mile.

"This is the road to Taylor, isn't it?" Gowan said.

"Yes," the first said.

"I've got to drive down there early in the morning," Gowan said. "Got to get there before the special does. You gentlemen not going to the game, you say."

"I reckon not," the first said. "Stop here."

35

A steep slope rose, crested by stunted black-
jacks. "You wait here," the first said. Gowan
switched off the lights. They could hear the
other scrambling the slope.

"Does Luke have good liquor?" Gowan said.

"Pretty good. Good as any, I reckon," the
third said.

"If you dont like it, you dont have to drink
it," Doc said. Gowan turned fatly and looked
at him.

"It's as good as that you had tonight," the
third said.

"You didn't have to drink that, neither," Doc
said.

"They cant seem to make good liquor down
here like they do up at school," Gowan said.

"Where you from?" the third said.

"Virgin—oh, Jefferson. I went to school at
Virginia. Teach you how to drink, there."

The other two said nothing. The first returned, preceded by a minute shaling of earth
down the slope. He had a fruit jar. Gowan
lifted it against the sky. It was pale, innocent looking. He removed the cap and extended it.

"Drink."

The first took it and extended it to them in
the rumble.

"Drink."

36

The third drank, but Doc refused. Gowan drank.

"Good God," he said, "how do you fellows drink this stuff?"

"We dont drink rotgut at Virginia," Doc said. Gowan turned in the seat and looked at him.

"Shut up, Doc," the third said. "Dont mind him," he said. "He's had a bellyache all night."

"Son bitch," Doc said.

"Did you call me that?" Gowan said.

" 'Course he didn't," the third said. "Doc's all right. Come on, Doc. Take a drink."

"I dont give a damn," Doc said. "Hand it here."

They returned to town. "The shack'll be open," the first said. "At the depot."

It was a confectionery-lunchroom. It was empty save for a man in a soiled apron. They went to the rear and entered an alcove with a table and four chairs. The man brought four glasses and coca-colas. "Can I have some sugar and water and a lemon, Cap?" Gowan said. The man brought them. The others watched Gowan make a whisky sour. "They taught me to drink it this way," he said. They watched him drink. "Hasn't got much kick, to me," he said, filling his glass from the jar. He drank that.

37

"You sure do drink it," the third said.

"I learned in a good school." There was a high window. Beyond it the sky was paler, fresher. "Have another, gentlemen," he said, filling his glass again. The others helped themselves moderately. "Up at school they consider it better to go down than to hedge," he said. They watched him drink that one. They saw his nostrils bead suddenly with sweat.

"That's all for him, too," Doc said.

"Who says so?" Gowan said. He poured an inch into the glass. "If we just had some decent liquor. I know a man in my county named Goodwin that makes—"

"That's what they call a drink up at school," Doc said.

Gowan looked at him. "Do you think so? Watch this." He poured into the glass. They watched the liquor rise.

"Look out, fellow," the third said. Gowan filled the glass level full and lifted it and emptied it steadily. He remembered setting the glass down carefully, then he became aware simultaneously of open air, of a chill gray freshness and an engine panting on a siding at the head of a dark string of cars, and that he was trying to tell someone that he had learned to drink like a gentleman. He was still trying to tell them, in a cramped dark place smelling of

38

ammonia and creosote, vomiting into a receptacle, trying to tell them that he must be at Taylor at six-thirty, when the special arrived. The paroxysm passed; he felt extreme lassitude, weakness, a desire to lie down which was forcibly restrained, and in the flare of a match he leaned against the wall, his eyes focusing slowly upon a name written there in pencil. He shut one eye, propped against the wall, swaying and drooling, and read the name. Then he looked at them, wagging his head.

"Girl name . . . Name girl I know. Good girl. Good sport. Got date take her to Stark . . . Starkville. No chap'rone, see?" Leaning there, drooling, mumbling, he went to sleep.

At once he began to fight himself out of sleep. It seemed to him that it was immediately, yet he was aware of time passing all the while, and that time was a factor in his need to wake; that otherwise he would be sorry. For a long while he knew that his eyes were open, waiting for vision to return. Then he was seeing again, without knowing at once that he was awake.

He lay quite still. It seemed to him that, by breaking out of sleep, he had accomplished the purpose that he had waked himself for. He was lying in a cramped position under a low canopy, looking at the front of an unfamiliar building above which small clouds rosy with sunlight

39

drove, quite empty of any sense. Then his abdominal muscles completed the retch upon which he had lost consciousness and he heaved himself up and sprawled into the foot of the car, banging his head on the door. The blow fetched him completely to and he opened the door and half fell to the ground and dragged himself up and turned toward the station at a stumbling run. He fell. On hands and knees he looked at the empty siding and up at the sun-filled sky with unbelief and despair. He rose and ran on, in his stained dinner jacket, his burst collar and broken hair. I passed out, he thought in a kind of rage, I passed out. *I passed out.*

The platform was deserted save for a negro with a broom. "Gret Gawd, white folks," he said.

"The train," Gowan said, "the special. The one that was on that track."

"Hit done lef. But five minutes ago." With the broom still in the arrested gesture of sweeping he watched Gowan turn and run back to the car and tumble into it.

The jar lay on the floor. He kicked it aside and started the engine. He knew that he needed something on his stomach, but there wasn't time. He looked down at the jar. His inside coiled coldly, but he raised the jar and drank, guzzling, choking the stuff down, clapping a cigarette into his mouth to restrain the paroxysm. Almost at once he felt better.

He crossed the square at forty miles an hour. It was six-fifteen. He took the Taylor road, increasing speed. He drank again from the jar without slowing down. When he reached Taylor the train was just pulling out of the station. He slammed in between two wagons as the last car passed. The vestibule opened; Temple sprang down and ran for a few steps beside the car while an official leaned down and shook his fist at her.

Gowan had got out. She turned and came toward him, walking swiftly. Then she paused, stopped, came on again, staring at his wild face and hair, at his ruined collar and shirt.

"You're drunk," she said. "You pig. You filthy pig."

"Had a big night. You dont know the half of it."

She looked about, at the bleak yellow station, the overalled men chewing slowly and watching her, down the track at the diminishing train, at the four puffs of vapor that had almost died away when the sound of the whistle came back. "You filthy pig," she said. "You cant go anywhere like this. You haven't even changed clothes." At the car she stopped again. "What's that behind you?"

"My canteen," Gowan said. "Get in."

She looked at him, her mouth boldly scarlet, her eyes watchful and cold beneath her brimless hat, a curled spill of red hair. She looked back at the station again, stark and ugly in the fresh morning. She sprang in, tucking her legs under her. "Let's get away from here." He started the car and turned it. "You'd better take me back to Oxford," she said. She looked back at the station. It now lay in shadow, in the shadow of a high scudding cloud. "You'd better," she said.

At two oclock that afternoon, running at good speed through a high murmurous desolation of pines, Gowan swung the car from the gravel into a narrow road between eroded banks, descending toward a bottom of cypress and gum. He wore a cheap blue workshirt beneath his dinner jacket. His eyes were bloodshot, puffed, his jowls covered by blue stubble, and looking at him, braced and clinging as the car leaped and bounced in the worn ruts, Temple thought His whiskers have grown since we left Dumfries. It was hair-oil he drank. He bought a bottle of hair-oil at Dumfries and drank it.

He looked at her, feeling her eyes. "Dont get

your back up, now. It wont take a minute to run up to Goodwin's and get a bottle. It wont take ten minutes. I said I'd get you to Starkville before the train does, and I will. Dont you believe me?"

She said nothing, thinking of the pennant-draped train already in Starkville; of the colorful stands; the band, the yawning glitter of the bass horn; the green diamond dotted with players, crouching, uttering short, yelping cries like marsh-fowl disturbed by an alligator, not certain of where the danger is, motionless, poised, encouraging one another with short meaningless cries, plaintive, wary and forlorn.

"Trying to come over me with your innocent ways. Dont think I spent last night with a couple of your barber-shop jellies for nothing. Dont think I fed them my liquor just because I'm big-hearted. You're pretty good, aren't you? Think you can play around all week with any badger-trimmed hick that owns a ford, and fool me on Saturday, dont you? Dont think I didn't see your name where it's written on that lavatory wall. Dont you believe me?"

She said nothing, bracing herself as the car lurched from one bank to the other of the cut, going too fast. He was still watching her, making no effort to steer it.

"By God, I want to see the woman that can—"

The road flattened into sand, arched completely over, walled completely by a jungle of cane and brier. The car lurched from side to side in the loose ruts.

She saw the tree blocking the road, but she only braced herself anew. It seemed to her to be the logical and disastrous end to the train of circumstance in which she had become involved. She sat and watched rigidly and quietly as Gowan, apparently looking straight ahead, drove into the tree at twenty miles an hour. The car struck, bounded back, then drove into the tree again and turned onto its side.

She felt herself flying through the air, carrying a numbing shock upon her shoulder and a picture of two men peering from the fringe of cane at the roadside. She scrambled to her feet, her head reverted, and saw them step into the road, the one in a suit of tight black and a straw hat, smoking a cigarette, the other bareheaded, in overalls, carrying a shotgun, his bearded face gaped in slow astonishment. Still running her bones turned to water and she fell flat on her face, still running.

Without stopping she whirled and sat up, her mouth open upon a soundless wail behind her lost breath. The man in overalls was still looking at her, his mouth open in innocent astonishment within a short soft beard. The other man was leaning over the upturned car, his tight coat ridged across his shoulders. Then the engine ceased, though the lifted front wheel continued to spin idly, slowing.

V

THE MAN IN OVERALLS WAS BAREFOOT ALSO.
He walked ahead of Temple and Gowan, the
shotgun swinging in his hand, his splay feet apparently effortless in the sand into which Temple
sank almost to the ankle at each step. From time
to time he looked over his shoulder at them, at
Gowan's bloody face and splotched clothes, at
Temple struggling and lurching on her high
heels.

"Putty hard walkin, aint it?" he said. "Ef
she'll take off them high heel shoes, she'll git
along better."

"Will I?" Temple said. She stopped and stood
on alternate legs, holding to Gowan, and removed her slippers. The man watched her, looking at the slippers.

"Durn ef I could git ere two of my fingers into
one of them things," he said. "Kin I look at em?"
She gave him one. He turned it slowly in his

16

hand. "Durn my hide," he said. He looked at Temple again with his pale, empty gaze. His hair grew innocent and straw-like, bleached on the crown, darkening about his ears and neck in untidy curls. "She's a right tall gal, too," he said. "With them skinny legs of hern. How much she weigh?" Temple extended her hand. He returned the slipper slowly, looking at her, at her belly and loins. "He aint laid no crop by yit, has he?"

"Come on," Gowan said, "let's get going. We've got to get a car and get back to Jefferson by night."

When the sand ceased Temple sat down and put her slippers on. She found the man watching her lifted thigh and she jerked her skirt down and sprang up. "Well," she said, "go on. Dont you know the way?"

The house came into sight, above the cedar grove beyond whose black interstices an apple orchard flaunted in the sunny afternoon. It was set in a ruined lawn, surrounded by abandoned grounds and fallen outbuildings. But nowhere was any sign of husbandry—plow or tool; in no direction was a planted field in sight—only a gaunt weather-stained ruin in a sombre grove through which the breeze drew with a sad, murmurous sound. Temple stopped.

"I dont want to go there," she said. "You go

47

on and get the car," she told the man. "We'll wait here."

"He said fer y'all to come on to the house," the man said.

"Who did?" Temple said. "Does that black man think he can tell me what to do?"

"Ah, come on," Gowan said. "Let's see Goodwin and get a car. It's getting late. Mrs. Goodwin's here, isn't she?"

"Hit's likely," the man said.

"Come on," Gowan said. They went on to the house. The man mounted to the porch and set the shotgun just inside the door.

"She's around somewher," he said. He looked at Temple again. "Hit aint no cause fer yo wife to fret," he said. "Lee'll git you to town, I reckon."

Temple looked at him. They looked at one another soberly, like two children or two dogs. "What's your name?"

"My name's Tawmmy," he said. "Hit aint no need to fret."

The hall was open through the house. She entered.

"Where you going?" Gowan said. "Why dont you wait out here?" She didn't answer. She went on down the hall. Behind her she could hear Gowan's and the man's voices. The back porch lay in sunlight, a segment of sunlight framed
48

by the door. Beyond, she could see a weed-choked slope and a huge barn, broken-backed, tranquil in sunny desolation. To the right of the door she could see the corner either of a detached building or of a wing of the house. But she could hear no sound save the voices from the front.

She went on, slowly. Then she stopped. On the square of sunlight framed by the door lay the shadow of a man's head, and she half spun, poised with running. But the shadow wore no hat, so she turned and on tiptoe she went to the door and peered around it. A man sat in a splint-bottom chair, in the sunlight, the back of his bald, white-fringed head toward her, his hands crossed on the head of a rough stick. She emerged onto the back porch.

"Good afternoon," she said. The man did not move. She advanced again, then she glanced quickly over her shoulder. With the tail of her eye she thought she had seen a thread of smoke drift out of the door in the detached room where the porch made an L, but it was gone. From a line between two posts in front of this door three square cloths hung damp and limp, as though recently washed, and a woman's undergarment of faded pink silk. It had been washed until the lace resembled a ragged, fibre-like fraying of the cloth itself. It bore a patch of pale calico, neatly sewn. Temple looked at the old man again.

49

For an instant she thought that his eyes were closed, then she believed that he had no eyes at all, for between the lids two objects like dirty yellowish clay marbles were fixed. "Gowan," she whispered, then she wailed "Gowan" and turned running, her head reverted, just as a voice spoke beyond the door where she had thought to have seen smoke:

"He cant hear you. What do you want?"

She whirled again and without a break in her stride and still watching the old man, she ran right off the porch and fetched up on hands and knees in a litter of ashes and tin cans and bleached bones, and saw Popeye watching her from the corner of the house, his hands in his pockets and a slanted cigarette curling across his face. Still without stopping she scrambled onto the porch and sprang into the kitchen, where a woman sat at a table, a burning cigarette in her hand, watching the door.

VI

POPEYE WENT ON AROUND THE HOUSE.
Gowan was leaning over the edge of the porch,
dabbing gingerly at his bloody nose. The bare-
footed man squatted on his heels against the
wall.

"For Christ's sake," Popeye said, "why cant
you take him out back and wash him off? Do you
want him sitting around here all day looking like
a damn hog with its throat cut?" He snapped
the cigarette into the weeds and sat on the top
step and began to scrape his muddy shoes with
a platinum penknife on the end of his watch
chain.

The barefoot man rose.

"You said something about—" Gowan said.

"Pssst!" the other said. He began to wink and
frown at Gowan, jerking his head at Popeye's
back.

"And then you get on back down that road,"
Popeye said. "You hear?"

"I thought you was fixin to watch down ther," the man said.

"Dont think," Popeye said, scraping at his trouser-cuffs. "You've got along forty years without it. You do what I told you."

When they reached the back porch the barefoot man said: "He jest caint stand fer nobody — Aint he a cur'us feller, now? I be dawg ef he aint better'n a circus to— He wont stand fer nobody drinkin hyer cep Lee. Wont drink none hisself, and jest let me take one sup and I be dawg ef hit dont look like he'll have a catfit."

"He said you were forty years old," Gowan said.

"'Taint that much," the other said.

"How old are you? Thirty?"

"I dont know. 'Taint as much as he said, though." The old man sat in the chair, in the sun. "Hit's jest Pap," the man said. The azure shadow of the cedars had reached the old man's feet. It was almost up to his knees. His hand came out and fumbled about his knees, dabbling into the shadow, and became still, wrist-deep in shadow. Then he rose and grasped the chair and, tapping ahead with the stick, he bore directly down upon them in a shuffling rush, so that they had to step quickly aside. He dragged the chair into the full sunlight and sat down again, his face lifted into the sun, his hands crossed on the head of the stick. "That's Pap," the man said. "Blind and deef both. I be dawg ef I wouldn't hate to be in a fix wher I couldn't tell and wouldn't even keer whut I was eatin."

On a plank fixed between two posts sat a galvanised pail, a tin basin, a cracked dish containing a lump of yellow soap. "To hell with water," Gowan said. "How about that drink?"

"Seems to me like you done already had too much. I be dawg ef you didn't drive that ere car straight into that tree."

"Come on. Haven't you got some hid out somewhere?"

"Mought be a little in the barn. But dont let him hyear us, er he'll find hit and po hit out." He went back to the door and peered up the hall. Then they left the porch and went toward the barn, crossing what had once been a kitchen garden choked now with cedar and blackjack saplings. Twice the man looked back over his shoulder. The second time he said:

"Yon's yo wife wantin somethin."

Temple stood in the kitchen door. "Gowan," she called.

"Wave yo hand er somethin," the man said. "Ef she dont hush, he's goin to hyear us." Gowan flapped his hand. They went on and entered the barn. Beside the entrance a crude ladder mounted. "Better wait twell I git up," the

53

man said. "Hit's putty rotten; mought not hold us both."

"Why dont you fix it, then? Dont you use it every day?"

"Hit's helt all right, so fur," the other said. He mounted. Then Gowan followed, through the trap, into yellow-barred gloom where the level sun fell through the broken walls and roof. "Walk wher I do," the man said. "You'll tromp on a loose boa'd and find yoself downstairs befo you know hit." He picked his way across the floor and dug an earthenware jug from a pile of rotting hay in the corner. "One place he wont look fer hit," he said. "Skeered of sp'ilin them gal's hands of hisn."

They drank. "I've seen you out hyer befo," the man said. "Caint call yo name, though."

"My name's Stevens. I've been buying liquor from Lee for three years. When'll he be back? We've got to get on to town."

"He'll be hyer soon. I've seen you befo. Nother feller fum Jefferson out hyer three-fo nights ago. I cant call his name neither. He sho was a talker, now. Kep on tellin how he up and quit his wife. Have some mo," he said; then he ceased and squatted slowly, the jug in his lifted hands, his head bent with listening. After a moment the voice spoke again, from the hallway beneath.

"Jack."

The man looked at Gowan. His jaw dropped into an expression of imbecile glee. What teeth he had were stained and ragged within his soft, tawny beard.

"You, Jack, up there," the voice said.

"Hyear him?" the man whispered, shaking with silent glee. "Callin me Jack. My name's Tawmmy."

"Come on," the voice said. "I know you're there."

"I reckon we better," Tommy said. "He jest lief take a shot up through the flo as not."

"For Christ's sake," Gowan said, "Why didn't you— Here," he shouted, "here we come!"

Popeye stood in the door, his forefingers in his vest. The sun had set. When they descended and appeared in the door Temple stepped from the back porch. She paused, watching them, then she came down the hill. She began to run.

"Didn't I tell you to get on down that road?" Popeye said.

"Me an him jest stepped down hyer a minute," Tommy said.

"Did I tell you to get on down that road, or didn't I?"

"Yeuh," Tommy said. "You told me." Popeye turned without so much as a glance at

Gowan. Tommy followed. His back still shook with secret glee. Temple met Popeye halfway to the house. Without ceasing to run she appeared to pause. Even her flapping coat did not overtake her, yet for an appreciable instant she faced Popeye with a grimace of taut, toothed coquetry. He did not stop; the finicking swagger of his narrow back did not falter. Temple ran again. She passed Tommy and clutched Gowan's arm.

"Gowan, I'm scared. She said for me not to — You've been drinking again; you haven't even washed the blood— She says for us to go away from here . . ." Her eyes were quite black, her face small and wan in the dusk. She looked toward the house. Popeye was just turning the corner. "She has to walk all the way to a spring for water; she— They've got the cutest little baby in a box behind the stove. Gowan, she said for me not to be here after dark. She said to ask him. He's got a car. She said she didn't think he—"

"Ask who?" Gowan said. Tommy was looking back at them. Then he went on.

"That black man. She said she didn't think he would, but he might. Come on." They went toward the house. A path led around it to the front. The car was parked between the path and the house, in the tall weeds. Temple faced

56

Gowan again, her hand lying upon the door of the car. "It wont take him any time, in this. I know a boy at home has one. It will run eighty. All he would have to do is just drive us to a town, because she said if we were married and I had to say we were. Just to a railroad. Maybe there's one closer than Jefferson," she whispered, staring at him, stroking her hand along the edge of the door.

"Oh," Gowan said, "I'm to do the asking. Is that it? You're all nuts. Do you think that ape will? I'd rather stay here a week than go anywhere with him."

"She said to. She said for me not to stay here."

"You're crazy as a loon. Come on here."

"You wont ask him? You wont do it?"

"No. Wait till Lee comes, I tell you. He'll get us a car."

They went on in the path. Popeye was leaning against a post, lighting a cigarette. Temple ran on up the broken steps. "Say," she said, "dont you want to drive us to town?"

He turned his head, the cigarette in his mouth, the match cupped between his hands Temple's mouth was fixed in that cringing grimace. Popeye leaned the cigarette to the match "No," he said.

"Come on," Temple said. "Be a sport. It

57

wont take you any time in that Packard. How
about it? We'll pay you."

Popeye inhaled. He snapped the match into
the weeds. He said, in his soft, cold voice:
"Make your whore lay off of me, Jack."

Gowan moved thickly, like a clumsy, good-
tempered horse goaded suddenly. "Look here,
now," he said. Popeye exhaled, the smoke jet-
ting downward in two thin spurts. "I dont like
that," Gowan said. "Do you know who you're
talking to?" He continued that thick movement,
like he could neither stop it nor complete it. "I
dont like that." Popeye turned his head and
looked at Gowan. Then he quit looking at him
and Temple said suddenly:

"What river did you fall in with that suit on?
Do you have to shave it off at night?" Then she
was moving toward the door with Gowan's hand
in the small of her back, her head reverted, her
heels clattering. Popeye leaned motionless
against the post, his head turned over his shoulder in profile.

"Do you want—" Gowan hissed.

"You mean old thing!" Temple cried. "You
mean old thing!"

Gowan shoved her into the house. "Do you
want him to slam your damn head off?" he said.

"You're scared of him!" Temple said.
"You're scared!"

58

"Shut your mouth!" Gowan said. He began to shake her. Their feet scraped on the bare floor as though they were performing a clumsy dance, and clinging together they lurched into the wall. "Look out," he said, "you're getting all that stuff stirred up in me again." She broke free, running. He leaned against the wall and watched her in silhouette run out the back door.

She ran into the kitchen. It was dark save for a crack of light about the fire-door of the stove. She whirled and ran out the door and saw Gowan going down the hill toward the barn. He's going to drink some more, she thought; he's getting drunk again. That makes three times today. Still more dusk had grown in the hall. She stood on tiptoe, listening, thinking I'm hungry. I haven't eaten all day; thinking of the school, the lighted windows, the slow couples strolling toward the sound of the supper bell, and of her father sitting on the porch at home, his feet on the rail, watching a negro mow the lawn. She moved quietly on tiptoe. In the corner beside the door the shotgun leaned and she crowded into the corner beside it and began to cry.

Immediately she stopped and ceased breathing. Something was moving beyond the wall against which she leaned. It crossed the room with minute, blundering sounds, preceded by a dry tapping. It emerged into the hall and she screamed, feeling her lungs emptying long after all the air was expelled, and her diaphragm laboring long after her chest was empty, and watched the old man go down the hall at a wide-legged shuffling trot, the stick in one hand and the other elbow cocked at an acute angle from his middle. Running, she passed him—a dim, spraddled figure standing at the edge of the porch—and ran on into the kitchen and darted into the corner behind the stove. Crouching, she drew the box out and drew it before her. Her hand touched the child's face, then she flung her arms around the box, clutching it, staring across it at the pale door and trying to pray. But she could not think of a single designation for the heavenly father, so she began to say "My father's a judge; my father's a judge" over and over until Goodwin ran lightly into the room. He struck a match and held it overhead and looked down at her until the flame reached his fingers.

"Hah," he said. She heard his light, swift feet twice, then his hand touched her cheek and he lifted her from behind the box by the scruff of the neck, like a kitten. "What are you doing in my house?" he said.

VII

FROM SOMEWHERE BEYOND THE LAMPLIT hall she could hear the voices—a word; now and then a laugh: the harsh, derisive laugh of a man easily brought to mirth by youth or by age, cutting across the spluttering of frying meat on the stove where the woman stood. Once she heard two of them come down the hall in their heavy shoes, and a moment later the clatter of the dipper in the galvanised pail and the voice that had laughed, cursing. Holding her coat close she peered around the door with the wide, abashed curiosity of a child, and saw Gowan and a second man in khaki breeches. He's getting drunk again, she thought. He's got drunk four times since we left Taylor.

"Is he your brother?" she said.

"Who?" the woman said. "My what?" she turned the meat on the hissing skillet.

"I thought maybe your young brother wa⸢ here."

61

"God," the woman said. She turned the meat with a wire fork. "I hope not."

"Where is your brother?" Temple said, peering around the door. "I've got four brothers. Two are lawyers and one's a newspaper man. The other's still in school. At Yale. My father's a judge. Judge Drake of Jackson." She thought of her father sitting on the veranda, in a linen suit, a palm leaf fan in his hand, watching the negro mow the lawn.

The woman opened the oven and looked in. "Nobody asked you to come out here. I didn't ask you to stay. I told you to go while it was daylight."

"How could I? I asked him. Gowan wouldn't, so I had to ask him."

The woman closed the oven and turned and looked at Temple, her back to the light. "How could you? Do you know how I get my water? I walk after it. A mile. Six times a day. Add that up. Not because I am somewhere I am afraid to stay." She went to the table and took up a pack of cigarettes and shook one out.

"May I have one?" Temple said. The woman flipped the pack along the table. She removed the chimney from the lamp and lit hers at the wick. Temple took up the pack and stood listening to Gowan and the other man go back into the house. "There are so many of them," she said in a wailing tone, watching the cigarette crush slowly in her fingers. "But maybe, with so many of them . . ." The woman had gone back to the stove. She turned the meat. "Gowan kept on getting drunk again. He got drunk three times today. He was drunk when I got off the train at Taylor and I am on probation and I told him what would happen and I tried to get him to throw the jar away and when we stopped at that little country store to buy a shirt he got drunk again. And so we hadn't eaten and we stopped at Dumfries and he went into the restaurant but I was too worried to eat and I couldn't find him and then he came up another street and I felt the bottle in his pocket before he knocked my hand away. He kept on saying I had his lighter and then when he lost it and I told him he had, he swore he never owned one in his life."

The meat hissed and spluttered in the skillet. "He got drunk three separate times," Temple said. "Three separate times in one day. Buddy —that's Hubert, my youngest brother—said that if he ever caught me with a drunk man, he'd beat hell out of me. And now I'm with one that gets drunk three times in one day." Leaning her hip against the table, her hand crushing the cigarette, she began to laugh. "Dont ₅ou think that's funny?" she said. Then she quit laughing by holding her breath, and she could hear the faint guttering the lamp made, and the meat in the skillet and the hissing of the kettle on the stove, and the voices, the harsh, abrupt, meaningless masculine sounds from the house. "And you have to cook for all of them every night. All those men eating here, the house full of them at night, in the dark . . ." She dropped the crushed cigarette. "May I hold the baby? I know how; I'll hold him good." She ran to the box, stooping, and lifted the sleeping child. It opened its eyes, whimpering. "Now, now; Temple's got it." She rocked it, held high and awkward in her thin arms. "Listen," she said, looking at the woman's back, "will you ask him? your husband, I mean. He can get a car and take me some-where. Will you? Will you ask him?" The child had stopped whimpering. Its lead-colored eye-lids showed a thin line of eyeball. "I'm not afraid," Temple said. "Things like that dont happen. Do they? They're just like other peo-ple. You're just like other people. With a little baby. And besides, my father's a ju-judge. The gu-govenor comes to our house to e-eat— What a cute little bu-ba-a-by," she wailed, lifting the child to her face; "if bad mans hurts Temple, us'll tell the governor's soldiers, wont us?"

"Like what people?" the woman said, turn-

64

ing the meat. "Do you think Lee hasn't anything better to do than chase after every one of you cheap little—" She opened the fire door and threw her cigarette in and slammed the door. In nuzzling at the child Temple had pushed her hat onto the back of her head at a precarious dissolute angle above her clotted curls. "Why did you come here?"

"It was Gowan. I begged him. We had already missed the ball game, but I begged him if he'd just get me to Starkville before the special started back, they wouldn't know I wasn't on it, because the ones that saw me get off wouldn't tell. But he wouldn't. He said we'd stop here just a minute and get some more whisky and he was already drunk then. He had gotten drunk again since we left Taylor and I'm on probation and Daddy would just die. But he wouldn't do it. He got drunk again while I was begging him to take me to a town anywhere and let me out."

"On probation?" the woman said.

"For slipping out at night. Because only town boys can have cars, and when you had a date with a town boy on Friday or Saturday or Sunday, the boys in school wouldn't have a date with you, because they cant have cars. So I had to slip out. And a girl that didn't like me told the Dean, because I had a date with a boy she

65

liked and he never asked her for another date. So I had to."

"If you didn't slip out, you wouldn't get to go riding," the woman said. "Is that it? And now when you slipped out once too often, you're squealing."

"Gowan's not a town boy. He's from Jefferson. He went to Virginia. He kept on saying how they had taught him to drink like a gentleman, and I begged him just to let me out anywhere and lend me enough money for a ticket because I only had two dollars, but he—"

"Oh, I know your sort," the woman said. "Honest women. Too good to have anything to do with common people. You'll slip out at night with the kids, but just let a man come along." She turned the meat. "Take all you can get, and give nothing. 'I'm a pure girl; I dont do that.' You'll slip out with the kids and burn their gasoline and eat their food, but just let a man so much as look at you and you faint away because your father the judge and your four brothers might not like it. But just let you get into a jam, then who do you come crying to? to us, the ones that are not good enough to lace the judge's almighty shoes." Across the child Temple gazed at the woman's back, her face like a small pale mask beneath the precarious hat.

66

"My brother said he would kill Frank. He didn't say he would give me a whipping if he caught me with him; he said he would kill the goddam son of a bitch in his yellow buggy and my father cursed my brother and said he could run his family a while longer and he drove me into the house and locked me in and went down to the bridge to wait for Frank. But I wasn't a coward. I climbed down the gutter and headed Frank off and told him. I begged him to go away, but he said we'd both go. When we got back in the buggy I knew it had been the last time. I knew it, and I begged him again to go away, but he said he'd drive me home to get my suitcase and we'd tell father. He wasn't a coward either. My father was sitting on the porch. He said 'Get out of that buggy' and I got out and I begged Frank to go on, but he got out too and we came up the path and father reached around inside the door and got the shotgun. I got in front of Frank and father said 'Do you want it too?' and I tried to stay in front but Frank shoved me behind him and held me and father shot him and said 'Get down there and sup your dirt, you whore.' "

"I have been called that," Temple whispered, holding the sleeping child in her high thin arms, gazing at the woman's back.

"But you good women. Cheap sports. Giv-

67

ing nothing, then when you're caught . . . Do you know what you've got into now?" she looked across her shoulder, the fork in her hand. "Do you think you're meeting kids now? kids that give a damn whether you like it or not? Let me tell you whose house you've come into without being asked or wanted; who you're expecting to drop everything and carry you back where you had no business ever leaving. When he was a soldier in the Philippines he killed another soldier over one of those nigger women and they sent him to Leavenworth. Then the war came and they let him out to go to it. He got two medals, and when it was over they put him back in Leavenworth until the lawyer got a congressman to get him out. Then I could quit jazzing again—"

"Jazzing?" Temple whispered, holding the child, looking herself no more than an elongated and leggy infant in her scant dress and uptilted hat.

"Yes, putty-face!" the woman said. "How do suppose I paid that lawyer? And that's the sort of man you think will care that much—" with the fork in her hand she came and snapped her fingers softly and viciously in Temple's face "—what happens to you. And you, you little doll-faced slut, that think you cant come into a room where a man is without him . . ." Be-
68

neath the faded garment her breast moved deep and full. With her hands on her hips she looked at Temple with cold, blazing eyes. "Man? You've never seen a real man. You dont know what it is to be wanted by a real man. And thank your stars you haven't and never will, for then you'd find just what that little putty face is worth, and all the rest of it you think you are jealous of when you're just scared of it. And if he is just man enough to call you whore, you'll say Yes Yes and you'll crawl naked in the dirt and the mire for him to call you that. . . . Give me that baby." Temple held the child, gazing at the woman, her mouth moving as if she were saying Yes Yes Yes. The woman threw the fork onto the table. "Turn loose," she said, lifting the child. It opened its eyes and wailed. The woman drew a chair out and sat down, the child upon her lap. "Will you hand me one of those diapers on the line yonder?" she said. Temple stood in the floor, her lips still moving. "You're scared to go out there, aren't you?" the woman said. She rose.

"No," Temple said; "I'll get—"

"I'll get it." The unlaced brogans scuffed across the kitchen. She returned and drew another chair up to the stove and spread the two remaining cloths and the undergarment on it, and sat again and laid the child across her lap. It wailed. "Hush," she said, "hush, now," her face in the lamplight taking a serene, brooding quality. She changed the child and laid it in the box. Then she took a platter down from a cupboard curtained by a split towsack and took up the fork and came and looked into Temple's face again.

"Listen. If I get a car for you, will you get out of here?" she said. Staring at her Temple moved her mouth as though she were experimenting with words, tasting them. "Will you go out the back and get into it and go away and never come back here?"

"Yes," Temple whispered, "anywhere. Anything."

Without seeming to move her cold eyes at all the woman looked Temple up and down. Temple could feel all her muscles shrinking like severed vines in the noon sun. "You poor little gutless fool," the woman said in her cold undertone. "Playing at it."

"I didn't. I didn't."

"You'll have something to tell them now, when you get back. Wont you?" Face to face, their voices were like shadows upon two close blank walls. "Playing at it."

"Anything. Just so I get away. Anywhere."

"It's not Lee I'm afraid of. Do you think he plays the dog after every hot little bitch that comes along? It's you."

"Yes. I'll go anywhere."

"I know your sort. I've seen them. All running, but not too fast. Not so fast you cant tell a real man when you see him. Do you think you've got the only one in the world?"

"Gowan," Temple whispered, "Gowan."

"I have slaved for that man," the woman whispered, her lips scarce moving, in her still, dispassionate voice. It was as though she were reciting a formula for bread. "I worked night shift as a waitress so I could see him Sundays at the prison. I lived two years in a single room, cooking over a gas-jet, because I promised him. I lied to him and made money to get him out of prison, and when I told him how I made it, he beat me. And now you must come here where you're not wanted. Nobody asked you to come here. Nobody cares whether you are afraid or not. Afraid? You haven't the guts to be really afraid, anymore than you have to be in love."

"I'll pay you," Temple whispered. "Anything you say. My father will give it to me." The woman watched her, her face motionless, as rigid as when she had been speaking. "I'll send you clothes. I have a new fur coat. I just wore it since Christmas. It's as good as new."

The woman laughed. Her mouth laughed, with no sound, no movement of her face. "Clothes? I had three fur coats once. I gave one of them to a woman in an alley by a saloon. Clothes? God." She turned suddenly. "I'll get a car. You get away from here and dont you ever come back. Do you hear?"

"Yes," Temple whispered. Motionless, pale, like a sleepwalker she watched the woman transfer the meat to the platter and pour the gravy over it. From the oven she took a pan of biscuits and put them on a plate. "Can I help you?" Temple whispered. The woman said nothing. She took up the two plates and went out. Temple went to the table and took a cigarette from the pack and stood staring stupidly at the lamp. One side of the chimney was blackened. Across it a crack ran in a thin silver curve. The lamp was of tin, coated about the neck with dirty grease. She lit hers at the lamp, someway, Temple thought, holding the cigarette in her hand, staring at the uneven flame. The woman returned. She caught up the corner of her skirt and lifted the smutty coffee-pot from the stove.

"Can I take that?" Temple said.

"No. Come on and get your supper." She went out.

72

Temple stood at the table, the cigarette in her hand. The shadow of the stove fell upon the box where the child lay. Upon the lumpy wad of bedding it could be distinguished only by a series of pale shadows in soft small curves, and she went and stood over the box and looked down at its putty-colored face and bluish eyelids. A thin whisper of shadow cupped its head and lay moist upon its brow; one thin arm, upflung, lay curl-palmed beside its cheek. Temple stooped above the box.

"He's going to die," Temple whispered. Bending, her shadow loomed high upon the wall, her coat shapeless, her hat tilted monstrously above a monstrous escaping of hair. "Poor little baby," she whispered, "poor little baby." The men's voices grew louder. She heard a trampling of feet in the hall, a rasping of chairs, the voice of the man who had laughed above them, laughing again. She turned, motionless again, watching the door. The woman entered.

"Go and eat your supper," she said.

"The car," Temple said. "I could go now, while they're eating."

"What car?" the woman said. "Go on and eat. Nobody's going to hurt you."

"I'm not hungry. I haven't eaten today. I'm not hungry at all."

"Go and eat your supper," she said.

"I'll wait and eat when you do."

"Go on and eat your supper. I've got to get done here some time tonight."

VIII

TEMPLE ENTERED THE DINING-ROOM FROM the kitchen, her face fixed in a cringing, placative expression; she was quite blind when she entered, holding her coat about her, her hat thrust upward and back at that dissolute angle. After a moment she saw Tommy. She went straight toward him, as if she had been looking for him all the while. Something intervened: a hard forearm; she attempted to evade it, looking at Tommy.

"Here," Gowan said across the table, his chair rasping back, "you come around here."

"Outside, brother," the one who had stopped her said, whom she recognised then as the one who had laughed so often; "you're drunk. Come here, kid." His hard forearm came across her middle. She thrust against it, grinning rigidly at Tommy. "Move down,

75

Tommy," the man said. "Aint you got no man-
ners, you mat-faced bastard?" Tommy guffawed, scraping his chair along the floor. The
man drew her toward him by the wrist. Across
the table Gowan stood up, propping himself
on the table. She began to resist, grinning at
Tommy, picking at the man's fingers.

"Quit that, Van," Goodwin said.

"Right on my lap here," Van said.

"Let her go," Goodwin said.

"Who'll make me?" Van said. "Who's big
enough?"

"Let her go," Goodwin said. Then she was
free. She began to back slowly away. Behind
her the woman, entering with a dish, stepped
aside. Still smiling her aching, rigid grimace
Temple backed from the room. In the hall she
whirled and ran. She ran right off the porch,
into the weeds, and sped on. She ran to the road
and down it for fifty yards in the darkness, then
without a break she whirled and ran back to the
house and sprang onto the porch and crouched
against the door just as someone came up the
hall. It was Tommy.

"Oh, hyer you are," he said. He thrust something awkwardly at her. "Hyer," he said.

"What is it?" she whispered.

"Little bite of victuals. I bet you aint et since
mawnin."

76

"No. Not then, even," she whispered.

"You eat a little mite and you'll feel better,'
he said, poking the plate at her. "You set
down hyer and eat a little bite wher wont nobody bother you. Durn them fellers."

Temple leaned around the door, past his dim
shape, her face wan as a small ghost in the re-
fracted light from the dining-room. "Mrs—
Mrs . . ." she whispered.

"She's in the kitchen. Want me to go back
there with you?" In the dining-room a chair
scraped. Between blinks Tommy saw Temple in
the path, her body slender and motionless for a
moment as though waiting for some laggard
part to catch up. Then she was gone like a
shadow around the corner of the house. He
stood in the door, the plate of food in his hand.
Then he turned his head and looked down the
hall just in time to see her flit across the darkness toward the kitchen. "Durn them fellers."

He was standing there when the others returned to the porch.

"He's got a plate of grub," Van said. "He's
trying to get his with a plate full of ham."

"Git my whut?" Tommy said.

"Look here," Gowan said.

Van struck the plate from Tommy's hand
He turned to Gowan. "Dont you like it?"

"No," Gowan said, "I dont."

"What are you going to do about it?" Van said.

"Van," Goodwin said.

"Do you think you're big enough to not like it?" Van said.

"I am," Goodwin said.

When Van went back to the kitchen Tommy followed him. He stopped at the door and heard Van in the kitchen.

"Come for a walk, little bit," Van said.

"Get out of here, Van," the woman said.

"Come for a little walk," Van said. "I'm a good guy. Ruby'll tell you."

"Get out of here, now," the woman said. "Do you want me to call Lee?" Van stood against the light, in a khaki shirt and breeches, a cigarette behind his ear against the smooth sweep of his blond hair. Beyond him Temple stood behind the chair in which the woman sat at the table, her mouth open a little, her eyes quite black.

When Tommy went back to the porch with the jug he said to Goodwin: "Why dont them fellers quit pesterin that gal?"

"Who's pestering her?"

"Van is. She's skeered. Whyn't they leave her be?"

"It's none of your business. You keep out of it. You hear?"

"Them fellers ought to quit pesterin her," Tommy said. He squatted against the wall. They were drinking, passing the jug back and forth, talking. With the top of his mind he listened to them, to Van's gross and stupid tales of city life with rapt interest, guffawing now and then, drinking in his turn. Van and Gowan were doing the talking, and Tommy listened to them. "Them two's fixin to have hit out with one another," he whispered to Goodwin in a chair beside him. "Hyear em?" They were talking quite loud; Goodwin moved swiftly and lightly from his chair, his feet striking the floor with light thuds; Tommy saw Van standing and Gowan holding himself erect by the back of his chair.

"I never meant—" Van said.

"Dont say it, then," Goodwin said.

Gowan said something. That durn feller, Tommy thought. Cant even talk no more.

"Shut up, you," Goodwin said.

"Think talk bout my—" Gowan said. He moved, swayed against the chair. It fell over. Gowan blundered into the wall.

"By God, I'll—" Van said.

"—ginia gentleman; I dont give a—" Gowan said. Goodwin flung him aside with a backhanded blow of his arm, and grasped Van. Gowan fell against the wall.

"When I say sit down, I mean it," Goodwin said.

After that they were quiet for a while. Goodwin returned to his chair. They began to talk again, passing the jug, and Tommy listened. But soon he began to think about Temple again. He would feel his feet scouring on the floor and his whole body writhing in an acute discomfort. "They ought to let that gal alone," he whispered to Goodwin. "They ought to quit pesterin her."

"It's none of your business," Goodwin said. "Let every damned one of them . . ."

"They ought to quit pesterin her."

Popeye came out the door. He lit a cigarette. Tommy watched his face flare out between his hands, his cheeks sucking; he followed with his eyes the small comet of the match into the weeds. Him too, he said. Two of em; his body writhing slowly. Pore little crittur. I be dawg ef I aint a mind to go down to the barn and stay there, I be dawg ef I aint. He rose, his feet making no sound on the porch. He stepped down into the path and went around the house. There was a light in the window there. Dont nobody never use in there, he said, stopping, then he said, That's where she'll be stayin, and he went to the window and looked in. The sash

80

was down. Across a missing pane a sheet of rusted tin was nailed.

Temple was sitting on the bed, her legs tucked under her, erect, her hands lying in her lap, her hat tilted on the back of her head. She looked quite small, her very attitude an outrage to muscle and tissue of more than seventeen and more compatible with eight or ten, her elbows close to her sides, her face turned toward the door against which a chair was wedged. There was nothing in the room save the bed, with its faded patchwork quilt, and the chair. The walls had been plastered once, but the plaster had cracked and fallen in places, exposing the lathing and molded shreds of cloth. On the wall hung a raincoat and a khaki-covered canteen.

Temple's head began to move. It turned slowly, as if she were following the passage of someone beyond the wall. It turned on to an excruciating degree, though no other muscle moved, like one of those papier-mâché Easter toys filled with candy, and became motionless in that reverted position. Then it turned back, slowly, as though pacing invisible feet beyond the wall, back to the chair against the door and became motionless there for a moment. Then she faced forward and Tommy watched her take a tiny watch from the top of her stocking and look at it. With the watch in her hand she lifted her head and looked directly at him, her eyes calm and empty as two holes. After a while she looked down at the watch again and returned it to her stocking.

She rose from the bed and removed her coat and stood motionless, arrowlike in her scant dress, her head bent, her hands clasped before her. She sat on the bed again. She sat with her legs close together, her head bent. She raised her head and looked about the room. Tommy could hear the voices from the dark porch. They rose again, then sank to the steady murmur.

Temple sprang to her feet. She unfastened her dress, her arms arched thin and high, her shadow anticking her movements. In a single motion she was out of it, crouching a little, match-thin in her scant undergarments. Her head emerged facing the chair against the door. She hurled the dress away, her hand reaching for the coat. She scrabbled it up and swept it about her, pawing at the sleeves. Then, the coat clutched to her breast, she whirled and looked straight into Tommy's eyes and whirled and ran and flung herself upon the chair. "Durn them fellers," Tommy whispered, "durn them fellers." He could hear them on the front porch and his body began again to writhe slowly in an acute unhap, piness. "Durn them fellers."

When he looked into the room again Temple was moving toward him, holding the coat about her. She took the raincoat from the nail and put it on over her own coat and fastened it. She lifted the canteen down and returned to the bed. She laid the canteen on the bed and picked her dress up from the floor and brushed it with her hand and folded it carefully and laid it on the bed. Then she turned back the quilt, exposing the mattress. There was no linen, no pillow, and when she touched the mattress it gave forth a faint dry whisper of shucks.

She removed her slippers and set them on the bed and got in beneath the quilt. Tommy could hear the mattress crackle. She didn't lie down at once. She sat upright, quite still, the hat tilted rakishly upon the back of her head. Then she moved the canteen, the dress and the slippers beside her head and drew the raincoat about her legs and lay down, drawing the quilt up, then she sat up and removed the hat and shook her hair out and laid the hat with the other garments and prepared to lie down again. Again she paused. She opened the raincoat and produced a compact from somewhere and, watching her motions in the tiny mirror, she spread and fluffed her hair

with her fingers and powdered her face and replaced the compact and looked at the watch
again and fastened the raincoat. She moved the
garments one by one under the quilt and lay
down and drew the quilt to her chin. The voices
had got quiet for a moment and in the silence
Tommy could hear a faint, steady chatter of the
shucks inside the mattress where Temple lay,
her hands crossed on her breast and her legs
straight and close and decorous, like an effigy on
an ancient tomb.

The voices were still; he had completely forgot them until he heard Goodwin say "Stop it.
Stop that!" A chair crashed over; he heard
Goodwin's light thudding feet; the chair clattered along the porch as though it had been
kicked aside, and crouching, his elbows out a
little in squat, bear-like alertness, Tommy heard
dry, light sounds like billiard balls. "Tommy,"
Goodwin said.

When necessary he could move with that
thick, lightning-like celerity of badgers or coons.
He was around the house and on the porch in
time to see Gowan slam into the wall and slump
along it and plunge full length off the porch into
the weeds, and Popeye in the door, his head
thrust forward. "Grab him there!" Goodwin
said. Tommy sprang upon Popeye in a sidling
rush.

"I got—hah!" he said as Popeye slashed savagely at his face; "you would, would you? Hole up hyer."

Popeye ceased. "Jesus Christ. You let them sit around here all night, swilling that goddam stuff; I told you. Jesus Christ."

Goodwin and Van were a single shadow, locked and hushed and furious. "Let go!" Van shouted. "I'll kill . . ." Tommy sprang to them. They jammed Van against the wall and held him motionless.

"Got him?" Goodwin said.

"Yeuh. I got him. Hole up hyer. You done whupped him."

"By God, I'll—"

"Now, now; whut you want to kill him fer? You caint eat him, kin you? You want Mr. Popeye to start guttin us all with that ere artermatic?"

Then it was over, gone like a furious gust of black wind, leaving a peaceful vacuum in which they moved quietly about, lifting Gowan out of the weeds with low-spoken, amicable directions to one another. They carried him into the hall, where the woman stood, and to the door of the room where Temple was.

"She's locked it," Van said. He struck the door, high. "Open the door," he shouted. "We're bringing you a customer."

"Hush," Goodwin said. "There's no lock on it. Push it."

"Sure," Van said; "I'll push it." He kicked it. The chair buckled and sprang into the room. Van banged the door open and they entered, carrying Gowan's legs. Van kicked the chair across the room. Then he saw Temple standing in the corner behind the bed. His hair was broken about his face, long as a girl's. He flung it back with a toss of his head. His chin was bloody and he deliberately spat blood onto the floor.

"Go on," Goodwin said, carrying Gowan's shoulders, "put him on the bed." They swung Gowan onto the bed. His bloody head lolled over the edge. Van jerked him over and slammed him into the mattress. He groaned, lifting his hand. Van struck him across the face with his palm.

"Lie still, you—"

"Let be," Goodwin said. He caught Van's hand. For an instant they glared at one another.

"I said, Let be," Goodwin said. "Get out of here."

"Got proteck . . ." Gowan muttered ". . . girl. 'Ginia gem . . . gemman got proteck . . ."

"Get out of here, now," Goodwin said.

The woman stood in the door beside Tommy, her back against the door frame. Beneath a cheap coat her nightdress dropped to her feet.

86

Van lifted Temple's dress from the bed. "Van," Goodwin said. "I said get out."

"I heard you," Van said. He shook the dress out. Then he looked at Temple in the corner, her arms crossed, her hands clutching her shoulders. Goodwin moved toward Van. He dropped the dress and went around the bed. Popeye came in the door, a cigarette in his fingers. Beside the woman Tommy drew his breath hissing through his ragged teeth.

He saw Van take hold of the raincoat upon Temple's breast and rip it open. Then Goodwin sprang between them; he saw Van duck, whirling, and Temple fumbling at the torn raincoat. Van and Goodwin were now in the middle of the floor, swinging at one another, then he was watching Popeye walking toward Temple. With the corner of his eye he saw Van lying on the floor and Goodwin standing over him, stooped a little, watching Popeye's back.

"Popeye," Goodwin said. Popeye went on, the cigarette trailing back over his shoulder, his head turned a little as though he were not looking where he was going, the cigarette slanted as though his mouth were somewhere under the turn of his jaw. "Dont touch her," Goodwin said.

Popeye stopped before Temple, his face turned a little aside. His right hand lay in his coat pocket. Beneath the raincoat on Temple's breast Tommy could see the movement of the other hand, communicating a shadow of movement to the coat.

"Take your hand away," Goodwin said. "Move it."

Popeye moved his hand. He turned, his hands in his coat pockets, looking at Goodwin. He crossed the room, watching Goodwin. Then he turned his back on him and went out the door.

"Here, Tommy," Goodwin said quietly, "grab hold of this." They lifted Van and carried him out. The woman stepped aside. She leaned against the wall, holding her coat together. Across the room Temple stood crouched into the corner, fumbling at the torn raincoat. Gowan began to snore.

Goodwin returned. "You'd better go back to bed," he said. The woman didn't move. He put his hand on her shoulder. "Ruby."

"While you finish the trick Van started and you wouldn't let him finish? You poor fool. You poor fool."

"Come on, now," he said, his hand on her shoulder. "Go back to bed."

"But dont come back. Dont bother to come back. I wont be there. You owe me nothing. Dont think you do."

Goodwin took her wrists and drew them

88

steadily apart. Slowly and steadily he carried her hands around behind her and held them in one of his. With the other hand he opened the coat. The nightdress was of faded pink crepe, lace-trimmed, laundered and laundered until, like the garment on the wire, the lace was a fibrous mass.

"Hah," he said. "Dressed for company."

"Whose fault is it if this is the only one I have? Whose fault is it? Not mine. I've given them away to nigger maids after one night. But do you think any nigger would take this and not laugh in my face?"

He let the coat fall to. He released her hands and she drew the coat together. With his hand on her shoulder he began to push her toward the door. "Go on," he said. Her shoulder gave. It alone moved, her body turning on her hips, her face reverted, watching him. "Go on," he said. But her torso alone turned, her hips and head still touching the wall. He turned and crossed the room and went swiftly around the bed and caught Temple by the front of the raincoat with one hand. He began to shake her. Holding her up by the gathered wad of coat he shook her, her small body clattering soundlessly inside the loose garment, her shoulders and thighs thumping against the wall. "You little fool!" he said. "You little fool!" Her eyes were quite wide, almost black, the lamplight on her face and two tiny reflections of his face in her pupils like peas in two inkwells.

He released her. She began to sink to the floor, the raincoat rustling about her. He caught her up and began to shake her again, looking over his shoulder at the woman. "Get the lamp," he said. The woman did not move. Her head was bent a little; she appeared to muse upon them. Goodwin swept his other arm under Temple's knees. She felt herself swooping, then she was lying on the bed beside Gowan, on her back, jouncing to the dying chatter of the shucks. She watched him cross the room and lift the lamp from the mantel. The woman had turned her head, following him also, her face sharpening out of the approaching lamp in profile. "Go on," he said. She turned, her face turning into shadow, the lamp now on her back and on his hand on her shoulder. His shadow blotted the room completely; his arm in silhouette back-reaching, drew to the door. Gowan snored, each respiration choking to a huddle fall, as though he would never breathe again.

Tommy was outside the door, in the hall.

"They gone down to the truck yet?" Goodwin said.

"Not yit," Tommy said.

"Better go and see about it," Goodwin said.

90

They went on. Tommy watched them enter another door. Then he went to the kitchen, silent on his bare feet, his neck craned a little with listening. In the kitchen Popeye sat, straddling a chair, smoking. Van stood at the table, before a fragment of mirror, combing his hair with a pocket comb. Upon the table lay a damp, blood-stained cloth and a burning cigarette. Tommy squatted outside the door, in the darkness.

He was there when Goodwin came out with the raincoat. Goodwin entered the kitchen without seeing him. "Where's Tommy?" he said. Tommy heard Popeye say something, then Goodwin emerged with Van following him, the raincoat on his arm now. "Come on, now," Goodwin said. "Let's get that stuff out of here."

Tommy's pale eye began to glow faintly, like those of a cat. The woman could see them in the darkness when he crept into the room after Popeye, and while Popeye stood over the bed where Temple lay. They glowed suddenly out of the darkness at her, then they went away and she could hear him breathing beside her; again they glowed up at her with a quality furious and questioning and sad and went away again and he crept behind Popeye from the room.

He saw Popeye return to the kitchen, but he did not follow at once. He stopped at the hall door and squatted there. His body began to writhe again in shocked indecision, his bare feet whispering on the floor with a faint, rocking movement as he swayed from side to side, his hands wringing slowly against his flanks. And Lee too, he said, And Lee too. Durn them fellers. Durn them fellers. Twice he stole along the porch until he could see the shadow of Popeye's hat on the kitchen floor, then returned to the hall and the door beyond which Temple lay and where Gowan snored. The third time he smelled Popeye's cigarette. Ef he'll jest keep that up, he said. And Lee too, he said, rocking from side to side in a dull, excruciating agony, And Lee too.

When Goodwin came up the slope and onto the back porch Tommy was squatting just outside the door again. "What in hell . . ." Goodwin said. "Why didn't you come on? I've been looking for you for ten minutes." He glared at Tommy, then he looked into the kitchen. "You ready?" he said. Popeye came to the door. Goodwin looked at Tommy again. "What have you been doing?"

Popeye looked at Tommy. Tommy stood now, rubbing his instep with the other foot, looking at Popeye.

"What're you doing here?" Popeye said.

"Aint doin nothin," Tommy said.

"Are you following me around?"

"I aint trailin nobody," Tommy said sullenly.

"Well, dont, then," Popeye said.

"Come on," Goodwin said. "Van's waiting." They went on. Tommy followed them. Once he looked back at the house, then he shambled on behind them. From time to time he would feel that acute surge go over him, like his blood was too hot all of a sudden, dying away into that warm unhappy feeling that fiddle music gave him. Durn them fellers, he whispered Durn them fellers.

IX

THE ROOM WAS DARK. THE WOMAN STOOD inside the door, against the wall, in the cheap coat, the lace-trimmed crepe nightgown, just inside the lockless door. She could hear Gowan snoring in the bed, and the other men moving about, on the porch and in the hall and in the kitchen, talking, their voices indistinguishable through the door. After a while they got quiet. Then she could hear nothing at all save Gowan as he choked and snored and moaned through his battered nose and face.

She heard the door open. The man came in, without trying to be silent. He entered, passing within a foot of her. She knew it was Goodwin before he spoke. He went to the bed. "I want the raincoat," he said. "Sit up and take it off.' The woman could hear the shucks in the mat tress as Temple sat up and Goodwin took the raincoat off of her. He returned across the floor and went out.

She stood just inside the door. She could tell all of them by the way they breathed. Then, without having heard, felt, the door open, she began to smell something: the brilliantine which Popeye used on his hair. She did not see Popeye at all when he entered and passed her; she did not know he had entered yet; she was waiting for him; until Tommy entered, following Popeye. Tommy crept into the room, also soundless; she would have been no more aware of his entrance than of Popeye's, if it hadn't been for his eyes. They glowed, breast-high, with a profound interrogation, then they disappeared and the woman could then feel him, squatting beside her; she knew that he too was looking toward the bed over which Popeye stood in the darkness, upon which Temple and Gowan lay, with Gowan snoring and choking and snoring. The woman stood just inside the door.

She could hear no sound from the shucks, so she remained motionless beside the door, with Tommy squatting beside her, his face toward the invisible bed. Then she smelled the brilliantine again. Or rather, she felt Tommy move from beside her, without a sound, as though the stealthy evacuation of his position blew soft and cold upon her in the black silence; without seeing or hearing him, she knew that he had crept again from the room, following Popeye.

She heard them go down the hall; the last sound died out of the house.

She went to the bed. Temple did not move until the woman touched her. Then she began to struggle. The woman found Temple's mouth and put her hand over it, though Temple had not attempted to scream. She lay on the shuck mattress, turning and thrashing her body from side to side, rolling her head, holding the coat together across her breast but making no sound.

"You fool!" the woman said in a thin, fierce whisper. "It's me. It's just me."

Temple ceased to roll her head, but she still thrashed from side to side beneath the woman's hand. "I'll tell my father!" she said. "I'll tell my father!"

The woman held her. "Get up," she said. Temple ceased to struggle. She lay still, rigid. The woman could hear her wild breathing. "Will you get up and walk quiet?" the woman said.

"Yes!" Temple said. "Will you get me out of here? Will you? Will you?"

"Yes," the woman said. "Get up." Temple got up, the shucks whispering. In the further darkness Gowan snored, savage and profound. At first Temple couldn't stand alone. The woman held her up. "Stop it," the woman said.

"You've got to stop it. You've got to be quiet."

"I want my clothes," Temple whispered. "I haven't got anything on but . . ."

"Do you want your clothes," the woman said, "or do you want to get out of here?"

"Yes," Temple said. "Anything. If you'll just get me out of here."

On their bare feet they moved like ghosts. They left the house and crossed the porch and went on toward the barn. When they were about fifty yards from the house the woman stopped and turned and jerked Temple up to her, and gripping her by the shoulders, their faces close together, she cursed Temple in a whisper, a sound no louder than a sigh and filled with fury. Then she flung her away and they went on. They entered the hallway. It was pitch dark. Temple heard the woman fumbling at the wall. A door creaked open; the woman took her arm and guided her up a single step into a floored room where she could feel walls and smell a faint, dusty odor of grain, and closed the door behind them. As she did so something rushed invisibly nearby in a scurrying scrabble, a dying whisper of fairy feet. Temple whirled, treading on something that rolled under her foot, and sprang toward the woman.

"It's just a rat," the woman said, but Temple hurled herself upon the other, flinging her arms about her, trying to snatch both feet from the floor.

"A rat?" she wailed, "a rat? Open the door! Quick!"

"Stop it! Stop it!" the woman hissed. She held Temple until she ceased. Then they knelt side by side against the wall. After a while the woman whispered: "There's some cottonseed-hulls over there. You can lie down." Temple didn't answer. She crouched against the woman, shaking slowly, and they squatted there in the black darkness, against the wall.

X

WHILE THE WOMAN WAS COOKING BREAK-
fast, the child still—or already—asleep in the
box behind the stove, she heard a blundering
sound approaching across the porch and stop
at the door. When she looked around she saw
the wild and battered and bloody apparition
which she recognised as Gowan. His face, beneath a two days' stubble, was marked, his lip
was cut. One eye was closed and the front of his
shirt and coat were blood-stained to the waist.
Through his swollen and stiffened lips he was
trying to say something. At first the woman could
not understand a word. "Go and bathe your
face," she said. "Wait. Come in here and sit
down. I'll get the basin."

He looked at her, trying to talk. "Oh," the
woman said. "She's all right. She's down there
in the crib, asleep." She had to repeat it three or
four times, patiently. "In the crib. Asleep. I

stayed with her until daylight. Go wash your face, now."

Gowan got a little calmer then. He began to talk about getting a car.

"The nearest one is at Tull's, two miles away," the woman said. "Wash your face and eat some breakfast."

Gowan entered the kitchen, talking about getting the car. "I'll get it and take her on back to school. One of the other girls will slip her in. It'll be all right then. Dont you think it'll be all right then?" He came to the table and took a cigarette from the pack and tried to light it with his shaking hands. He had trouble putting it into his mouth, and he could not light it at all until the woman came and held the match. But he took but one draw, then he stood, holding the cigarette in his hand, looking at it with his one good eye in a kind of dull amazement. He threw the cigarette away and turned toward the door, staggering and catching himself. "Go get car," he said.

"Get something to eat first," the woman said. "Maybe a cup of coffee will help you."

"Go get car," Gowan said. When he crossed the porch he paused long enough to splash some water upon his face, without helping his appearance much.

When he left the house he was still groggy

and he thought that he was still drunk. He could remember only vaguely what had happened. He had got Van and the wreck confused and he did not know that he had been knocked out twice. He only remembered that he had passed out some time early in the night, and he thought that he was still drunk. But when he reached the wrecked car and saw the path and followed it to the spring and drank of the cold water, he found that it was a drink he wanted, and he knelt there, bathing his face in the cold water and trying to examine his reflection in the broken surface, whispering Jesus Christ to himself in a kind of despair. He thought about returning to the house for a drink, then he thought of having to face Temple, the men; of Temple there among them.

When he reached the highroad the sun was well up, warm. I'll get cleaned up some, he said. And coming back with a car. I'll decide what to say to her on the way to town; thinking of Temple returning among people who knew him, who might know him. I passed out twice, he said. *I passed out twice.* Jesus Christ, Jesus Christ he whispered, his body writhing inside his disreputable and bloody clothes in an agony of rage and shame.

His head began to clear with air and motion, but as he began to feel better physically the blackness of the future increased. Town, the world, began to appear as a black cul-de-sac; a place in which he must walk forever more, his whole body cringing and flinching from whispering eyes when he had passed, and when in midmorning he reached the house he sought, the prospect of facing Temple again was more than he could bear. So he engaged the car and directed the man and paid him and went on. A little later a car going in the opposite direction stopped and picked him up.

XI

TEMPLE WAKED LYING IN A TIGHT BALL, with narrow bars of sunlight falling across her face like the tines of a golden fork, and while the stiffened blood trickled and tingled through her cramped muscles she lay gazing quietly up at the ceiling. Like the walls, it was of rough planks crudely laid, each plank separated from the next by a thin line of blackness; in the corner a square opening above a ladder gave into a gloomy loft shot with thin pencils of sun also. From nails in the walls broken bits of desiccated harness hung, and she lay plucking tentatively at the substance in which she lay. She gathered a handful of it and lifted her head, and saw within her fallen coat naked flesh between brassiere and knickers and knickers and stockings. Then she remembered the rat and scrambled up and sprang to the door, clawing at it, stil' clutching the fist full of cottonseed-hulls, hei

face puffed with the hard slumber of seventeen.

She had expected the door to be locked and
for a time she could not pull it open, her numb
hands scoring at the undressed planks until she
could hear her finger nails. It swung back and
she sprang out. At once she sprang back into
the crib and banged the door to. The blind
man was coming down the slope at a scuffling
trot, tapping ahead with the stick, the other
hand at his waist, clutching a wad of his trousers. He passed the crib with his braces dangling
about his hips, his gymnasium shoes scuffing in
the dry chaff of the hallway, and passed from
view, the stick rattling lightly along the rank
of empty stalls.

Temple crouched against the door, clutching
her coat about her. She could hear him back there
in one of the stalls. She opened the door and
peered out, at the house in the bright May sun-
shine, the sabbath peace, and she thought about
the girls and men leaving the dormitories in
their new Spring clothes, strolling along the
shaded streets toward the cool, unhurried sound
of bells. She lifted her foot and examined the
soiled sole of her stocking, brushing at it with
her palm, then at the other one.

The blind man's stick clattered again. She
jerked her head back and closed the door to a

crack and watched him pass, slower now, hunching his braces onto his shoulders. He mounted the slope and entered the house. Then she opened the door and stepped gingerly down.

She walked swiftly to the house, her stockinged feet flinching and cringing from the rough earth, watching the house. She mounted to the porch and entered the kitchen and stopped, listening into the silence. The stove was cold. Upon it the blackened coffee-pot sat, and a soiled skillet; upon the table soiled dishes were piled at random. I haven't eaten since . . . since . . . Yesterday was one day, she thought, but I didn't eat then. I haven't eaten since . . . and that night was the dance, and I didn't eat any supper. I haven't eaten since dinner Friday, she thought. And now it's Sunday, thinking about the bells in cool steeples against the blue, and pigeons crooning about the belfries like echoes of the organ's bass. She returned to the door and peered out. Then she emerged, clutching the coat about her.

She entered the house and sped up the hall. The sun lay now on the front porch and she ran with a craning motion of her head, watching the patch of sun framed in the door. It was empty. She reached the door to the right of the entrance and opened it and sprang into the room and shut the door and leaned her back against it. The bed was empty. A faded patch-work quilt was wadded across it. A khaki-covered canteen and one slipper lay on the bed. On the floor her dress and hat lay.

She picked up the dress and hat and tried to brush them with her hand and with the corner of her coat. Then she sought the other slipper, moving the quilt, stooping to look under the bed. At last she found it in the fireplace, in a litter of wood ashes between an iron fire-dog and an overturned stack of bricks, lying on its side, half full of ashes, as though it had been flung or kicked there. She emptied it and wiped it on her coat and laid it on the bed and took the canteen and hung it on a nail in the wall. It bore the letters U S and a blurred number in black stencil. Then she removed the coat and dressed.

Long legged, thin armed, with high small buttocks—a small childish figure no longer quite a child, not yet quite a woman—she moved swiftly, smoothing her stockings and writhing into her scant, narrow dress. Now I can stand anything, she thought quietly, with a kind of dull, spent astonishment; I can stand just anything. From the top of one stocking she removed a watch on a broken black ribbon. Nine oclock. With her fingers she combed her matted curls, combing out three or four cotton-seed-hulls. She took up the coat and hat and listened again at the door.

She returned to the back porch. In the basin was a residue of dirty water. She rinsed it and filled it and bathed her face. A soiled towel hung from a nail. She used it gingerly, then she took a compact from her coat and was using it when she found the woman watching her in the kitchen door.

"Good morning," Temple said. The woman held the child on her hip. It was asleep. "Hello, baby," Temple said, stooping; "you wan s'eep all day? Look at Temple." They entered the kitchen. The woman poured coffee into a cup.

"It's cold, I expect," she said. "Unless you want to make up the fire." From the oven she took a pan of bread.

"No," Temple said, sipping the lukewarm coffee, feeling her insides move in small, tickling clots, like loose shot. "I'm not hungry. I haven't eaten in two days, but I'm not hungry. Isn't that funny? I haven't eaten in . . ." She looked at the woman's back with a fixed placative grimace. "You haven't got a bathroom, have you?"

"What?" the woman said. She looked at Temple across her shoulder while Temple stared at her with that grimace of cringing and placative assurance. From a shelf the woman took a mail-order catalogue and tore out a few leaves and handed them to Temple. "You'll have to go to the barn, like we do."

"Will I?" Temple said, holding the paper. "The barn."

"They're all gone," the woman said. "They wont be back this morning."

"Yes," Temple said. "The barn."

"Yes; the barn," the woman said. "Unless you're too pure to have to."

"Yes," Temple said. She looked out the door, across the weed-chocked clearing. Between the sombre spacing of the cedars the orchard lay bright in the sunlight. She donned the coat and hat and went toward the barn, the torn leaves in her hand, splotched over with small cuts of clothes-pins and patent wringers and washing-powder, and entered the hallway. She stopped, folding and folding the sheets, then she went on, with swift, cringing glances at the empty stalls. She walked right through the barn. It was open at the back, upon a mass of jimson weed in savage white-and-lavender bloom. She walked on into the sunlight again, into the weeds. Then she began to run, snatching her feet up almost before they touched the earth, the weeds slashing at her with huge, moist, malodorous blossoms. She stooped and

108

twisted through a fence of sagging rusty wire and ran downhill among trees.

At the bottom of the hill a narrow scar of sand divided the two slopes of a small valley, winding in a series of dazzling splotches where the sun found it. Temple stood in the sand, listening to the birds among the sunshot leaves, listening, looking about. She followed the dry runlet to where a jutting shoulder formed a nook matted with briers. Among the new green last year's dead leaves from the branches overhead clung, not yet fallen to earth. She stood here for a while, folding and folding the sheets in her fingers, in a kind of despair. When she rose she saw, upon the glittering mass of leaves along the crest of the ditch, the squatting outline of a man.

For an instant she stood and watched herself run out of her body, out of one slipper. She watched her legs twinkle against the sand, through the flecks of sunlight, for several yards, then whirl and run back and snatch up the slipper and whirl and run again.

When she caught a glimpse of the house she was opposite the front porch. The blind man sat in a chair, his face lifted into the sun. At the edge of the woods she stopped and put on the slipper. She crossed the ruined lawn and sprang onto the porch and ran down the hall.

When she reached the back porch she saw a man in the door of the barn, looking toward the house. She crossed the porch in two strides and entered the kitchen, where the woman sat at the table, smoking, the child on her lap.

"He was watching me!" Temple said. "He was watching me all the time!" She leaned beside the door, peering out, then she came to the woman, her face small and pale, her eyes like holes burned with a cigar, and laid her hand on the cold stove.

"Who was?" the woman said.

"Yes," Temple said. "He was there in the bushes, watching me all the time." She looked toward the door, then back at the woman, and saw her hand lying on the stove. She snatched it up with a wailing shriek, clapping it against her mouth, and turned and ran toward the door. The woman caught her arm, still carrying the child on the other, and Temple sprang back into the kitchen. Goodwin was coming toward the house. He looked once at them and went on into the hall.

Temple began to struggle. "Let go," she whispered, "let go! Let go!" She surged and plunged, grinding the woman's hand against the door jamb until she was free. She sprang from the porch and ran toward the barn and into the hallway and climbed the ladder and scrambled through the trap and to her feet again, running toward the pile of rotting hay.

Then suddenly she ran upside down in a rushing interval; she could see her legs still running in space, and she struck lightly and solidly on her back and lay still, staring up at an oblong yawn that closed with a clattering vibration of loose planks. Faint dust sifted down across the bars of sunlight.

Her hand moved in the substance in which she lay, then she remembered the rat a second time. Her whole body surged in an involuted spurning movement that brought her to her feet in the loose hulls, so that she flung her hands out and caught herself upright, a hand on either angle of the corner, her face not twelve inches from the cross beam on which the rat crouched. For an instant they stared eye to eye, then its eyes glowed suddenly like two tiny electric bulbs and it leaped at her head just as she sprang backward, treading again on something that rolled under her foot.

She fell toward the opposite corner, on her face in the hulls and a few scattered corn-cobs gnawed bone-clean. Something thudded against the wall and struck her hand in ricochet. The rat was in that corner now, on the floor. Again their faces were not twelve inches apart, the rat's eyes glowing and fading as though worked by lungs. Then it stood erect, its back to the corner, its forepaws curled against its chest, and began to squeak at her in tiny plaintive gasps. She backed away on hands and knees, watching it. Then she got to her feet and sprang at the door, hammering at it, watching the rat over her shoulder, her body arched against the door, rasping at the planks with her bare hands.

XII

THE WOMAN STOOD IN THE KITCHEN DOOR, holding the child, until Goodwin emerged from the house. The lobes of his nostrils were quite white against his brown face, and she said: "God, are you drunk too?" He came along the porch. "She's not here," the woman said. "You cant find her." He brushed past her, trailing a reek of whisky. She turned, watching him. He looked swiftly about the kitchen, then he turned and looked at her standing in the door, blocking it. "You wont find her," she said. "She's gone." He came toward her, lifting his hand. "Dont put your hand on me," she said. He gripped her arm, slowly. His eyes were a little bloodshot. The lobes of his nostrils looked like wax.

"Take your hand off me," she said. "Take it off." Slowly he drew her out of the door. She began to curse him. "Do you think you can?

Do you think I'll let you? Or any other little slut?" Motionless, facing one another like the first position of a dance, they stood in a mounting terrific muscular hiatus.

With scarce any movement at all he flung her aside in a complete revolution that fetched her up against the table, her arm flung back for balance, her body bent and her hand fumbling behind her among the soiled dishes, watching him across the inert body of the child. He walked toward her. "Stand back," she said, lifting her hand slightly, bringing the butcher knife into view. "Stand back." He came steadily toward her, then she struck at him with the knife.

He caught her wrist. She began to struggle. He plucked the child from her and laid it on the table and caught her other hand as it flicked at his face, and holding both wrists in one hand, he slapped her. It made a dry, flat sound. He slapped her again, first on one cheek, then the other, rocking her head from side to side. "That's what I do to them," he said, slapping her. "See?" He released her. She stumbled backward against the table and caught up the child and half crouched between the table and the wall, watching him as he turned and left the room.

She knelt in the corner, holding the child. It had not stirred. She laid her palm first on one cheek, then on the other. She rose and laid the child in the box and took a sunbonnet from a nail and put it on. From another nail she took a coat trimmed with what had once been white fur, and took up the child and left the room.

Tommy was standing in the barn, beside the crib, looking toward the house. The old man sat on the front porch, in the sun. She went down the steps and followed the path to the road and went on without looking back. When she came to the tree and the wrecked car she turned from the road, into a path. After a hundred yards or so she reached the spring and sat down beside it, the child on her lap and the hem of her skirt turned back over its sleeping face.

Popeye came out of the bushes, walking gingerly in his muddy shoes, and stood looking down at her across the spring. His hand flicked to his coat and he fretted and twisted a cigarette and put it into his mouth and snapped a match with his thumb. "Jesus Christ," he said, "I told him about letting them sit around all night, swilling that goddam stuff. There ought to be a law." He looked away in the direction in which the house lay. Then he looked at the woman, at the top of her sunbonnet. "Goofy house," he said. "That's what it is. It's not four days ago I find a bastard squatting here, asking me if I read books. Like he would jump me with a book or something. Take me for a ride with the telephone directory." Again he looked off toward the house, jerking his neck forth as if his collar were too tight. He looked down at the top of the sunbonnet. "I'm going to town, see?" he said. "I'm clearing out. I've got enough of this." She did not look up. She adjusted the hem of the skirt above the child's face. Popeye went on, with light, finicking sounds in the underbrush. Then they ceased. Somewhere in the swamp a bird sang.

Before he reached the house Popeye left the road and followed a wooded slope. When he emerged he saw Goodwin standing behind a tree in the orchard, looking toward the barn. Popeye stopped at the edge of the wood and looked at Goodwin's back. He put another cigarette into his mouth and thrust his fingers into his vest. He went on across the orchard, walking gingerly. Goodwin heard him and looked over his shoulder. Popeye took a match from his vest, flicked it into flame and lit the cigarette. Goodwin looked toward the barn again and Popeye stood at his shoulder, looking toward the barn.

"Who's down there?" he said. Goodwin said nothing. Popeye jetted smoke from his nostrils.

"I'm clearing out," he said. Goodwin said nothing, watching the barn. "I said, I'm getting out of here," Popeye said. Without turning his head Goodwin cursed him. Popeye smoked quietly, the cigarette wreathing across his still, soft, black gaze. Then he turned and went toward the house. The old man sat in the sun. Popeye did not enter the house. Instead he went on across the lawn and into the cedars until he was hidden from the house. Then he turned and crossed the garden and the weed-choked lot and entered the barn from the rear.

Tommy squatted on his heels beside the crib door, looking toward the house. Popeye looked at him a while, smoking. Then he snapped the cigarette away and entered a stall quietly. Above the manger was a wooden rack for hay, just under an opening in the loft floor. Popeye climbed into the rack and drew himself silently into the loft, his tight coat strained into thin ridges across his narrow shoulders and back.

XIII

TOMMY WAS STANDING IN THE HALLWAY OF the barn when Temple at last got the door of the crib open. When she recognised him she was half spun, leaping back, then she whirled and ran toward him and sprang down, clutching his arm. Then she saw Goodwin standing in the back door of the house and she whirled and leaped back into the crib and leaned her head around the door, her voice making a thin eeeeeeeeeeeeee sound like bubbles in a bottle. She leaned there, scrabbling her hands on the door, trying to pull it to, hearing Tommy's voice.

". . . Lee says hit wont hurt you none. All you got to do is lay down . . ." It was a dry sort of sound, not in her consciousness at all, nor his pale eyes beneath the shaggy thatch. She leaned in the door, wailing, trying to shut it. Then she felt his hand clumsily on her thigh. ". . . says hit wont hurt you none. All you got to do is . . ."

118

She looked at him, his diffident, hard hand on her hip. "Yes," she said, "all right. Dont you let him in here."

"You mean fer me not to let none of them in hyer?"

"All right. I'm not scared of rats. You stay there and dont let him in."

"All right. I'll fix hit so caint nobody git to you. I'll be right hyer."

"All right. Shut the door. Dont let him in here."

"All right." He shut the door. She leaned in it, looking toward the house. He pushed her back so he could close the door. "Hit aint goin to hurt you none, Lee says. All you got to do is lay down."

"All right. I will. Dont you let him in here." The door closed. She heard him drive the hasp to. Then he shook the door.

"Hit's fastened," he said. "Caint nobody git to you now. I'll be right hyer."

He squatted on his heels in the chaff, looking at the house. After a while he saw Goodwin come to the back door and look toward him, and squatting, clasping his knees, Tommy's eyes glowed again, the pale irises appearing for an instant to spin on the pupils like tiny wheels. He squatted there, his lip lifted a little, until Goodwin went back into the house. Then he sighed, expelling his breath, and he looked at the blank door of the crib and again his eyes glowed with a diffident, groping, hungry fire and he began to rub his hands slowly on his shanks, rocking a little from side to side. Then he ceased, became rigid, and watched Goodwin move swiftly across the corner of the house and into the cedars. He squatted rigid, his lip lifted a little upon his ragged teeth.

Sitting in the cottonseed-hulls, in the litter of gnawed corn-cobs, Temple lifted her head suddenly toward the trap at the top of the ladder. She heard Popeye cross the floor of the loft, then his foot appeared, groping gingerly for the step. He descended, watching her over his shoulder.

She sat quite motionless, her mouth open a little. He stood looking at her. He began to thrust his chin out in a series of jerks, as though his collar were too tight. He lifted his elbows and brushed them with his palm, and the skirt of his coat, then he crossed her field of vision, moving without a sound, his hand in his coat pocket. He tried the door. Then he shook it.

"Open the door," he said.

There was no sound. Then Tommy whispered: "Who's that?"

"Open the door," Popeye said. The door opened. Tommy looked at Popeye. He blinked.

"I didn't know you was in hyer," he said. He made to look past Popeye, into the crib. Popeye laid his hand flat on Tommy's face and thrust him back and leaned past him and looked up at the house. Then he looked at Tommy.

"Didn't I tell you about following me?"

"I wasn't following you," Tommy said. "I was watching him," jerking his head toward the house.

"Watch him, then," Popeye said. Tommy turned his head and looked toward the house and Popeye drew his hand from his coat pocket.

To Temple, sitting in the cottonseed-hulls and the corn-cobs, the sound was no louder than the striking of a match: a short, minor sound shutting down upon the scene, the instant, with a profound finality, completely isolating it, and she sat there, her legs straight before her, her hands limp and palm-up on her lap, looking at Popeye's tight back and the ridges of his coat across the shoulders as he leaned out the door, the pistol behind him, against his flank, wisping thinly along his leg.

He turned and looked at her. He waggled the pistol slightly and put it back in his coat, then he walked toward her. Moving, he made no sound at all; the released door yawned and clapped against the jamb, but it made no sound either; it was as though sound and silence had become inverted. She could hear silence in a thick rustling as he moved toward her through it, thrusting it aside, and she began to say Something is going to happen to me. She was saying it to the old man with the yellow clots for eyes. "Something is happening to me!" she screamed at him, sitting in his chair in the sunlight, his hands crossed on the top of the stick. "I told you it was!" she screamed, voiding the words like hot silent bubbles into the bright silence about them until he turned his head and the two phlegm-clots above her where she lay tossing and thrashing on the rough, sunny boards. "I told you! I told you all the time!"

XIV

WHILE SHE WAS SITTING BESIDE THE SPRING, with the sleeping child upon her knees, the woman discovered that she had forgot its bottle. She sat there for about an hour after Popeye left her. Then she returned to the road and turned back toward the house. When she was about halfway back to the house, carrying the child in her arms, Popeye's car passed her. She heard it coming and she got out of the road and stood there and watched it come dropping down the hill. Temple and Popeye were in it. Popeye did not make any sign, though Temple looked full at the woman. From beneath her hat Temple looked the woman full in the face, without any sign of recognition whatever. The face did not turn, the eyes did not wake; to the woman beside the road it was like a small, dead-colored mask drawn past her on a string and then away. The car went on, lurching and jolting in the ruts. The woman went on to the house.

The blind man was sitting on the front porch, in the sun. When she entered the hall, she was walking fast. She was not aware of the child's thin weight. She found Goodwin in their bedroom. He was in the act of putting on a frayed tie; looking at him, she saw that he had just shaved.

"Yes," she said. "What is it? What is it?"

"I've got to walk up to Tull's and telephone for the sheriff," he said.

"The sheriff," she said. "Yes. All right." She came to the bed and laid the child carefully down. "To Tull's," she said. "Yes. He's got a phone."

"You'll have to cook," Goodwin said. "There's Pap."

"You can give him some cold bread. He wont mind. There's some left in the stove. He wont mind."

"I'll go," Goodwin said. "You stay here."

"To Tull's," she said. "All right." Tull was the man at whose house Gowan had found a car. It was two miles away. Tull's family was at dinner. They asked her to stop. "I just want to use the telephone," she said. The telephone was in the dining-room, where they were eating. She called, with them sitting about the table. She didn't know the number. "The Sheriff," she said patiently into the mouthpiece. Then she got the sheriff, with Tull's family sitting about the table, about the Sunday dinner. "A dead man. You pass Mr Tull's about a mile and turn off to the right. . . . Yes, the Old Frenchman place. Yes. This is Mrs Goodwin talking . . . Good-vin. Yes."

XV

BENBOW REACHED HIS SISTER'S HOME IN THE middle of the afternoon. It was four miles from town, Jefferson. He and his sister were born in Jefferson, seven years apart, in a house which they still owned, though his sister had wanted to sell the house when Benbow married the divorced wife of a man named Mitchell and moved to Kinston. Benbow would not agree to sell, though he had built a new bungalow in Kinston on borrowed money upon which he was still paying interest.

When he arrived, there was no one about. He entered the house and he was sitting in the dim parlor behind the closed blinds, when he heard his sister come down the stairs, still unaware of his arrival. He made no sound. She had almost crossed the parlor door and vanished when she paused and looked full at him, without outward surprise, with that serene and

126

stupid impregnability of heroic statuary; she was in white. "Oh, Horace," she said.

He did not rise. He sat with something of the air of a guilty small boy. "How did you—" he said. "Did Belle—"

"Of course. She wired me Saturday. That you had left, and if you came here, to tell you that she had gone back home to Kentucky and had sent for Little Belle."

"Ah, damnation," Benbow said.

"Why?" his sister said. "You want to leave home yourself, but you dont want her to leave."

He stayed at his sister's two days. She had never been given to talking, living a life of serene vegetation like perpetual corn or wheat in a sheltered garden instead of a field, and during those two days she came and went about the house with an air of tranquil and faintly ludicrous tragic disapproval.

After supper they sat in Miss Jenny's room, where Narcissa would read the Memphis paper before taking the boy off to bed. When she went out of the room, Miss Jenny looked at Benbow.

"Go back home, Horace," she said.

"Not to Kinston," Benbow said. "I hadn't intended to stay here, anyway. It wasn't Narcissa I was running to. I haven't quit one woman to run to the skirts of another."

"If you keep on telling yourself that you may

believe it, someday," Miss Jenny said. "Then what'll you do?"

"You're right," Benbow said. "Then I'd have to stay at home."

His sister returned. She entered the room with a definite air. "Now for it," Benbow said. His sister had not spoken directly to him all day.

"What are you going to do, Horace?" she said. "You must have business of some sort there in Kinston that should be attended to."

"Even Horace must have," Miss Jenny said. "What I want to know is, why he left. Did you find a man under the bed, Horace?"

"No such luck," Benbow said. "It was Friday, and all of a sudden I knew that I could not go to the station and get that box of shrimp and—"

"But you have been doing that for ten years," his sister said.

"I know. That's how I know that I will never learn to like smelling shrimp."

"Was that why you left Belle?" Miss Jenny said. She looked at him. "It took you a long time to learn that, if a woman dont make a very good wife for one man, she aint likely to for another, didn't it?"

"But to walk out just like a nigger," Narcissa said. "And to mix yourself up with moonshiners and street-walkers."

"Well, he's gone and left the street-walker

too," Miss Jenny said. "Unless you're going to walk the streets with that orange-stick in your pocket until she comes to town."

"Yes," Benbow said. He told again about the three of them, himself and Goodwin and Tommy sitting on the porch, drinking from the jug and talking, and Popeye lurking about the house, coming out from time to time to ask Tommy to light a lantern and go down to the barn with him and Tommy wouldn't do it and Popeye would curse him, and Tommy sitting on the floor, scouring his bare feet on the boards with a faint, hissing noise, chortling: "Aint he a sight, now?"

"You could feel the pistol on him just like you knew he had a navel," Benbow said. "He wouldn't drink, because he said it made him sick to his stomach like a dog; he wouldn't stay and talk with us; he wouldn't do anything: just lurking about, smoking his cigarettes, like a sullen and sick child.

"Goodwin and I were both talking. He had been a cavalry sergeant in the Philippines and on the Border, and in an infantry regiment in France; he never told me why he changed, trans ferred to infantry and lost his rank. He might have killed someone, might have deserted. He was talking about Manila and Mexican girls, and that halfwit chortling and glugging at the jug and shoving it at me: 'Take some mo'; and then I knew that the woman was just behind the door, listening to us. They are not married. I know that just like I know that that little black man had that flat little pistol in his coat pocket. But she's out there, doing a nigger's work, that's owned diamonds and automobiles too in her day, and bought them with a harder currency than cash. And that blind man, that old man sitting there at the table, waiting for somebody to feed him, with that immobility of blind people, like it was the backs of their eyeballs you looked at while they were hearing music you couldn't hear; that Goodwin led out of the room and completely off the earth, as far as I know. I never saw him again. I never knew who he was, who he was kin to. Maybe not to anybody. Maybe that old Frenchman that built the house a hundred years ago didn't want him either and just left him there when he died or moved away."

The next morning Benbow got the key to the house from his sister, and went into town. The house was on a side street, unoccupied now for ten years. He opened the house, drawing the nails from the windows. The furniture had not been moved. In a pair of new overalls, with mops and pails, he scoured the floors. At noon he went down town and bought bedding and

130

some tinned food. He was still at work at six oclock when his sister drove up in her car.

"Come on home, Horace," she said. "Dont you see you cant do this?"

"I found that out right after I started," Benbow said. "Until this morning I thought that anybody with one arm and a pail of water could wash a floor."

"Horace," she said.

"I'm the older, remember," he said. "I'm going to stay here. I have some covers." He went to the hotel for supper. When he returned, his sister's car was again in the drive. The negro driver had brought a bundle of bedclothing.

"Miss Narcissa say for you to use them," the negro said. Benbow put the bundle into a closet and made a bed with the ones which he had bought.

Next day at noon, eating his cold food at the kitchen table, he saw through the window a wagon stop in the street. Three women got down and standing on the curb they made unabashed toilets, smoothing skirts and stockings, brushing one another's back, opening parcels and donning various finery. The wagon had gone on. They followed, on foot, and he remembered that it was Saturday. He removed the overalls and dressed and left the house.

The street opened into a broader one. To

131

the left it went on to the square, the opening between two buildings black with a slow, continuous throng, like two streams of ants, above which the cupola of the courthouse rose from a clump of oaks and locusts covered with ragged snow. He went on toward the square. Empty wagons still passed him and he passed still more women on foot, black and white, unmistakable by the unease of their garments as well as by their method of walking, believing that town dwellers would take them for town dwellers too, not even fooling one another.

The adjacent alleys were choked with tethered wagons, the teams reversed and nuzzling gnawed corn-ears over the tail-boards. The square was lined two-deep with ranked cars, while the owners of them and of the wagons thronged in slow overalls and khaki, in mail-order scarves and parasols, in and out of the stores, soiling the pavement with fruit- and peanut-hulls. Slow as sheep they moved, tranquil, impassable, filling the passages, contemplating the fretful hurrying of those in urban shirts and collars with the large, mild inscrutability of cattle or of gods, functioning outside of time, having left time lying upon the slow and imponderable land green with corn and cotton in the yellow afternoon.

Horace moved among them, swept here and

132

there by the deliberate current, without impatience. Some of them he knew; most of the merchants and professional men remembered him as a boy, a youth, a brother lawyer—beyond a foamy screen of locust branches he could see the dingy second-story windows where he and his father had practised, the glass still innocent of water and soap as then—and he stopped now and then and talked with them in unhurried backwaters.

The sunny air was filled with competitive radios and phonographs in the doors of drug- and music-stores. Before these doors a throng stood all day, listening. The pieces which moved them were ballads simple in melody and theme, of bereavement and retribution and repentance metallically sung, blurred, emphasised by stactic or needle—disembodied voices blaring from imitation wood cabinets or pebble-grain horn-mouths above the rapt faces, the gnarled slow hands long shaped to the imperious earth, lugubrious, harsh, and sad.

That was Saturday, in May: no time to leave the land. Yet on Monday they were back again, most of them, in clumps about the courthouse and the square, and trading a little in the stores since they were here, in their khaki and overalls and collarless shirts. All day long a knot of them stood about the door to the undertaker's parlor, and boys and youths with and without schoolbooks leaned with flattened noses against the glass, and the bolder ones and the younger men of the town entered in twos and threes to look at the man called Tommy. He lay on a wooden table, barefoot, in overalls, the sun-bleached curls on the back of his head matted with dried blood and singed with powder, while the coroner sat over him, trying to ascertain his last name. But none knew it, not even those who had known him for fifteen years about the countryside, nor the merchants who on infrequent Saturdays had seen him in town, barefoot, hatless, with his rapt, empty gaze and his cheek bulged innocently by a peppermint jawbreaker. For all general knowledge, he had none.

XVI

On the day when the sheriff brought
Goodwin to town, there was a negro murderer
in the jail, who had killed his wife; slashed her
throat with a razor so that, her whole head
tossing further and further backward from the
bloody regurgitation of her bubbling throat, she
ran out the cabin door and for six or seven steps
up the quiet moonlit lane. He would lean in the
window in the evening and sing. After supper a
few negroes gathered along the fence below—
natty, shoddy suits and sweat-stained overalls
shoulder to shoulder—and in chorus with the
murderer, they sang spirituals while white people slowed and stopped in the leafed darkness
that was almost summer, to listen to those who
were sure to die and him who was already dead
singing about heaven and being tired; or perhaps in the interval between songs a rich, sourceless voice coming out of the high darkness where

135

the ragged shadow of the heaven-tree which snooded the street lamp at the corner fretted and mourned: "Fo days mo! Den dey ghy stroy de bes ba'ytone singer in nawth Mississippi!"

Sometimes during the day he would lean there, singing alone then, though after a while one or two ragamuffin boys or negroes with delivery baskets like as not, would halt at the fence, and the white men sitting in tilted chairs along the oil-foul wall of the garage across the street would listen above their steady jaws. "One day mo! Den Ise a gawn po sonnen bitch. Say, Aint no place fer you in heavum! Say, Aint no place fer you in hell! Say, Aint no place fer you in jail!"

"Damn that fellow," Goodwin said, jerking up his black head, his gaunt, brown, faintly harried face. "I aint in any position to wish any man that sort of luck, but I'll be damned. . . ." He wouldn't talk. "I didn't do it. You know that, yourself. You know I wouldn't have. I aint going say what I think. I didn't do it. They've got to hang it on me first. Let them do that. I'm clear. But if I talk, if I say what I think or believe, I wont be clear." He was sitting on the cot in his cell. He looked up at the windows: two orifices not much larger than sabre slashes.

"Is he that good a shot?" Benbow said. "To hit a man through one of those windows?"

Goodwin looked at him. "Who?"

"Popeye," Benbow said.

"Did Popeye do it?" Goodwin said.

"Didn't he?" Benbow said.

"I've told all I'm going to tell. I dont have to clear myself; it's up to them to hang it on me."

"Then what do you want with a lawyer?" Benbow said. "What do you want me to do?"

Goodwin was not looking at him. "If you'll just promise to get the kid a good newspaper grift when he's big enough to make change," he said. "Ruby'll be all right. Wont you, old gal?" He put his hand on the woman's head, scouring her hair with his hand. She sat on the cot beside him, holding the child on her lap. It lay in a sort of drugged immobility, like the children which beggars on Paris streets carry, its pinched face slick with faint moisture, its hair a damp whisper of shadow across its gaunt, veined skull, a thin crescent of white showing beneath its lead-colored eyelids.

The woman wore a dress of gray crepe, neatly brushed and skilfully darned by hand. Parallel with each seam was that faint, narrow, glazed imprint which another woman would recognise at a hundred yards with one glance. On the shoulder was a purple ornament of the sort that may be bought in ten cent stores or by mail order; on the cot beside her lay a gray hat

137

with a neatly darned veil; looking at it, Benbow could not remember when he had seen one before, when women ceased to wear veils.

He took the woman to his house. They walked, she carrying the child while Benbow carried a bottle of milk and a few groceries, food in tin cans. The child still slept. "Maybe you hold it too much," he said. "Suppose we get a nurse for it."

He left her at the house and returned to town, to a telephone, and he telephoned out to his sister's, for the car. The car came for him. He told his sister and Miss Jenny about the case over the supper table.

"You're just meddling!" his sister said, her serene face, her voice, furious. "When you took another man's wife and child away from him I thought it was dreadful, but I said At least he will not have the face to ever come back here again. And when you just walked out of the house like a nigger and left her I thought that was dreadful too, but I would not let myself believe you meant to leave her for good. And then when you insisted without any reason at all on leaving here and opening the house, scrubbing it yourself and all the town looking on and living there like a tramp, refusing to stay here where everybody would expect you to stay and think it funny when you wouldn't; and now to de-

liberately mix yourself up with a woman you
said yourself was a street-walker, a murderer's
woman."

"I cant help it. She has nothing, no one. In a
made-over dress all neatly about five years out
of mode, and that child that never has been more
than half alive, wrapped in a piece of blanket
scrubbed almost cotton-white. Asking nothing
of anyone except to be let alone, trying to make
something out of her life when all you sheltered
chaste women—"

"Do you mean to say a moonshiner hasn't got
the money to hire the best lawyer in the country?" Miss Jenny said.

"It's not that," Horace said. "I'm sure he
could get a better lawyer. It's that—"

"Horace," his sister said. She had been watching him. "Where is that woman?" Miss Jenny
was watching him too, sitting a little forward in
the wheel chair. "Did you take that woman into
my house?"

"It's my house too, honey." She did not know
that for ten years he had been lying to his wife
in order to pay interest on a mortgage on the
stucco house he had built for her in Kinston,
so that his sister might not rent to strangers
that other house in Jefferson which his wife did
not know he still owned any share in. "As long
as it's vacant, and with that child—"

139

"The house where my father and mother and your father and mother, the house where I— I wont have it. I wont have it."

"Just for one night, then. I'll take her to the hotel in the morning. Think of her, alone, with that baby. . . . Suppose it were you and Bory, and your husband accused of a murder you knew he didn't—"

"I dont want to think about her. I wish I had never heard of the whole thing. To think that my brother— Dont you see that you are always having to clean up after yourself? It's not that there's a litter left; it's that you—that— But to bring a street-walker, a murderess, into the house where I was born."

"Fiddlesticks," Miss Jenny said. "But, Horace, aint that what the lawyers call collusion? connivance?" Horace looked at her. "It seems to me you've already had a little more to do with these folks than the lawyer in the case should have. You were out there where it happened yourself not long ago. Folks might begin to think you know more than you've told."

"That's so," Horace said, "Mrs. Blackstone. And sometimes I have wondered why I haven't got rich at the law. Maybe I will, when I get old enough to attend the same law school you did."

"If I were you," Miss Jenny said, "I'd drive

back to town now and take her to the hotel and get her settled. It's not late."

"And go on back to Kinston until the whole thing is over," Narcissa said. "These people are not your people. Why must you do such things?"

"I cannot stand idly by and see injustice—"

"You wont ever catch up with injustice, Horace," Miss Jenny said.

"Well, that irony which lurks in events, then."

"Hmmph," Miss Jenny said. "It must be because she is one woman you know that dont know anything about that shrimp."

"Anyway, I've talked too much, as usual," Horace said. "So I'll have to trust you all—"

"Fiddlesticks," Miss Jenny said. "Do you think Narcissa'd want anybody to know that any of her folks could know people that would do anything as natural as make love or rob or steal?" There was that quality about his sister During all the four days between Kinston and Jefferson he had counted on that imperviousness. He hadn't expected her—any woman— to bother very much over a man she had neither married nor borne when she had one she did bear to cherish and fret over. But he had expected that imperviousness, since she had had it thirty-six years.

When he reached the house in town a light

burned in one room. He entered, crossing floors which he had scrubbed himself, revealing at the time no more skill with a mop than he had expected, than he had with the lost hammer with which he nailed the windows down and the shutters to ten years ago, who could not even learn to drive a motor car. But that was ten years ago, the hammer replaced by the new one with which he had drawn the clumsy nails, the windows open upon scrubbed floor spaces still as dead pools within the ghostly embrace of hooded furniture.

The woman was still up, dressed save for the hat. It lay on the bed where the child slept. Lying together there, they lent to the room a quality of transience more unmistakable than the makeshift light, the smug paradox of the made bed in a room otherwise redolent of long unoccupation. It was as though femininity were a current running through a wire along which a certain number of identical bulbs were hung.

"I've got some things in the kitchen," she said. "I wont be but a minute."

The child lay on the bed, beneath the unshaded light, and he wondered why women, in quitting a house, will remove all the lamp shades even though they touch nothing else; looking down at the child, at its bluish eyelids showing a faint crescent of bluish white against its lead-

142

colored cheeks, the moist shadow of hair capping its skull, its hands uplifted, curl-palmed, sweating too, thinking Good God. Good God.

He was thinking of the first time he had seen it, lying in a wooden box behind the stove in that ruined house twelve miles from town; of Popeye's black presence lying upon the house like the shadow of something no larger than a match falling monstrous and portentous upon something else otherwise familiar and everyday and twenty times its size; of the two of them —himself and the woman—in the kitchen lighted by a cracked and smutty lamp on a table of clean, spartan dishes and Goodwin and Popeye somewhere in the outer darkness peaceful with insects and frogs yet filled too with Popeye's presence in black and nameless threat. The woman drew the box out from behind the stove and stood above it, her hands still hidden in her shapeless garment. "I have to keep him in this so the rats cant get to him," she said.

"Oh," Horace said, "you have a son." Then she showed him her hands, flung them out in a gesture at once spontaneous and diffident and self-conscious and proud, and told him he might bring her an orange-stick.

She returned, with something wrapped discreetly in a piece of newspaper. He knew that it was a diaper, freshly washed, even before she said: "I made a fire in the stove. I guess I over-stepped."

"Of course not," he said. "It's merely a matter of legal precaution, you see," he said. "Better to put everybody to a little temporary discomfort than to jeopardize our case." She did not appear to be listening. She spread the blanket on the bed and lifted the child onto it. "You understand how it is," Horace said. "If the judge suspected that I knew more about it than the facts would warrant—I mean, we must try to give everybody the idea that holding Lee for that killing is just—"

"Do you live in Jefferson?" she said, wrapping the blanket about the child.

"No. I live in Kinston. I used to—I have practised here, though."

"You have kinfolks here, though. Women. That used to live in this house." She lifted the child, tucking the blanket about it. Then she looked at him. "It's all right. I know how it is. You've been kind."

"Damn it," he said, "do you think— Come on. Let's go on to the hotel. You get a good night's rest, and I'll be in early in the morning. Let me take it."

"I've got him," she said. She started to say something else, looking at him quietly for a moment, but she went on. He turned out the
144

light and followed and locked the door. She was already in the car. He got in.

"Hotel, Isom," he said. "I never did learn to drive one," he said. "Sometimes, when I think of all the time I have spent not learning to do things . . ."

The street was narrow, quiet. It was paved now, though he could remember when, after a rain, it had been a canal of blackish substance half earth, half water, with murmuring gutters in which he and Narcissa paddled and splashed with tucked-up garments and muddy bottoms, after the crudest of whittled boats, or made lob-lollies by treading and treading in one spot with the intense oblivion of alchemists. He could remember when, innocent of concrete, the street was bordered on either side by paths of red brick tediously and unevenly laid and worn in rich, random maroon mosaic into the black earth which the noon sun never reached; at that moment, pressed into the concrete near the entrance of the drive, were the prints of his and his sister's naked feet in the artificial stone.

The infrequent lamps mounted to crescendo beneath the arcade of a filling-station at the corner. The woman leaned suddenly forward. "Stop here, please, boy," she said. Isom put on the brakes. "I'll get out here and walk," she said.

"You'll do nothing of the kind," Horace said. "Go on, Isom."

"No; wait," the woman said. "We'll be passing people that know you. And then the square."

"Nonsense," Horace said. "Go on, Isom."

"You get out and wait, then," she said. "He can come straight back."

"You'll do no such thing," Horace said. "By heaven, I— Drive on, Isom!"

"You'd better," the woman said. She sat back in the seat. Then she leaned forward again. "Listen. You've been kind. You mean all right, but—"

"You dont think I am lawyer enough, you mean?"

"I guess I've got just what was coming to me. There's no use fighting it."

"Certainly not, if you feel that way about it. But you dont. Or you'd have told Isom to drive you to the railroad station. Wouldn't you?" She was looking down at the child, fretting the blanket about its face. "You get a good night's rest and I'll be in early tomorrow." They passed the jail—a square building slashed harshly by pale slits of light. Only the central window was wide enough to be called a window, criss-crossed by slender bars. In it the negro murderer leaned; below along the fence a row of heads hatted and bare above work-thickened shoulders, and

146

the blended voices swelled rich and sad into the soft, depthless evening, singing of heaven and being tired. "Dont you worry at all, now. Everybody knows Lee didn't do it."

They drew up to the hotel, where the drummers sat in chairs along the curb, listening to the singing. "I must—" the woman said. Horace got down and held the door open. She didn't move. "Listen. I've got to tell—"

"Yes," Horace said, extending his hand. "I know. I'll be in early tomorrow." He helped her down. They entered the hotel, the drummers turning to watch her legs, and went to the desk. The singing followed them, dimmed by the walls, the lights.

The woman stood quietly nearby, holding the child, until Horace had done.

"Listen," she said. The porter went on with the key, toward the stairs. Horace touched her arm, turning her that way. "I've got to tell you," she said.

"In the morning," he said. "I'll be in early," he said, guiding her toward the stairs. Still she hung back, looking at him; then she freed her arm by turning to face him.

"All right, then," she said. She said, in a low, level tone, her face bent a little toward the child: "We haven't got any money. I'll tell you now. That last batch Popeve didn't—"

"Yes, yes," Horace said; "first thing in the morning. I'll be in by the time you finish breakfast. Goodnight." He returned to the car, into the sound of the singing. "Home, Isom," he said. They turned and passed the jail again and the leaning shape beyond the bars and the heads along the fence. Upon the barred and slitted wall the splotched shadow of the heaven-tree shuddered and pulsed monstrously in scarce any wind; rich and sad, the singing fell behind. The car went on, smooth and swift, passing the narrow street. "Here," Horace said, "where are you—" Isom clapped on the brakes.

"Miss Narcissa say to bring you back out home," he said.

"Oh, she did?" Horace said. "That was kind of her. You can tell her I changed her mind."

Isom backed and turned into the narrow street and then into the cedar drive, the lights lifting and boring ahead into the unpruned tunnel as though into the most profound blackness of the sea, as though among straying rigid shapes to which not even light could give color. The car stopped at the door and Horace got out. "You might tell her it was not to her I ran," he said. "Can you remember that?"

148

XVII

THE LAST TRUMPET-SHAPED BLOOM HAD
fallen from the heaven tree at the corner of
the jail yard. They lay thick, viscid underfoot,
sweet and oversweet in the nostrils with a
sweetness surfeitive and moribund, and at night
now the ragged shadow of full-fledged leaves
pulsed upon the barred window in shabby rise
and fall. The window was in the general room,
the white-washed walls of which were stained
with dirty hands, scribbled and scratched over
with names and dates and blasphemous and obscene doggerel in pencil or nail or knife-blade.
Nightly the negro murderer leaned there, his
face checkered by the shadow of the grating
in the restless interstices of leaves, singing in
chorus with those along the fence below.

Sometimes during the day he sang also, alone
then save for the slowing passerby and ragamuffin boys and the garage men across the way.

149

"One day mo! Aint no place fer you in heavum! Aint no place fer you in hell! Aint no place fer you in whitefolks' jail! Nigger, whar you gwine to? Whar you gwine to, nigger?"

Each morning Isom fetched in a bottle of milk, which Horace delivered to the woman at the hotel, for the child. On Sunday afternoon he went out to his sister's. He left the woman sitting on the cot in Goodwin's cell, the child on her lap. Heretofore it had lain in that drugged apathy, its eyelids closed to thin crescents, but today it moved now and then in frail, galvanic jerks, whimpering.

Horace went up to Miss Jenny's room. His sister had not appeared. "He wont talk," Horace said. "He just says they will have to prove he did it. He said they had nothing on him, no more than on the child. He wouldn't even consider bond, if he could have got it. He says he is better off in the jail. And I suppose he is. His business out there is finished now, even if the sheriff hadn't found his kettles and destroyed—"

"Kettles?"

"His still. After he surrendered, they hunted around until they found the still. They knew what he was doing, but they waited until he was down. Then they all jumped on him. The good customers, that had been buying whiskey from him and drinking all that he would give them free and maybe trying to make love to his wife behind his back. You should hear them down town. This morning the Baptist minister took him for a text. Not only as a murderer, but as an adulterer; a polluter of the free Democratico-Protestant atmosphere of Yoknapatawpha county. I gathered that his idea was that Goodwin and the woman should both be burned as a sole example to that child; the child to be reared and taught the English language for the sole end of being taught that it was begot in sin by two people who suffered by fire for having begot it. Good God, can a man, a civilised man, seriously . . ."

"They're just Baptists," Miss Jenny said. "What about the money?"

"He had a little, almost a hundred and sixty dollars. It was buried in a can in the barn. They let him dig that up. 'That'll keep her' he says 'until it's over. Then we'll clear out. We've been intending to for a good while. If I'd listened to her, we'd have been gone already. You've been a good girl' he says. She was sitting on the cot beside him, holding the baby, and he took her chin in his hand and shook her head a little."

"It's a good thing Narcissa aint going to be on that jury," Miss Jenny said.

151

"Yes. But the fool wont even let me mention that that gorilla was ever on the place. He said 'They cant prove anything on me. I've been in a jam before. Everybody that knows anything about me knows that I wouldn't hurt a feeb.' But that wasn't the reason he doesn't want it told about that thug. And he knew I knew it wasn't, because he kept on talking, sitting there in his overalls, rolling his cigarettes with the sack hanging in his teeth. 'I'll just stay here until it blows over. I'll be better off here; cant do anything outside, anyway. And this will keep her, with maybe something for you until you're better paid.'

"But I knew what he was thinking. 'I didn't know you were a coward' I said.

" 'You do like I say' he said. 'I'll be all right here.' But he doesn't . . ." He sat forward, rubbing his hands slowly. "He doesn't realise. . . . Dammit, say what you want to, but there's a corruption about even looking upon evil, even by accident; you cannot haggle, traffic, with putrefaction— You've seen how Narcissa, just hearing about it, how it's made her restless and suspicious. I thought I had come back here of my own accord, but now I see that— Do you suppose she thought I was bringing that woman into the house at night, or something like that?"

"I did too, at first," Miss Jenny said. "But I reckon now she's learned that you'll work harder for whatever reason you think you have, than for anything anybody could offer you or give you."

"You mean, she'd let me think they never had any money, when she——"

"Why not? Aint you doing all right without it?"

Narcissa entered.

"We were just talking about murder and crime," Miss Jenny said.

"I hope you're through, then," Narcissa said. She did not sit down.

"Narcissa has her sorrows too," Miss Jenny said. "Dont you, Narcissa?"

"What now?" Horace said. "She hasn't caught Bory with alcohol on his breath, has she?"

"She's been jilted. Her beau's gone and left her."

"You're such a fool," Narcissa said.

"Yes, sir," Miss Jenny said, "Gowan Stevens has thrown her down. He didn't even come back from that Oxford dance to say goodbye. He just wrote her a letter." She began to search about her in the chair. "And now I flinch everytime the doorbell rings, thinking that his mother——"

"Miss Jenny," Narcissa said, "you give me my letter."

"Wait," Miss Jenny said, "here it is. Now, what do you think of that for a delicate operation on the human heart without anaesthetic? I'm beginning to believe all this I hear, about how young folks learn all the things in order to get married, that we had to get married in order to learn."

Horace took the single sheet.

Narcissa my dear

This has no heading. I wish it could have no date. But if my heart were as blank as this page, this would not be necessary at all. I will not see you again. I cannot write it, for I have gone through with an experience which I cannot face. I have but one rift in the darkness, that is that I have injured no one save myself by my folly, and that the extent of that folly you will never learn. I need not say that the hope that you never learn it is the sole reason why I will not see you again. Think as well of me as you can. I wish I had the right to say, if you learn of my folly think not the less of me. G.

Horace read the note, the single sheet. He held it between his hands. He did not say anything for a while.

"Good Lord," Horace said. "Someone mis-took him for a Mississippi man on the dance floor."

"I think, if I were you—" Narcissa said. After a moment she said: "How much longer is this going to last, Horace?"

"Not any longer than I can help. If you know of any way in which I can get him out of that jail by tomorrow . . ."

"There's only one way," she said. She looked at him a moment. Then she turned toward the door. "Which way did Bory go? Dinner'll be ready soon." She went out.

"And you know what that way is," Miss Jenny said. "If you aint got any backbone."

"I'll know whether or not I have any back-bone when you tell me what the other way is."

"Go back to Belle," Miss Jenny said. "Go back home."

The negro murderer was to be hung on a Saturday without pomp, buried without circum-stance: one night he would be singing at the barred window and yelling down out of the soft myriad darkness of a May night; the next night he would be gone, leaving the window for Good-win. Goodwin had been bound over for the June term of court, without bail. But still he would not agree to let Horace divulge Popeye's presence at the scene of the murder.

"I tell you, they've got nothing on me," Goodwin said.

"How do you know they haven't?" Horace said.

"Well, no matter what they think they have on me, I stand a chance in court. But just let it get to Memphis that I said he was anywhere around there, what chance do you think I'd have to get back to this cell after I testified?"

"You've got the law, justice, civilization."

"Sure, if I spend the rest of my life squatting in that corner yonder. Come here." He led Horace to the window. "There are five windows in that hotel yonder that look into this one. And I've seen him light matches with a pistol at twenty feet. Why, damn it all, I'd never get back here from the courtroom the day I testified that."

"But there's such a thing as obstruct—"

"Obstructing damnation. Let them prove I did it. Tommy was found in the barn, shot from behind. Let them find the pistol. I was there, waiting. I didn't try to run. I could have, but I didn't. It was me notified the sheriff. Of course my being there alone except for her and Pap looked bad. If it was a stall, dont common sense tell you I'd have invented a better one?"

156

"You're not being tried by common sense," Horace said. "You're being tried by a jury."

"Then let them make the best of it. That's all they'll get. The dead man is in the barn, hadn't been touched; me and my wife and child and Pap in the house; nothing in the house touched; me the one that sent for the sheriff. No, no; I know I run a chance this way, but let me just open my head about that fellow, and there's no chance to it. I know what I'll get."

"But you heard the shot," Horace said. "You have already told that."

"No," he said, "I didn't. I didn't hear anything. I dont know anything about it. . . . Do you mind waiting outside a minute while I talk to Ruby?"

It was five minutes before she joined him. He said:

"There's something about this that I dont know yet; that you and Lee haven't told me. Something he just warned you not to tell me. Isn't there?" She walked beside him, carrying the child. It was still whimpering now and then, tossing its thin body in sudden jerks. She tried to soothe it, crooning to it, rocking it in her arms. "Maybe you carry it too much," Horace said; "maybe if you could leave it at the hotel . . ."

"I guess Lee knows what to do," she said.

"But the lawyer should know all the facts, everything. He is the one to decide what to tell and what not to tell. Else, why have one? That's like paying a dentist to fix your teeth and then refusing to let him look into your mouth, dont you see? You wouldn't treat a dentist or a doctor this way." She said nothing, her head bent over the child. It wailed.

"Hush," she said, "hush, now."

"And worse than that, there's such a thing called obstructing justice. Suppose he swears there was nobody else there, suppose he is about to be cleared—which is not likely—and somebody turns up who saw Popeye about the place, or saw his car leaving. Then they'll say, if Lee didn't tell the truth about an unimportant thing, why should we believe him when his neck's in danger?"

They reached the hotel. He opened the door for her. She did not look at him. "I guess Lee knows best," she said, going in. The child wailed, a thin, whimpering, distressful cry. "Hush," she said. "Shhhhhhhhhhhh."

Isom had been to fetch Narcissa from a party; it was late when the car stopped at the corner and picked him up. A few of the lights were beginning to come on, and men were already drifting back toward the square after supper, but it was still too early for the negro murderer to begin to sing. "And he'd better sing fast, too," Horace said. "He's only got two days more." But he was not there yet. The jail faced west; a last faint copper-colored light lay upon the dingy grating and upon the small, pale blob of a hand, and in scarce any wind a blue wisp of tobacco floated out and dissolved raggedly away. "If it wasn't bad enough to have her husband there, without that poor brute counting his remaining breaths at the top of his voice. . . ."

"Maybe they'll wait and hang them both to-gether," Narcissa said. "They do that some-times, dont they?"

That night Horace built a small fire in the grate. It was not cool. He was using only one room now, taking his meals at the hotel; the rest of the house was locked again. He tried to read, then he gave up and undressed and went to bed, watching the fire die in the grate. He heard the town clock strike twelve. "When this is over, I think I'll go to Europe," he said. "I need a change. Either I, or Mississippi, one."

Maybe a few of them would still be gathered along the fence, since this would be his last night; the thick, small-headed shape of him would be clinging to the bars, gorilla-like, sing-ing, while upon his shadow, upon the checkered

orifice of the window, the ragged grief of the
heaven tree would pulse and change, the last
bloom fallen now in viscid smears upon the sidewalk. Horace turned again in the bed. "They
ought to clean that damn mess off the sidewalk,"
he said. "Damn. Damn. Damn."

He was sleeping late the next morning; he
had seen daylight. He was wakened by someone
knocking at the door. It was half-past six. He
went to the door. The negro porter of the hotel
stood there.

"What?" Horace said. "Is it Mrs Goodwin?"

"She say for you to come when you up," the
negro said.

"Tell her I'll be there in ten minutes."

As he entered the hotel he passed a young
man with a small black bag, such as doctors
carry. Horace went on up. The woman was
standing in the half-open door, looking down
the hall.

"I finally got the doctor," she said. "But I
wanted anyway. . . ." The child lay on the
bed, its eyes shut, flushed and sweating, its
curled hands above its head in the attitude of
one crucified, breathing in short, whistling
gasps. "He was sick all last night. I went and
got some medicine and I tried to keep him quiet
until daylight. At last I got the doctor." She
stood beside the bed, looking down at the child.

160

"There was a woman there," she said. "A young girl."

"A—" Horace said. "Oh," he said. "Yes. You'd better tell me about it."

Popeye drove swiftly but without any quality of haste or of flight, down the clay road and into the sand. Temple was beside him. Her hat was jammed onto the back of her head, her hair escaping beneath the crumpled brim in matted clots. Her face looked like a sleepwalker's as she swayed limply to the lurching of the car. She lurched against Popeye, lifting her hand in limp reflex. Without releasing the wheel he thrust her back with his elbow. "Brace yourself," he said. "Come on, now."

Before they came to the tree they passed the woman. She stood beside the road, carrying the child, the hem of her dress folded back over its face, and she looked at them quietly from beneath the faded sunbonnet, flicking swiftly in and out of Temple's vision without any motion, any sign.

When they reached the tree Popeye swung the car out of the road and drove it crashing

162

into the undergrowth and through the prone tree-top and back into the road again in a running popping of cane-stalks like musketry along a trench, without any diminution of speed. Beside the tree Gowan's car lay on its side. Temple looked vaguely and stupidly at it as it too shot behind.

Popeye swung back into the sandy ruts. Yet there was no flight in the action: he performed it with a certain vicious petulance, that was all. It was a powerful car. Even in the sand it held forty miles an hour, and up the narrow gulch to the highroad, where he turned north. Sitting beside him, braced against jolts that had already given way to a smooth increasing hiss of gravel, Temple gazed dully forward as the road she had traversed yesterday began to flee backward under the wheels as onto a spool, feeling her blood seeping slowly inside her loins. She sat limp in the corner of the seat, watching the steady backward rush of the land—pines in opening vistas splashed with fading dogwood; sedge; fields green with new cotton and empty of any movement, peaceful, as though Sunday were a quality of atmosphere, of light and shade—sitting with her legs close together, listening to the hot minute seeping of her blood, saying dully to herself, I'm still bleeding. I'm still bleeding.

163

It was a bright, soft day, a wanton morning filled with that unbelievable soft radiance of May, rife with a promise of noon and of heat, with high fat clouds like gobs of whipped cream floating lightly as reflections in a mirror, their shadows scudding sedately across the road. It had been a lavender spring. The fruit trees, the white ones, had been in small leaf when the blooms matured; they had never attained that brilliant whiteness of last spring, and the dogwood had come into full bloom after the leaf also, in green retrograde before crescendo. But lilac and wistaria and redbud, even the shabby heaven-trees, had never been finer, fulgent, with a burning scent blowing for a hundred yards along the vagrant air of April and May. The bougainvillea against the veranda would be large as basketballs and lightly poised as balloons, and looking vacantly and stupidly at the rushing roadside Temple began to scream.

It started as a wail, raising, cut suddenly off by Popeye's hand. With her hands lying on her lap, sitting erect, she screamed, tasting the gritty acridity of his fingers while the car slewed squealing in the gravel, feeling her secret blood. Then he gripped her by the back of the neck and she sat motionless, her mouth round and open like a small empty cave. He shook her head.

"Shut it," he said, "shut it;" gripping her silent. "Look at yourself. Here." With the other hand he swung the mirror on the windshield around and she looked at her image, at the up-tilted hat and her matted hair and her round mouth. She began to fumble at her coat pockets, looking at her reflection. He released her and she produced the compact and opened it and peered into the mirror, whimpering a little. She powdered her face and rouged her mouth and straightened her hat, whimpering into the tiny mirror on her lap while Popeye watched her. He lit a cigarette. "Aint you ashamed of yourself?" he said.

"It's still running," she whimpered. "I can feel it." With the lipstick poised she looked at him and opened her mouth again. He gripped her by the back of the neck.

"Stop it, now. You going to shut it?"

"Yes," she whimpered.

"See you do, then. Come on. Get yourself fixed."

She put the compact away. He started the car again.

The road began to thicken with pleasure cars Sunday-bent—small, clay-crusted Fords and Chevrolets; an occasional larger car moving swiftly, with swathed women, and dust-covered hampers; trucks filled with wooden-faced country people in garments like a colored wood me-

ticulously carved; now and then a wagon or a
buggy. Before a weathered frame church on a
hill the grove was full of tethered teams and
battered cars and trucks. The woods gave away
to fields; houses became more frequent. Low
above the skyline, above roofs and a spire or
two, smoke hung. The gravel became asphalt
and they entered Dumfries.

Temple began to look about, like one waking
from sleep. "Not here!" she said. "I cant—"

"Hush it, now," Popeye said.

"I cant—I might—" she whimpered. "I'm
hungry," she said. "I haven't eaten since . . ."

"Ah, you aint hungry. Wait till we get to
town."

She looked about with dazed, glassy eyes.
"There might be people here . . ." He swung
in toward a filling station. "I cant get out," she
whimpered. "It's still running, I tell you!"

"Who told you to get out?" He descended
and looked at her across the wheel. "Dont you
move." She watched him go up the street and
enter a door. It was a dingy confectionery. He
bought a pack of cigarettes and put one in his
mouth. "Gimme a couple of bars of candy," he
said.

"What kind?"

"Candy," he said. Under a glass bell on the
counter a plate of sandwiches sat. He took one
166

and flipped a dollar on the counter and turned toward the door.

"Here's your change," the clerk said.

"Keep it," he said. "You'll get rich faster."

When he saw the car it was empty. He stopped ten feet away and changed the sandwich to his left hand, the unlighted cigarette slanted beneath his chin. The mechanic, hanging the hose up, saw him and jerked his thumb toward the corner of the building.

Beyond the corner the wall made an offset. In the niche was a greasy barrel half full of scraps of metal and rubber. Between the barrel and the wall Temple crouched. "He nearly saw me!" she whispered. "He was almost looking right at me!"

"Who?" Popeye said. He looked back up the street. "Who saw you?"

"He was coming right toward me! A boy. At school. He was looking right toward—"

"Come on. Come out of it."

"He was look—" Popeye took her by the arm. She crouched in the corner, jerking at the arm he held, her wan face craned around the corner.

"Come on, now." Then his hand was at the back of her neck, gripping it.

"Oh," she wailed in a choked voice. It was as though he were lifting her slowly erect by that

167

one hand. Excepting that, there was no movement between them. Side by side, almost of a height, they appeared as decorous as two acquaintances stopped to pass the time of day before entering church.

"Are you coming?" he said. "Are you?"

"I cant. It's down to my stocking now. Look." She lifted her skirt away in a shrinking gesture, then she dropped the skirt and rose again, her torso arching backward, her soundless mouth open as he gripped her. He released her.

"Will you come now?"

She came out from behind the barrel. He took her arm.

"It's all over the back of my coat," she whimpered. "Look and see."

"You're all right. I'll get you another coat tomorrow. Come on."

They returned to the car. At the corner she hung back again. "You want some more of it, do you?" he whispered, not touching her. "Do you?" She went on and got into the car quietly. He took the wheel. "Here, I got you a sandwich." He took it from his pocket and put it in her hand. "Come on, now. Eat it." She took a bite obediently. He started the car and took the Memphis road. Again, the bitten sandwich in her hand, she ceased chewing and opened her mouth in that round, hopeless expression of a child; again his hand left the wheel and gripped the back of her neck and she sat motionless, gazing straight at him, her mouth open and the half chewed mass of bread and meat lying upon her tongue.

They reached Memphis in midafternoon. At the foot of the bluff below Main Street Popeye turned into a narrow street of smoke-grimed frame houses with tiers of wooden galleries, set a little back in grassless plots, with now and then a forlorn and hardy tree of some shabby species—gaunt, lopbranched magnolias, a stunted elm or a locust in grayish, cadaverous bloom—interspersed by rear ends of garages; a scrap-heap in a vacant lot; a low doored cavern of an equivocal appearance where an oilcloth-covered counter and a row of backless stools, a metal coffee-urn and a fat man in a dirty apron with a toothpick in his mouth, stood for an instant out of the gloom with an effect as of a sinister and meaningless photograph poorly made. From the bluff, beyond a line of office buildings terraced sharply against the sunfilled sky, came a sound of traffic—motor horns, trolleys—passing high overhead on the river breeze; at the end of the street a trolley materialised in the narrow gap with an effect as of magic and vanished with a stupendous clatter.

On a second storey gallery a young negress in her underclothes smoked a cigarette sullenly, her arms on the balustrade.

Popeye drew up before one of the dingy three-storey houses, the entrance of which was hidden by a dingy lattice cubicle leaning a little awry. In the grimy grassplot before it two of those small, woolly, white, worm-like dogs, one with a pink, the other a blue, ribbon about its neck, moved about with an air of sluggish and obscene paradox. In the sunlight their coats looked as though they had been cleaned with gasoline.

Later Temple could hear them outside her door, whimpering and scuffing, or, rushing thickly in when the negro maid opened the door, climbing and sprawling onto the bed and into Miss Reba's lap with wheezy, flatulent sounds, billowing into the rich pneumasis of her breast and tonguing along the metal tankard which she waved in one ringed hand as she talked.

"Anybody in Memphis can tell you who Reba Rivers is. Ask any man on the street, cop or not. I've had some of the biggest men in Memphis right here in this house, bankers, lawyers, doctors—all of them. I've had two police captains drinking beer in my dining-room and the commissioner himself upstairs with one of my girls. They got drunk and crashed the door in
170

on him and found him buck-nekkid, dancing the highland fling. A man fifty years old, seven foot tall, with a head like a peanut. He was a fine fellow. He knew me. They all know Reba Rivers. Spent their money here like water, they have. They know me. I aint never double-crossed nobody, honey." She drank beer, breathing thickly into the tankard, the other hand, ringed with yellow diamonds as large as gravel, lost among the lush billows of her breast.

Her slightest movement appeared to be accomplished by an expenditure of breath out of all proportion to any pleasure the movement could afford her. Almost as soon as they entered the house she began to tell Temple about her asthma, toiling up the stairs in front of them, planting her feet heavily in worsted bedroom slippers, a wooden rosary in one hand and the tankard in the other. She had just returned from church, in a black silk gown and a hat savagely flowered; the lower half of the tankard was still frosted with inner chill. She moved heavily from big thigh to thigh, the two dogs moiling underfoot, talking steadily back across her shoulder in a harsh, expiring, maternal voice.

"Popeye knew better than to bring you anywhere else but to my house. I been after him for, how many years I been after you to get you a girl, honey? What I say, a young fellow

171

cant no more live without a girl than . . ."
Panting, she fell to cursing the dogs under her feet, stopping to shove them aside. "Get back down there," she said, shaking the rosary at them. They snarled at her in vicious falsetto, baring their teeth, and she leaned against the wall in a thin aroma of beer, her hand to her breast, her mouth open, her eyes fixed in a glare of sad terror of all breathing as she sought breath, the tankard a squat soft gleam like dull silver lifted in the gloom.

The narrow stairwell turned back upon itself in a succession of niggard reaches. The light, falling through a thickly-curtained door at the front and through a shuttered window at the rear of each stage, had a weary quality. A spent quality; defunctive, exhausted—a protracted weariness like a vitiated backwater beyond sunlight and the vivid noises of sunlight and day. There was a defunctive odor of irregular food, vaguely alcoholic, and Temple even in her ignorance seemed to be surrounded by a ghostly promiscuity of intimate garments, of discreet whispers of flesh stale and oft-assailed and impregnable beyond each silent door which they passed. Behind her, about hers and Miss Reba's feet the two dogs scrabbled in nappy gleams, their claws clicking on the metal strips which bound the carpet to the stairs.

172

Later, lying in bed, a towel wrapped about her naked loins, she could hear them sniffing and whining outside the door. Her coat and hat hung on nails on the door, her dress and stockings lay upon a chair, and it seemed to her that she could hear the rhythmic splash-splash of the washing-board somewhere and she flung herself again in an agony for concealment as she had when they took her knickers off.

"Now, now," Miss Reba said. "I bled for four days, myself. It aint nothing. Doctor Quinn'll stop it in two minutes, and Minnie'll have them all washed and pressed and you wont never know it. That blood'll be worth a thousand dollars to you, honey." She lifted the tankard, the flowers on her hat rigidly moribund, nodding in macabre was hael. "Us poor girls," she said. The drawn shades, cracked into a myriad pattern like old skin, blew faintly on the bright air, breathing into the room on waning surges the sound of Sabbath traffic, festive, steady, evanescent. Temple lay motionless in the bed, her legs straight and close, in covers to her chin and her face small and wan, framed in the rich sprawl of her hair. Miss Reba lowered the tankard, gasping for breath. In her hoarse, fainting voice she began to tell Temple how lucky she was.

"Every girl in the district has been trying to

get him, honey. There's one, a little married woman slips down here sometimes, she offered Minnie twenty-five dollars just to get him into the room, that's all. But do you think he'd so much as look at one of them? Girls that have took in a hundred dollars a night. No, sir. Spend his money like water, but do you think he'd look at one of them except to dance with her? I always knowed it wasn't going to be none of these here common whores he'd take. I'd tell them, I'd say, the one of yez that gets him'll wear diamonds, I says, but it aint going to be none of you common whores, and now Minnie'll have them washed and pressed until you wont know it."

"I cant wear it again," Temple whispered. "I cant."

"No more you'll have to, if you dont want. You can give them to Minnie, though I dont know what she'll do with them except maybe—" At the door the dogs began to whimper louder. Feet approached. The door opened. A negro maid entered, carrying a tray bearing a quart bottle of beer and a glass of gin, the dogs surging in around her feet. "And tomorrow the stores'll be open and me and you'll go shopping, like he said for us to. Like I said, the girl that gets him'll wear diamonds: you just see if I wasn't- -" she turned, mountainous, the tankard lifted, as the two dogs scrambled onto the bed and then onto her lap, snapping viciously at one another. From their curled shapeless faces bead-like eyes glared with choleric ferocity, their mouths gaped pinkly upon needle-like teeth. "Reba!" Miss Reba said, "get down! You, Mr Binford!" flinging them down, their teeth clicking about her hands. "You just bite me, you— Did you get Miss— What's your name, honey? I didn't quite catch it."

"Temple," Temple whispered.

"I mean, your first name, honey. We dont stand on no ceremony here."

"That's it. Temple. Temple Drake."

"You got a boy's name, aint you?—Miss Temple's things washed, Minnie?"

"Yessum," the maid said. "Hit's dryin now hind the stove." She came with the tray, shoving the dogs gingerly aside while they clicked their teeth at her ankles.

"You wash it out good?"

"I had a time with it," Minnie said. "Seem like that the most hardest blood of all to get—" With a convulsive movement Temple flopped over, ducking her head beneath the covers. She felt Miss Reba's hand.

"Now, now. Now, now. Here, take your drink. This one's on me. I ain't going to let no girl of Popeye's—"

175

"I dont want anymore," Temple said.

"Now, now," Miss Reba said. "Drink it and you'll feel better." She lifted Temple's head. Temple clutched the covers to her throat. Miss Reba held the glass to her lips. She gulped it, writhed down again, clutching the covers about her, her eyes wide and black above the covers. "I bet you got that towel disarranged," Miss Reba said, putting her hand on the covers.

"No," Temple whispered. "It's all right. It's still there." She shrank, cringing; they could see the cringing of her legs beneath the covers.

"Did you get Dr Quinn, Minnie?" Miss Reba said.

"Yessum." Minnie was filling the tankard from the bottle, a dull frosting pacing the rise of liquor within the metal. "He say he dont make no Sunday afternoon calls."

"Did you tell him who wanted him? Did you tell him Miss Reba wanted him?"

"Yessum. He say he dont—"

"You go back and tell that suh— You tell him I'll— No; wait." She rose heavily. "Sending a message like that back to me, that can put him in jail three times over." She waddled toward the door, the dogs crowding about the felt slippers. The maid followed and closed the door. Temple could hear Miss Reba cursing the dogs as she descended the stairs with terrific slowness. The sounds died away.

The shades blew steadily in the windows with faint rasping sounds. Temple began to hear a clock. It sat on the mantel above a grate filled with fluted green paper. The clock was of flowered china, supported by four china nymphs. It had only one hand, scrolled and gilded, half-way between ten and eleven, lending to the otherwise blank face a quality of unequivocal assertion, as though it had nothing whatever to do with time.

Temple rose from the bed. Holding the towel about her she stole toward the door, her ears acute, her eyes a little blind with the strain of listening. It was twilight; in a dim mirror, a pellucid oblong of dusk set on end, she had a glimpse of herself like a thin ghost, a pale shadow moving in the uttermost profundity of shadow. She reached the door. At once she began to hear a hundred conflicting sounds in a single converging threat and she clawed furiously at the door until she found the bolt, dropping the towel to drive it home. Then she caught up the towel, her face averted, and ran back and sprang into the bed and clawed the covers to her chin and lay there, listening to the secret whisper of her blood.

They knocked at the door for some time before she made any sound. "It's the doctor, honey," Miss Reba panted harshly. "Come on, now. Be a good girl."

"I cant," Temple said, her voice faint and small. "I'm in bed."

"Come on, now. He wants to fix you up." She panted harshly. "My God, if I could just get one full breath again. I aint had a full breath since . . ." Low down beyond the door Temple could hear the dogs. "Honey."

She rose from the bed, holding the towel about her. She went to the door, silently.

"Honey," Miss Reba said.

"Wait," Temple said. "Let me get back to the bed before Let me get."

"There's a good girl," Miss Reba said. "I knowed she was going to be good."

"Count ten, now," Temple said. "Will you count ten, now?" she said against the wood. She slipped the bolt soundlessly, then she turned and sped back to the bed, her naked feet in pattering diminuendo.

The doctor was a fattish man with thin, curly hair. He wore horn-rimmed glasses which lent to his eyes no distortion at all, as though they were of clear glass and worn for decorum's sake. Temple watched him across the covers, holding

178

them to her throat. "Make them go out," she whispered; "if they'll just go out."

"Now, now," Miss Reba said, "he's going to fix you up."

Temple clung to the covers.

"If the little lady will just let . . ." the doctor said. His hair evaporated finely from his brow. His mouth nipped in at the corners, his lips full and wet and red. Behind the glasses his eyes looked like little bicycle wheels at dizzy speed; a metallic hazel. He put out a thick, white hand bearing a masonic ring, haired over with fine reddish fuzz to the second knuckle-joints. Cold air slipped down her body, below her thighs; her eyes were closed. Lying on her back, her legs close together, she began to cry, hopelessly and passively, like a child in a dentist's waiting-room.

"Now, now," Miss Reba said, "take another sup of gin, honey. It'll make you feel better."

In the window the cracked shade, yawning now and then with a faint rasp against the frame, let twilight into the room in fainting surges. From beneath the shade the smoke-colored twilight emerged in slow puffs like signal smoke from a blanket, thickening in the room. The china figures which supported the clock

179

gleamed in hushed smooth flexions: knee, elbow, flank, arm and breast in additudes of voluptuous lassitude. The glass face, become mirror-like, appeared to hold all reluctant light, holding in its tranquil depths a quiet gesture of moribund time, one-armed like a veteran from the wars. Half past ten oclock. Temple lay in the bed, looking at the clock, thinking about half-past-ten-oclock.

She wore a too-large gown of cerise crepe, black against the linen. Her hair was a black sprawl, combed out now; her face, throat and arms outside the covers were gray. After the others left the room she lay for a time, head and all beneath the covers. She lay so until she heard the door shut and the descending feet, the doctor's light, unceasing voice and Miss Reba's labored breath grow twilight-colored in the dingy hall and die away. Then she sprang from the bed and ran to the door and shot the bolt and ran back and hurled the covers over her head again, lying in a tight knot until the air was exhausted.

A final saffron-colored light lay upon the ceiling and the upper walls, tinged already with purple by the serrated palisade of Main Street high against the western sky. She watched it fade as the successive yawns of the shade consumed it. She watched the final light condense

180

into the clock face, and the dial change from a round orifice in the darkness to a disc suspended in nothingness, the original chaos, and change in turn to a crystal ball holding in its still and cryptic depths the ordered chaos of the intricate and shadowy world upon whose scarred flanks the old wounds whirl onward at dizzy speed into darkness lurking with new disasters.

She was thinking about half-past-ten-oclock. The hour for dressing for a dance, if you were popular enough not to have to be on time. The air would be steamy with recent baths, and perhaps powder in the light like chaff in barn-lofts, and they looking at one another, comparing, talking whether you could do more damage if you could just walk out on the floor like you were now. Some wouldn't, mostly ones with short legs. Some of them were all right, but they just wouldn't. They wouldn't say why. The worst one of all said boys thought all girls were ugly except when they were dressed. She said the Snake had been seeing Eve for several days and never noticed her until Adam made her put on a fig leaf. How do you know? they said, and she said because the Snake was there before Adam, because he was the first one thrown out of heaven; he was there all the time. But that wasn't what they meant and they said, How do you know? and Temple thought of her kind of backed up against the dressing table and the rest of them in a circle around her with their combed hair and their shoulders smelling of scented soap and the light powder in the air and their eyes like knives until you could almost watch her flesh where the eyes were touching it, and her eyes in her ugly face courageous and frightened and daring, and they all saying, How do you know? until she told them and held up her hand and swore she had. That was when the youngest one turned and ran out of the room. She locked herself in the bath and they could hear her being sick.

She thought about half-past-ten-oclock in the morning. Sunday morning, and the couples strolling toward church. She remembered it was still Sunday, the same Sunday, looking at the fading peaceful gesture of the clock. Maybe it was half-past-ten this morning, that half-past-ten-oclock. Then I'm not here, she thought. This is not me. Then I'm at school. I have a date tonight with . . . thinking of the student with whom she had the date. But she couldn't remember who it would be. She kept the dates written down in her Latin 'pony,' so she didn't have to bother about who it was. She'd just dress, and after a while somebody would call for her. So I better get up and dress, she said, looking at the clock.

She rose and crossed the room quietly. She watched the clock face, but although she could see a warped turmoil of faint light and shadow in geometric miniature swinging across it, she could not see herself. It's this nightie, she thought, looking at her arms, her breast rising out of a dissolving pall beneath which her toes peeped in pale, fleet intervals as she walked. She drew the bolt quietly and returned to the bed and lay with her head cradled in her arms.

There was still a little light in the room. She found that she was hearing her watch; had been hearing it for some time. She discovered that the house was full of noises, seeping into the room muffled and indistinguishable, as though from a distance. A bell rang faintly and shrilly somewhere; someone mounted the stairs in a swishing garment. The feet went on past the door and mounted another stair and ceased. She listened to the watch. A car started beneath the window with a grind of gears; again the faint bell rang, shrill and prolonged. She found that the faint light yet in the room was from a street lamp. Then she realised that it was night and that the darkness beyond was full of the sound of the city.

She heard the two dogs come up the stairs in a furious scrabble. The noise passed the door and stopped, became utterly still; so still that she could almost see them crouching there in the dark against the wall, watching the stairs. One of them was named Mister something, Temple thought, waiting to hear Miss Reba's feet on the stairs. But it was not Miss Reba; they came too steadily and too lightly. The door opened; the dogs surged in in two shapeless blurs and scuttled under the bed and crouched, whimpering. "You, dawgs!" Minnie's voice said. "You make me spill this." The light came on. Minnie carried a tray. "I got you some supper," she said. "Where them dawgs gone to?"

"Under the bed," Temple said. "I don't want any."

Minnie came and set the tray on the bed and looked down at Temple, her pleasant face knowing and placid. "You want me to——" she said, extending her hand. Temple turned her face quickly away. She heard Minnie kneel, cajoling the dogs, the dogs snarling back at her with whimpering, asthmatic snarls and clicking teeth. "Come outen there, now," Minnie said. "They know fo Miss Reba do when she fixing to get drunk. You, Mr Binford!"

Temple raised her head. "Mr Binford?"

"He the one with the blue ribbon," Minnie said. Stooping, she flapped her arm at the dogs. They were backed against the wall at the head of the bed, snapping and snarling at her in mad
184

terror. "Mr Binford was Miss Reba's man. Was landlord here eleven years until he die bout two years ago. Next day Miss Reba get these dawgs, name one Mr Binford and other Miss Reba. Whenever she go to the cemetery she start drinking like this evening, then they both got to run. But Mr Binford ketch it sho nough. Last time she throw him outen upstair window and go down and empty Mr Binford's clothes closet and throw everything out in the street except what he buried in."

"Oh," Temple said. "No wonder they're scared. Let them stay under there. They wont bother me."

"Reckon I have to. Mr Binford aint going to leave this room, not if he know it." She stood again, looking at Temple. "Eat that supper," she said. "You feel better. I done slip you a drink of gin, too."

"I don't want any," Temple said, turning her face away. She heard Minnie leave the room. The door closed quietly. Under the bed the dogs crouched against the wall in that rigid and furious terror.

The light hung from the center of the ceiling, beneath a fluted shade of rose-colored paper browned where the bulb bulged it. The floor was covered by a figured maroon-tinted carpet tacked down in strips; the olive-tinted walls bore two framed lithographs. From the two windows curtains of machine lace hung, dust-colored, like strips of lightly congealed dust set on end. The whole room had an air of musty stoginess, decorum; in the wavy mirror of a cheap varnished dresser, as in a stagnant pool, there seemed to linger spent ghosts of voluptuous gestures and dead lusts. In the corner, upon a faded scarred strip of oilcloth tacked over the carpet, sat a washstand bearing a flowered bowl and pitcher and a row of towels; in the corner behind it sat a slop jar dressed also in fluted rose-colored paper.

Beneath the bed the dogs made no sound. Temple moved slightly; the dry complaint of mattress and springs died into the terrific silence in which they crouched. She thought of them, woolly, shapeless; savage, petulant, spoiled, the flatulent monotony of their sheltered lives snatched up without warning by an incomprehensible moment of terror and fear of bodily annihilation at the very hands which symbolised by ordinary the licensed tranquillity of their lives.

The house was full of sounds. Indistinguishable, remote, they came in to her with a quality of awakening, resurgence, as though the house itself had been asleep, rousing itself with dark; she heard something which might have been a burst of laughter in a shrill woman voice. Steamy odors from the tray drifted across her face. She turned her head and looked at it, at the covered and uncovered dishes of thick china. In the midst of them sat the glass of pale gin, a pack of cigarettes and a box of matches. She rose on her elbow, catching up the slipping gown. She lifted the covers upon a thick steak, potatoes, green peas; rolls; an anonymous pinkish mass which some sense—elimination, perhaps—identified as a sweet. She drew the slipping gown up again, thinking about them eating down at school in a bright uproar of voices and clattering forks; of her father and brothers at the supper table at home; thinking about the borrowed gown and Miss Reba saying that they would go shopping tomorrow. And I've just got two dollars, she thought.

When she looked at the food she found that she was not hungry at all, didn't even want to look at it. She lifted the glass and gulped it empty, her face wry, and set it down and turned her face hurriedly from the tray, fumbling for the cigarettes. When she went to strike the match she looked at the tray again and took up a strip of potato gingerly in her fingers and ate it. She ate another, the unlighted cigarette in her other hand. Then she put the cigarette down and took up the knife and fork and began to eat,

187

pausing from time to time to draw the gown up onto her shoulder.

When she finished eating she lit the cigarette. She heard the bell again, then another in a slightly different key. Across a shrill rush of a woman's voice a door banged. Two people mounted the stairs and passed the door; she heard Miss Reba's voice booming from somewhere and listened to her toiling slowly up the stairs. Temple watched the door until it opened and Miss Reba stood in it, the tankard in her hand. She now wore a bulging house dress and a widow's bonnet with a veil. She entered on the flowered felt slippers. Beneath the bed the two dogs made a stifled concerted sound of utter despair.

The dress, unfastened in the back, hung lumpily about Miss Reba's shoulders. One ringed hand lay on her breast, the other held the tankard high. Her open mouth, studded with gold fillings gaped upon the harsh labor of her breathing.

"Oh God oh God," she said. The dogs surged out from beneath the bed and hurled themselves toward the door in a mad scrabble. As they rushed past her she turned and flung the tankard at them. It struck the door jamb, splashing up the wall, and rebounded with a forlorn clatter. She drew her breath whistling, clutching her
188

breast. She came to the bed and looked down at Temple through the veil. "We was happy as two doves," she wailed, choking, her rings smoldering in hot glints within her billowing breast. "Then he had to go and die on me." She drew her breath whistling, her mouth gaped, shaping the hidden agony of her thwarted lungs, her eyes pale and round with striken bafflement, protuberant. "As two doves," she roared in a harsh, choking voice.

Again time had overtaken the dead gesture behind the clock crystal: Temple's watch on the table beside the bed said half-past-ten. For two hours she had lain undisturbed, listening. She could distinguish voices now from below stairs. She had been hearing them for some time, lying in the room's musty isolation. Later a mechanical piano began to play. Now and then she heard automobile brakes in the street beneath the window; once two voices quarreling bitterly came up and beneath the shade.

She heard two people—a man and a woman —mount the stairs and enter the room next hers. Then she heard Miss Reba toil up the stairs and pass her door, and lying in the bed, her eyes wide and still, she heard Miss Reba hammering at the next door with the metal tankard and shouting into the wood. Beyond the door the

189

man and woman were utterly quiet, so quiet that Temple thought of the dogs again, thought of them crouching against the wall under the bed in that rigid fury of terror and despair. She listened to Miss Reba's voice shouting hoarsely into the blank wood. It died away into terrific gasping, then it rose again in the gross and virile cursing of a man. Beyond the wall the man and woman made no sound. Temple lay staring at the wall beyond which Miss Reba's voice rose again as she hammered at the door with the tankard.

Temple neither saw nor heard her door when it opened. She just happened to look toward it after how long she did not know, and saw Popeye standing there, his hat slanted across his face. Still without making any sound he entered and shut the door and shot the bolt and came toward the bed. As slowly she began to shrink into the bed, drawing the covers up to her chin, watching him across the covers. He came and looked down at her. She writhed slowly in a cringing movement, cringing upon herself in as complete an isolation as though she were bound to a church steeple. She grinned at him, her mouth warped over the rigid, placative porcelain of her grimace.

When he put his hand on her she began to whimper. "No. no." she whispered, "he said I cant now he said . . . ' He jerked the covers back and flung them aside. She lay motionless, her palms lifted, her flesh beneath the envelope of her loins cringing rearward in furious disintegration like frightened people in a crowd. When he advanced his hand again she thought he was going to strike her. Watching his face, she saw it beginning to twitch and jerk like that of a child about to cry, and she heard him begin to make a whimpering sound. He gripped the top of the gown. She caught his wrists and began to toss from side to side, opening her mouth to scream. His hand clapped over her mouth, and gripping his wrist, the saliva drooling between his fingers, her body thrashing furiously from thigh to thigh, she saw him crouching beside the bed, his face wrung above his absent chin, his bluish lips protruding as though he were blowing upon hot soup, making a high whinnying sound like a horse. Beyond the wall Miss Reba filled the hall, the house, with a harsh choking uproar of obscene cursing.

XIX

"**B**UT THAT GIRL," HORACE SAID. "SHE WAS
all right. You know she was all right when you
left the house. When you saw her in the car with
him. He was just giving her a lift to town. She
was all right. You know she was all right."

The woman sat on the edge of the bed, looking down at the child. It lay beneath the faded,
clean blanket, its hands upflung beside its head,
as though it had died in the presence of an un-
bearable agony which had not had time to touch
it. Its eyes were half open, the balls rolled back
into the skull so that only the white showed, in
color like weak milk. Its face was still damp
with perspiration, but its breathing was easier.
It no longer breathed in those weak, whistling
gasps as it had when Horace entered the room.
On a chair beside the bed sat a tumbler half full
of faintly discolored water, with a spoon in it.
Through the open window came the myriad

192

noises of the square—cars, wagons, footsteps on the pavement beneath—and through it Horace could see the courthouse, with men pitching dollars back and forth between holes in the bare earth beneath the locust and water oaks.

The woman brooded above the child. "Nobody wanted her out there. Lee has told them and told them they must not bring women out there, and I told her before it got dark they were not her kind of people and to get away from there. It was that fellow that brought her. He was out there on the porch with them, still drinking, because when he came in to supper he couldn't hardly walk, even. He hadn't even tried to wash the blood off of his face. Little shirt-tail boys that think because Lee breaks the law, they can come out there and treat our house like a . . . Grown people are bad, but at least they take buying whisky like buying anything else; it's the ones like him, the ones that are too young to realise that people dont break the law just for a holiday." Horace could see her clenched hands writhing in her lap. "God, if I had my way, I'd hang every man that makes it or buys it or drinks it, every one of them.

"But why must it have been me, us? What had I ever done to her, to her kind? I told her to get away from there. I told her not to stay there until dark. But that fellow that brought her was getting drunk again, and him and Van picking at each other. If she'd just stopped running around where they had to look at her. She wouldn't stay anywhere. She'd just dash out one door, and in a minute she'd come running in from the other direction. And if he'd just let Van alone, because Van had to go back on the truck at midnight, and so Popeye would have made him behave. And Saturday night too, and them sitting up all night drinking anyway, and I had gone through it and gone through it and I'd tell Lee to let's get away, that he was getting nowhere, and he would have these spells like last night, and no doctor, no telephone. And then she had to come out there, after I had slaved for him, slaved for him." Motionless, her head bent and her hands still in her lap, she had that spent immobility of a chimney rising above the ruin of a house in the aftermath of a cyclone.

"Standing there in the corner behind the bed, with that raincoat on. She was that scared, when they brought the fellow in, all bloody again. They laid him on the bed and Van hit him again and Lee caught Van's arm, and her standing there with her eyes like the holes in one of these masks. The raincoat was hanging

194

on the wall, and she had it on, over her coat. Her dress was all folded up on the bed. They threw the fellow right on top of it, blood and all, and I said 'God, are you drunk too?' But Lee just looked at me and I saw that his nose was white already, like it gets when he's drunk.

"There wasn't any lock on the door, but I thought that pretty soon they'd have to go and see about the truck and then I could do something. Then Lee made me go out too, and he took the lamp out, so I had to wait until they went back to the porch before I could go back. I stood just inside the door. The fellow was snoring, in the bed there, breathing hard, with his nose and mouth all battered up again, and I could hear them on the porch. Then they would be outdoors, around the house and at the back too I could hear them. Then they got quiet.

"I stood there, against the wall. He would snore and choke and catch his breath and moan, sort of, and I would think about that girl lying there in the dark, with her eyes open, listening to them, and me having to stand there, waiting for them to go away so I could do something. I told her to go away. I said 'What fault is it of mine if you're not married? I dont want you here a bit more than you want to be here.' I said 'I've lived my life without any help from people of your sort; what right have you got to look to me for help?' Because I've done everything for him. I've been in the dirt for him. I've put everything behind me and all I asked was to be let alone.

"Then I heard the door open. I could tell Lee by the way he breathes. He went to the bed and said 'I want the raincoat. Sit up and take it off' and I could hear the shucks rattling while he took it off of her, then he went out. He just got the raincoat and went out. It was Van's coat.

"And I have walked around that house so much at night, with those men there, men living off of Lee's risk, men that wouldn't lift a finger for him if he got caught, until I could tell any of them by the way they breathed, and I could tell Popeye by the smell of that stuff on his hair. Tommy was following him. He came in the door behind Popeye and looked at me and I could see his eyes, like a cat. Then his eyes went away and I could feel him sort of squatting against me, and we could hear Popeye over where the bed was and that fellow snoring and snoring.

"I could just hear little faint sounds, from the shucks, so I knew it was all right yet, and in a minute Popeye came on back, and Tommy followed him out, creeping along behind him, and I stood there until I heard them go down

106

to the truck. Then I went to the bed. When I touched her she began to fight. I was trying to put my hand over her mouth so she couldn't make a noise, but she didn't anyway. She just lay there, thrashing about, rolling her head from one side to the other, holding to the coat.

" 'You fool!' I says 'It's me—the woman.' "

"But that girl," Horace said. "She was all right. When you were coming back to the house the next morning after the baby's bottle, you saw her and knew she was all right." The room gave onto the square. Through the window he could see the young men pitching dollars in the courthouse yard, and the wagons passing or tethered about the hitching chains, and he could hear the footsteps and voices of people on the slow and unhurried pavement below the window; the people buying comfortable things to take home and eat at quiet tables. "You know she was all right."

"That night Horace went out to his sister's, in a hired car; he did not telephone. He found Miss Jenny in her room. "Well," she said. "Narcissa will—"

"I don't want to see her," Horace said. "Her nice, well-bred young man. Her Virginia gentleman. I know why he didn't come back."

"Who? Gowan?"

197

"Yes; Gowan. And, by the Lord, ne'd better not come back. By God, when I think that I had the opportunity—"

"What? What did he do?"

"He carried a little fool girl out there with him that day and got drunk and ran off and left her. That's what he did. If it hadn't been for that woman—And when I think of people like that walking the earth with impunity just because he has a balloon-tailed suit and went through the astonishing experience of having attended Virginia . . . On any train or in any hotel, on the street; anywhere, mind you—"

"Oh," Miss Jenny said. "I didn't understand at first who you meant. Well," she said. "You remember that last time he was here, just after you came? the day he wouldn't stay for supper and went to Oxford?"

"Yes. And when I think how I could have—"

"He asked Narcissa to marry him. She told him that one child was enough for her."

"I said she has no heart. She cannot be satisfied with less than insult."

"So he got mad and said he would go to Oxford, where there was a woman he was reasonably confident he would not appear ridiculous to: something like that. Well." She looked at him, her neck bowed to see across her spectacles. "I'll declare, a male parent is a funny thing, but just let a man have a hand in the affairs of a female that's no kin to him . . . What is it that makes a man think that the female flesh he marries or begets might misbehave, but all he didn't marry or get is bound to?"

"Yes," Horace said, "and thank God she isn't my flesh and blood. I can reconcile myself to her having to be exposed to a scoundrel now and then, but to think that at any moment she may become involved with a fool."

"Well, what are you going to do about it? Start some kind of roach campaign?"

"I'm going to do what she said; I'm going to have a law passed making it obligatory upon everyone to shoot any man less than fifty years old that makes, buys, sells or thinks whisky . . . scoundrel I can face, but to think of her being exposed to any fool. . . ."

He returned to town. The night was warm, the darkness filled with the sound of new-fledged cicadas. He was using a bed, one chair, a bureau on which he had spread a towel and upon which lay his brushes, his watch, his pipe and tobacco pouch, and, propped against a book, a photograph of his step-daughter, Little Belle. Upon the glazed surface a highlight lay. He shifted the photograph until the face came clear. He stood before it, looking at the sweet, inscrutable face which looked in turn at something just beyond his shoulder, out of the dead cardboard. He was thinking of the grape arbor in Kinston, of summer twilight and the murmur of voices darkening into silence as he approached, who meant them, her, no harm; who meant her less than harm, good God; darkening into the pale whisper of her white dress, of the delicate and urgent mammalian whisper of that curious small flesh which he had not begot and in which appeared to be vatted delicately some seething sympathy with the blossoming grape.

He moved, suddenly. As of its own accord the photograph had shifted, slipping a little from its precarious balancing against the book. The image blurred into the highlight, like something familiar seen beneath disturbed though clear water; he looked at the familiar image with a kind of quiet horror and despair, at a face suddenly older in sin than he would ever be, a face more blurred than sweet, at eyes more secret than soft. In reaching for it, he knocked it flat; whereupon once more the face mused tenderly behind the rigid travesty of the painted mouth, contemplating something beyond his shoulder. He lay in bed, dressed, with the light burning, until he heard the court-house clock strike three. Then he left the house, putting his watch and his tobacco pouch into his pocket.

The railroad station was three quarters of a

mile away. The waiting room was lit by a single weak bulb. It was empty save for a man in overalls asleep on a bench, his head on his folded coat, snoring, and a woman in a calico dress, in a dingy shawl and a new hat trimmed with rigid and moribund flowers set square and awkward on her head. Her head was bent; she may have been asleep; her hands crossed on a paper-wrapped parcel upon her lap, a straw suit case at her feet. It was then that Horace found that he had forgot his pipe.

The train came, finding him tramping back and forth along the cinder-packed right-of-way. The man and woman got on, the man carrying his rumpled coat, the woman the parcel and the suit case. He followed them into the day coach filled with snoring, with bodies sprawled half into the aisle as though in the aftermath of a sudden and violent destruction, with dropped heads, open-mouthed, their throats turned profoundly upward as though waiting the stroke of knives.

He dozed. The train clicked on, stopped, jolted. He waked and dozed again. Someone shook him out of sleep into a primrose dawn, among unshaven puffy faces washed lightly over as though with the paling ultimate stain of a holocaust, blinking at one another with dead eyes into which personality returned in secret opaque waves. He got off, had breakfast, and took another accommodation, entering a car where a child wailed hopelessly, crunching peanut-shells under his feet as he moved up the car in a stale ammoniac odor until he found a seat beside a man. A moment later the man leaned forward and spat tobacco juice between his knees. Horace rose quickly and went forward into the smoking car. It was full too, the door between it and the jim crow car swinging open. Standing in the aisle he could look forward into a diminishing corridor of green plush seat-backs topped by hatted cannonballs swaying in unison, while gusts of talk and laughter blew back and kept in steady motion the blue acrid air in which white men sat, spitting into the aisle.

He changed again. The waiting crowd was composed half of young men in collegiate clothes with small cryptic badges on their shirts and vests, and two girls with painted small faces and scant bright dresses like identical artificial flowers surrounded each by bright and restless bees. When the train came they pushed gaily forward, talking and laughing, shouldering aside older people with gay rudeness, clashing and slamming seats back and settling themselves, turning their faces up out of laughter, their cold faces still toothed with it, as three middle-aged women moved down the car, looking tentatively left and right at the filled seats.

The two girls sat together, removing a fawn and a blue hat, lifting slender hands and preening not-quite-formless fingers about their close heads seen between the sprawled elbows and the leaning heads of two youths hanging over the back of the seat and surrounded by colored hat bands at various heights where the owners sat on the seat arms or stood in the aisle; and presently the conductor's cap as he thrust among them with plaintive, fretful cries, like a bird.

"Tickets. Tickets, please," he chanted. For an instant they held him there, invisible save for his cap. Then two young men slipped swiftly back and into the seat behind Horace. He could hear them breathing. Forward the conductor's punch clicked twice. He came on back. "Tickets," he chanted. "Tickets." He took Horace's and stopped where the youths sat.

"You already got mine," one said. "Up there."

"Where's your check?" the conductor said.

"You never gave us any. You got our tickets, though. Mine was number—" he repeated a number glibly, in a frank, pleasant tone. "Did you notice the number of yours, Shack?"

The second one repeated a number in a frank, pleasant tone. "Sure you got ours. Look and

203

see." He began to whistle between his teeth, a broken dance rhythm, unmusical.

"Do you eat at Gordon hall?" the other said.

"No. I have natural halitosis." The conductor went on. The whistle reached crescendo, clapped off by his hands on his knees, ejaculating duh-duh-duh. Then he just squalled, meaningless, vertiginous; to Horace it was like sitting before a series of printed pages turned in furious snatches, leaving a series of cryptic, headless and tailless evocations on the mind.

"She's travelled a thousand miles without a ticket."

"Marge too."

"Beth too."

"Duh-duh-duh."

"Marge too."

"I'm going to punch mine Friday night."

"Eeeeyow."

"Do you like liver?"

"I cant reach that far."

"Eeeeeyow."

They whistled, clapping their heels on the floor to furious crescendo, saying duh-duh-duh. The first jolted the seat back against Horace's head. He rose. "Come on," he said. "He's done gone." Again the seat jarred into Horace and he watched them return and join the group that blocked the aisle, saw one of them lay his bold,

204

rough hand flat upon one of the bright, soft faces uptilted to them. Beyond the group a countrywoman with an infant in her arms stood braced against a seat. From time to time she looked back at the blocked aisle and the empty seats beyond.

At Oxford he descended into a throng of them at the station, hatless, in bright dresses, now and then with books in their hands and surrounded still by swarms of colored shirts. Impassable, swinging hands with their escorts, objects of casual and puppyish pawings, they dawdled up the hill toward the college, swinging their little hips, looking at Horace with cold, blank eyes as he stepped off the walk in order to pass them.

At the top of the hill three paths diverged through a broad grove beyond which, in green vistas, buildings in red brick or gray stone gleamed, and where a clear soprano bell began to ring. The procession became three streams, thinning rapidly upon the dawdling couples, swinging hands, strolling in erratic surges, lurching into one another with puppyish squeals, with the random intense purposelessness of children.

The broader path led to the postoffice. He entered and waited until the window was clear.

"I'm trying to find a young lady, Miss Temple Drake. I probably just missed her, didn't I?"

"She's not here any longer," the clerk said. "She quit school about two weeks ago." He was young: a dull, smooth face behind horn glasses, the hair meticulous. After a time Horace heard himself asking quietly:

"You dont know where she went?"

The clerk looked at him. He leaned, lowering his voice: "Are you another detective?"

"Yes," Horace said, "yes. No matter. It doesn't matter." Then he was walking quietly down the steps, into the sunlight again. He stood there while on both sides of him they passed in a steady stream of little colored dresses, bare-armed, with close bright heads, with that identical cool, innocent, unabashed expression which he knew well in their eyes, above the savage identical paint upon their mouths; like music moving, like honey poured in sunlight, pagan and evanescent and serene, thinly evocative of all lost days and outpaced delights, in the sun. Bright, trembling with heat, it lay in open glades of miragelike glimpses of stone or brick: columns without tops, towers apparently floating above a green cloud in slow ruin against the southwest wind, sinister, imponderable, bland; and he standing there listening to the sweet cloistral bell, thinking Now what? What now? and answering himself: Why, nothing. Nothing. It's finished.

He returned to the station an hour before the train was due, a filled but unlighted cob pipe in his hand. In the lavatory he saw, scrawled on the foul, stained wall, her pencilled name. Temple Drake. He read it quietly, his head bent, slowly fingering the unlighted pipe.

A half hour before the train came they began to gather, strolling down the hill and gathering along the platform with thin, bright, raucous laughter, their blonde legs monotonous, their bodies moving continually inside their scant garments with that awkward and voluptuous purposelessness of the young.

The return train carried a pullman. He went on through the day coach and entered it. There was only one other occupant: a man in the center of the car, next the window, bareheaded, leaning back, his elbow on the window sill and an unlighted cigar in his ringed hand. When the train drew away, passing the sleek crowns in increasing reverse, the other passenger rose and went forward toward the day coach. He carried an overcoat on his arm, and a soiled, light-colored felt hat. With the corner of his eye Horace saw his hand fumbling at his breast pocket, and he remarked the severe trim of hair across the man's vast, soft, white neck. Like with a guillotine, Horace thought, watching the man sidle past the porter in the aisle and vanish, passing out of his sight and his mind in the act of flinging the hat onto his head. The train sped on, swaying on the curves, flashing past an occasional house, through cuts and across valleys where young cotton wheeled slowly in fanlike rows.

The train checked speed; a jerk came back, and four whistle-blasts. The man in the soiled hat entered, taking a cigar from his breast pocket. He came down the aisle swiftly, looking at Horace. He slowed, the cigar in his fingers. The train jolted again. The man flung his hand out and caught the back of the seat facing Horace.

"Aint this Judge Benbow?" he said. Horace looked up into a vast, puffy face without any mark of age or thought whatever—a majestic sweep of flesh on either side of a small blunt nose, like looking out over a mesa, yet withal some indefinable quality of delicate paradox, as though the Creator had completed his joke by lighting the munificent expenditure of putty with something originally intended for some weak, acquisitive creature like a squirrel or a rat. "Dont I address Judge Benbow?" he said, offering his hand. "I'm Senator Snopes, Cla'ence Snopes."

"Oh," Horace said, "yes. Thanks," he said,

"but I'm afraid you anticipate a little. Hope, rather."

The other waved the cigar, the other hand, palm-up, the third finger discolored faintly at the base of a huge ring, in Horace's face. Horace shook it and freed his hand. "I thought I recognised you when you got on at Oxford," Snopes said, "but I— May I set down?" he said, already shoving at Horace's knee with his leg. He flung the overcoat—a shoddy blue garment with a greasy velvet collar—on the seat and sat down as the train stopped. "Yes, sir, I'm always glad to see any of the boys, any time . . ." He leaned across Horace and peered out the window at a small dingy station with its cryptic bulletin board chalked over, an express truck bearing a wire chicken coop containing two forlorn fowls, at three or four men in overalls gone restfully against the wall, chewing. " 'Course you aint in my county no longer, but what I say a man's friends is his friends, whichever way they vote. Because a friend is a friend, and whether he can do anything for me or not . . ." He leaned back, the unlighted cigar in his fingers. "You aint come all the way up from the big town, then."

"No," Horace said.

"Anytime you're in Jackson, I'll be glad to

accommodate you as if you was still in my county. Dont no man stay so busy he aint got time for his old friends, what I say. Let's see, you're in Kinston, now, aint you? I know your senators. Fine men, both of them, but I just caint call their names."

"I really couldn't say, myself," Horace said. The train started. Snopes leaned into the aisle, looking back. His light gray suit had been pressed but not cleaned. "Well," he said. He rose and took up the overcoat. "Any time you're in the city . . . You going to Jefferson, I reckon?"

"Yes," Horace said.

"I'll see you again, then."

"Why not ride back here?" Horace said. "You'll find it more comfortable."

"I'm going up and have a smoke," Snopes said, waving the cigar. "I'll see you again."

"You can smoke here. There aren't any ladies."

"Sure," Snopes said. "I'll see you at Holly Springs." He went on back toward the day coach and passed out of sight with the cigar in his mouth. Horace remembered him ten years ago as a hulking, dull youth, son of a restaurant-owner, member of a family which had been moving from the Frenchman's Bend neighborhood into Jefferson for the past twenty years, in sections; a family of enough ramifications to have elected him to the legislature without recourse to a public polling.

He sat quite still, the cold pipe in his hand. He rose and went forward through the day coach, then into the smoker. Snopes was in the aisle, his thigh draped over the arm of a seat where four men sat, using the unlighted cigar to gesture with. Horace caught his eye and beckoned from the vestibule. A moment later Snopes joined him, the overcoat on his arm.

"How are things going at the capital?" Horace said.

Snopes began to speak in his harsh, assertive voice. There emerged gradually a picture of stupid chicanery and petty corruption for stupid and petty ends, conducted principally in hotel rooms into which bellboys whisked with bulging jackets upon discreet flicks of skirts in swift closet doors. "Anytime you're in town," he said. "I always like to show the boys around. Ask anybody in town; they'll tell you if it's there, Cla'ence Snopes'll know where it is. You got a pretty tough case up home there, what I hear."

"Cant tell yet," Horace said. He said: "I stopped off at Oxford today, at the university, speaking to some of my step-daughter's friends.

One of her best friends is no longer in school there. A young lady from Jackson named Temple Drake."

Snopes was watching him with thick, small, opaque eyes. "Oh, yes; Judge Drake's gal," he said. "The one that ran away."

"Ran away?" Horace said. "Ran back home, did she? What was the trouble? Fail in her work?"

"I dont know. When it come out in the paper folks thought she'd run off with some fellow. One of them companionate marriages."

"But when she turned up at home, they knew it wasn't that, I reckon. Well, well, Belle'll be surprised. What's she doing now? Running around Jackson, I suppose?"

"She aint there."

"Not?" Horace said. He could feel the other watching him. "Where is she?"

"Her paw sent her up north somewhere, with an aunt. Michigan. It was in the papers couple days later."

"Oh," Horace said. He still held the cold pipe, and he discovered his hand searching his pocket for a match. He drew a deep breath. "That Jackson paper's a pretty good paper. It's considered the most reliable paper in the state, isn't it?"

212

"Sure," Snopes said. "You was at Oxford trying to locate her?"

"No, no. I just happened to meet a friend of my daughter who told me she had left school. Well, I'll see you at Holly Springs."

"Sure," Snopes said. Horace returned to the pullman and sat down and lit the pipe.

When the train slowed for Holly Springs he went to the vestibule, then he stepped quickly back into the car. Snopes emerged from the day coach as the porter opened the door and swung down the step, stool in hand. Snopes descended. He took something from his breast pocket and gave it to the porter. "Here, George," he said, "have a cigar."

Horace descended. Snopes went on, the soiled hat towering half a head above any other. Horace looked at the porter.

"He gave it to you, did he?"

The porter chucked the cigar on his palm. He put it in his pocket.

"What're you going to do with it?" Horace said.

"I wouldn't give it to nobody I know," the porter said.

"Does he do this very often?"

"Three-four times a year. Seems like I always git him, too . . . Thank' suh."

Horace saw Snopes enter the waiting-room; the soiled hat, the vast neck, passed again out of his mind. He filled the pipe again.

From a block away he heard the Memphis-bound train come in. It was at the platform when he reached the station. Beside the open vestibule Snopes stood, talking with two youths in new straw hats, with something vaguely mentorial about his thick shoulders and his gestures. The train whistled. The two youths got on. Horace stepped back around the corner of the station.

When his train came he saw Snopes get on ahead of him and enter the smoker. Horace knocked out his pipe and entered the day coach and found a seat at the rear, facing backward.

XX

As HORACE WAS LEAVING THE STATION AT Jefferson a townward-bound car slowed beside him. It was the taxi which he used to go out to his sister's. "I'll give you a ride, this time," the driver said.

"Much obliged," Horace said. He got in. When the car entered the square, the courthouse clock said only twenty minutes past eight, yet there was no light in the hotel room window. "Maybe the child's asleep," Horace said. He said. "If you'll just drop me at the hotel—" Then he found that the driver was watching him, with a kind of discreet curiosity.

"You been out of town today," the driver said.

"Yes," Horace said. "What is it? What happened here today?"

"She aint staying at the hotel anymore. I heard Mrs Walker taken her in at the jail."

"Oh," Horace said. "I'll get out at the hotel."

The lobby was empty. After a moment the proprietor appeared: a tight, iron-gray man with a toothpick, his vest open upon a neat paunch. The woman was not there. "It's these church ladies," he said. He lowered his voice, the toothpick in his fingers. "They come in this morning. A committee of them. You know how it is, I reckon."

"You mean to say you let the Baptist church dictate who your guests shall be?"

"It's them ladies. You know how it is, once they get set on a thing. A man might just as well give up and do like they say. Of course, with me—"

"By God, if there was a man—"

"Shhhhhh," the proprietor said. "You know how it is when them—"

"But of course there wasn't a man who would— And you call yourself one, that'll let—"

"I got a certain position to keep up myself," the proprietor said in a placative tone. "If you come right down to it." He stepped back a little, against the desk. "I reckon I can say who'll stay in my house and who wont," he said. "And I know some more folks around here that better do the same thing. Not no mile off, neither. I

216

aint beholden to no man. Not to you, noways."

"Where is she now? or did they drive her out of town?"

"That aint my affair, where folks go after they check out," the proprietor said, turning his back. He said: "I reckon somebody took her in, though."

"Yes," Horace said. "Christians. Christians." He turned toward the door. The proprietor called him. He turned. The other was taking a paper down from a pigeon-hole. Horace returned to the desk. The paper lay on the desk. The proprietor leaned with his hands on the desk, the toothpick tilted in his mouth.

"She said you'd pay it," he said.

He paid the bill, counting the money down with shaking hands. He entered the jail yard and went to the door and knocked. After a while a lank, slattern woman came with a lamp, holding a man's coat across her breast. She peered at him and said before he could speak:

"You're lookin fer Miz Goodwin, I reckon."

"Yes. How did— Did—"

"You're the lawyer. I've seed you befo. She's hyer. Sleepin now."

"Thanks," Horace said, "Thanks. I knew that someone— I didn't believe that—"

"I reckon I kin always find a bed fer a woman and child," the woman said. "I dont keer whut

Ed says. Was you wantin her special? She's sleepin now."

"No, no; I just wanted to—"

The woman watched him across the lamp. " 'Taint no need botherin her, then. You kin come around in the mawnin and git her a boa'din-place. 'Taint no hurry."

On the next afternoon Horace went out to his sister's, again in a hired car. He told her what had happened. "I'll have to take her home now."

"Not into my house," Narcissa said.

He looked at her. Then he began to fill his pipe slowly and carefully. "It's not a matter of choice, my dear. You must see that."

"Not in my house," Narcissa said. "I thought we settled that."

He struck the match and lit the pipe and put the match carefully into the fireplace. "Do you realise that she has been practically turned into the streets? That—"

"That shouldn't be a hardship. She ought to be used to that."

He looked at her. He put the pipe in his mouth and smoked it to a careful coal, watching his hand tremble upon the stem. "Listen. By to-morrow they will probably ask her to leave town.

Just because she happens not to be married to the man whose child she carries about these sanctified streets. But who told them? That's what I want to know. I know that nobody in Jefferson knew it except—"

"You were the first I heard tell it," Miss Jenny said. "But, Narcissa, why—"

"Not in my house," Narcissa said.

"Well," Horace said. He drew the pipe to an even coal. "That settles it, of course," he said, in a dry, light voice.

She rose. "Will you stay here tonight?"

"What? No. No. I'll—I told her I'd come for her at the jail and . . ." He sucked at his pipe. "Well, I dont suppose it matters. I hope it doesn't."

She was still paused, turning. "Will you stay or not?"

"I could even tell her I had a puncture," Horace said. "Time's not such a bad thing after all. Use it right, and you can stretch anything out, like a rubber band, until it busts somewhere, and there you are, with all tragedy and despair in two little knots between thumb and finger of each hand."

"Will you stay, or wont you stay, Horace?" Narcissa said.

"I think I'll stay," Horace said.

He was in bed. He had been lying in the dark for about an hour, when the door of the room opened, felt rather than seen or heard. It was his sister. He rose to his elbow. She took shape vaguely, approaching the bed. She came and looked down at him. "How much longer are you going to keep this up?" she said.

"Just until morning," he said. "I'm going back to town. You need not see me again."

She stood beside the bed, motionless. After a moment her cold unbending voice came down to him: "You know what I mean."

"I promise not to bring her into your house again. You can send Isom in to hide in the canna bed." She said nothing. "Surely you dont object to my living there, do you?"

"I dont care where you live. The question is, where I live. I live here, in this town. I'll have to stay here. But you're a man. It doesn't matter to you. You can go away."

"Oh," he said. He lay quite still. She stood above him, motionless. They spoke quietly, as though they were discussing wall-paper, food.

"Dont you see, this is my home, where I must spend the rest of my life. Where I was born. I dont care where else you go nor what you do. I dont care how many women you have nor who they are. But I cannot have my brother mixed up with a woman people are talking about.

I dont expect you to have consideration for me; I ask you to have consideration for our father and mother. Take her to Memphis. They say you refused to let the man have bond to get out of jail; take her on to Memphis. You can think of a lie to tell him about that, too."

"Oh. So you think that, do you?"

"I dont think anything about it. I dont care. That's what people in town think. So it doesn't matter whether it's true or not. What I do mind is, everyday you force me to have to tell lies for you. Go away from here, Horace. Anybody but you would realise it's a case of cold-blooded murder."

"And over her, of course. I suppose they say that too, out of their odorous and omnipotent sanctity. Do they say yet that it was I killed him?"

"I dont see that it makes any difference who did it. The question is, are you going to stay mixed up with it? When people already believe you and she are slipping into my house at night." Her cold, unbending voice shaped the words in the darkness above him. Through the window, upon the blowing darkness, came the drowsy dissonance of cicada and cricket.

"Do you believe that?" he said.

"It doesn't matter what I believe. Go on away, Horace. I ask it."

221

"And leave her—them, flat?"

"Hire a lawyer, if he still insists he's innocent. I'll pay for it. You can get a better criminal lawyer than you are. She wont know it. She
wont even care. Cant you see that she is just
leading you on to get him out of jail for nothing? Dont you know that woman has got money
hidden away somewhere? You're going back
into town tomorrow, are you?" She turned, began to dissolve into the blackness. "You wont
leave before breakfast."

The next morning at breakfast, his sister
said: "Who will be the lawyer on the other side
of the case?"

"District Attorney. Why?"

She rang the bell and sent for fresh bread.
Horace watched her. "Why do you ask that?"
Then he said: "Damn little squirt." He was talking about the district attorney, who had also
been raised in Jefferson and who had gone to the
town school with them. "I believe he was at
the bottom of that business night before last.
The hotel. Getting her turned out of the hotel
for public effect, political capital. By God, if I
knew that, believed that he had done that just to
get elected to Congress . . ."

After Horace left, Narcissa went up to Miss

222

Jenny's room. "Who is the District Attorney?" she said.

"You've known him all your life," Miss Jenny said. "You even elected him. Eustace Graham. What do you want to know for? Are you looking around for a substitute for Gowan Stevens?"

"I just wondered," Narcissa said.

"Fiddlesticks," Miss Jenny said. "You dont wonder. You just do things and then stop until the next time to do something comes around."

Horace met Snopes emerging from the barber-shop, his jowls gray with powder, moving in an effluvium of pomade. In the bosom of his shirt, beneath his bow tie, he wore an imitation ruby stud which matched his ring. The tie was of blue polka-dots; the very white spots on it appeared dirty when seen close; the whole man with his shaved neck and pressed clothes and gleaming shoes emanated somehow the idea that he had been dry-cleaned rather than washed.

"Well, Judge," he said, "I hear you're having some trouble gittin a boarding-place for that client of yourn. Like I always say—" he leaned, his voice lowered, his mud-colored eyes roving aside "—the church aint got no place in politics, and women aint got no place in neither

223

one, let alone the law. Let them stay at home and they'll find plenty to do without upsetting a man's law-suit. And besides, a man aint no more than human, and what he does aint nobody's business but his. What you done with her?"

"She's at the jail," Horace said. He spoke shortly, making to pass on. The other blocked his way with an effect of clumsy accident.

"You got them all stirred up, anyhow. Folks is saying you wouldn't git Goodwin no bond, so he'd have to stay—" again Horace made to pass on. "Half the trouble in this world is caused by women, I always say. Like that girl gittin her paw all stirred up, running off like she done. I reckon he done the right thing sending her clean outen the state."

"Yes," Horace said in a dry, furious voice.

"I'm mighty glad to hear your case is going all right. Between you and me, I'd like to see a good lawyer make a monkey outen that District Attorney. Give a fellow like that a little county office and he gits too big for his pants right away. Well, glad to've saw you. I got some business up town for a day or two. I dont reckon you'll be going up that-a-way?"

"What?" Horace said. "Up where?"

"Memphis. Anything I can do for you?"

"No," Horace said. He went on. For a short

distance he could not see at all. He tramped steadily, the muscles beside his jaws beginning to ache, passing people who spoke to him, unawares.

XXI

As THE TRAIN NEARED MEMPHIS VIRGIL Snopes ceased talking and began to grow quieter and quieter, while on the contrary his companion, eating from a parrafin-paper package of popcorn and molasses, grew livelier and livelier with a quality something like intoxication, seeming not to notice the inverse state of his friend. He was still talking away when, carrying their new, imitation leather suit cases, their new hats slanted above their shaven necks, they descended at the station. In the waiting room Fonzo said:

"Well, what're we going to do first?" Virgil said nothing. Someone jostled them; Fonzo caught at his hat. "What we going to do?" he said. Then he looked at Virgil, at his face. "What's the matter?"

"Aint nothing the matter," Virgil said.

"Well, what're we going to do? You been here before. I aint."

"I reckon we better kind of look around," Virgil said.

Fonzo was watching him, his blue eyes like china. "What's the matter with you? All the time on the train you was talking about how many times you been to Memphis. I bet you aint never bu—" Someone jostled them, thrust them apart; a stream of people began to flow between them. Clutching his suit case and hat Fonzo fought his way back to his friend.

"I have, too," Virgil said, looking glassily about.

"Well, what we going to do then? It wont be open till eight oclock in the morning."

"What you in such a rush for, then?"

"Well, I don't aim to stay here all night. . . . What did you do when you was here before?"

"Went to the hotel," Virgil said.

"Which one? They got more than one here. You reckon all these folks could stay in one hotel? Which one was it?"

Virgil's eyes were also a pale, false blue. He looked glassily about. "The Gayoso hotel," he said.

"Well, let's go to it," Fonzo said. They moved toward the exit. A man shouted "taxi" at them; a redcap tried to take Fonzo's bag. "Look out," he said, drawing it back. On the street more cabmen barked at them.

"So this is Memphis," Fonzo said. "Which way is it, now?" He had no answer. He looked around and saw Virgil in the act of turning away from a cabman. "What you—"

"Up this way," Virgil said. "It aint far."

It was a mile and a half. From time to time they swapped hands with the bags. "So this is Memphis," Fonzo said. "Where have I been all my life?" When they entered the Gayoso a porter offered to take the bags. They brushed past him and entered, walking gingerly on the tile floor. Virgil stopped.

"Come on," Fonzo said.

"Wait," Virgil said.

"Thought you was here before," Fonzo said.

"I was. This hyer place is too high. They'll want a dollar a day here."

"What we going to do, then?"

"Let's kind of look around."

They returned to the street. It was five oclock. They went on, looking about, carrying the suit cases. They came to another hotel. Looking in they saw marble, brass cuspidors, hurrying bell-boys, people sitting among potted plants.

"That un'll be just as bad," Virgil said.

"What we going to do then? We caint walk around all night."

"Let's git off this hyer street," Virgil said. They left Main Street. At the next corner Virgil
228

turned again. "Let's look down this-a-way. Git away from all that ere plate glass and monkey niggers. That's what you have to pay for in them places."

"Why? It's already bought when we got there. How come we have to pay for it?"

"Suppose somebody broke it while we was there. Suppose they couldn't ketch who done it. Do you reckon they'd let us out withouten we paid our share?"

At five-thirty they entered a narrow dingy street of frame houses and junk yards. Presently they came to a three storey house in a small grassless yard. Before the entrance a lattice-work false entry leaned. On the steps sat a big woman in a mother hubbard, watching two fluffy white dogs which moved about the yard.

"Let's try that un," Fonzo said.

"That aint no hotel. Where's ere sign?"

"Why aint it?" Fonzo said. " 'Course it is. Who ever heard of anybody just living in a three storey house?"

"We cant go in this-a-way," Virgil said. "This hyer's the back. Don't you see that privy?" jerking his head toward the lattice.

"Well, let's go around to the front, then," Fonzo said. "Come on."

They went around the block. The opposite side was filled by a row of automobile salesrooms. They stood in the middle of the block, their suit cases in their right hands.

"I dont believe you was ever here before, noways," Fonzo said.

"Let's go back. That must a been the front."

"With the privy built onto the front door?" Fonzo said.

"We can ask that lady."

"Who can? I aint."

"Let's go back and see, anyway."

They returned. The woman and the dogs were gone.

"Now you done it," Fonzo said. "Aint you?"

"Let's wait a while. Maybe she'll come back."

"It's almost seven oclock," Fonzo said.

They set the bags down beside the fence. The lights had come on, quivering high in the serried windows against the tall serene western sky.

"I can smell ham, too," Fonzo said.

A cab drew up. A plump blonde woman got out, followed by a man. They watched them go up the walk and enter the lattice. Fonzo sucked his breath across his teeth. "Durned if they didn't," he whispered.

"Maybe it's her husband," Virgil said.

Fonzo picked up his bag. "Come on."

"Wait," Virgil said. "Give them a little time."

They waited. The man came out and got in the cab and went away.

"Caint be her husband," Fonzo said. "I wouldn't a never left. Come on." He entered the gate.

"Wait," Virgil said.

"You can," Fonzo said. Virgil took his bag and followed. He stopped while Fonzo opened the lattice gingerly and peered in. "Aw, hell," he said. He entered. There was another door, with curtained glass. Fonzo knocked.

"Why didn't you push that ere button?" Virgil said. "Dont you know city folks dont answer no knock?"

"All right," Fonzo said. He rang the bell. The door opened. It was the woman in the mother hubbard; they could hear the dogs behind her.

"Got ere extra room?" Fonzo said.

Miss Reba looked at them, at their new hats and the suit cases.

"Who sent you here?" she said.

"Didn't nobody. We just picked it out." Miss Reba looked at him. "Them hotels is too high."

Miss Reba breathed harshly. "What you boys doing?"

"We come hyer on business," Fonzo said. "We aim to stay a good spell."

231

"If it aint too high," Virgil said.

Miss Reba looked at him. "Where you from, honey?"

They told her, and their names. "We aim to be hyer a month or more, if it suits us."

"Why, I reckon so," she said after a while. She looked at them. "I can let you have a room, but I'll have to charge you extra whenever you do business in it. I got my living to make like everbody else."

"We aint," Fonzo said. 'We'll do our business at the college."

"What college?" Miss Reba said.

"The barber's college," Fonzo said.

"Look here," Miss Reba said, "you little whipper-snapper." Then she began to laugh, her hand at her breast. They watched her soberly while she laughed in harsh gasps. "Lord, Lord," she said. "Come in here."

The room was at the top of the house, at the back. Miss Reba showed them the bath. When she put her hand on the door a woman's voice said: "Just a minute, dearie" and the door opened and she passed them, in a kimono. They watched her go up the hall, rocked a little to their young foundations by a trail of scent which she left. Fonzo nudged Virgil surreptitiously. In their room again he said:

"That was another one. She's got two daugh-

232

ters. Hold me, big boy; I'm heading for the hen-house."

They didn't go to sleep for some time that first night, what with the strange bed and room and the voices. They could hear the city, evocative and strange, imminent and remote; threat and promise both—a deep, steady sound upon which invisible lights glittered and wavered: colored coiling shapes of splendor in which already women were beginning to move in suave attitudes of new delights and strange nostalgic promises. Fonzo thought of himself surrounded by tier upon tier of drawn shades, rose-colored, beyond which, in a murmur of silk, in panting whispers, the apotheosis of his youth assumed a thousand avatars. Maybe it'll begin tomorrow, he thought; maybe by tomorrow night . . . A crack of light came over the top of the shade and sprawled in a spreading fan upon the ceiling. Beneath the window he could hear a voice, a woman's, then a man's: they blended, murmured; a door closed. Someone came up the stairs in swishing garments, on the swift hard heels of a woman.

He began to hear sounds in the house: voices, laughter; a mechanical piano began to play. "Hear them?" he whispered.

"She's got a big family, I reckon," Virgil said, his voice already dull with sleep.

233

"Family, hell," Fonzo said. "It's a party. Wish I was to it."

On the third day as they were leaving the house in the morning, Miss Reba met them at the door. She wanted to use their room in the afternoons while they were absent. There was to be a detective's convention in town and business would look up some, she said. "Your things'll be all right. I'll have Minnie lock everything up before hand. Aint nobody going to steal nothing from you in my house."

"What business you reckon she's in?" Fonzo said when they reached the street.

"Don't know," Virgil said.

"Wish I worked for her, anyway," Fonzo said. "With all them women in kimonos and such running around."

"Wouldn't do you no good," Virgil said. "They're all married. Aint you heard them?"

The next afternoon when they returned from the school they found a woman's undergarment under the washstand . . . Fonzo picked it up. "She's a dress-maker," he said.

"Reckon so," Virgil said. "Look and see if they taken anything of yourn."

The house appeared to be filled with people who did not sleep at night at all. They could hear them at all hours, running up and down the stairs, and always Fonzo would be conscious of women, of female flesh. It got to where he seemed to lie in his celibate bed surrounded by women, and he would lie beside the steadily snoring Virgil, his ears strained for the murmurs, the whispers of silk that came through the walls and the floor, that seemed to be as much a part of both as the planks and the plaster, thinking that he had been in Memphis ten days, yet the extent of his acquaintance was a few of his fellow pupils at the school. After Virgil was asleep he would rise and unlock the door and leave it ajar, but nothing happened.

On the twelfth day he told Virgil they were going visiting, with one of the barber-students.

"Where?" Virgil said.

"That's all right. You come on. I done found out something. And when I think I been here two weeks without knowing about it—"

"What's it going to cost?" Virgil said.

"When'd you ever have any fun for nothing?" Fonzo said. "Come on."

"I'll go," Virgil said. "But I aint going to promise to spend nothing."

"You wait and say that when we get there," Fonzo said.

The barber took them to a brothel. When they came out Fonzo said. "And to think I been here two weeks without never knowing about that house."

235

"I wisht you hadn't never learned," Virgil said. "It cost three dollars."

"Wasn't it worth it?" Fonzo said.

"Aint nothing worth three dollars you caint tote off with you," Virgil said.

When they reached home Fonzo stopped. "We got to sneak in, now," he said. "If she was to find out where we been and what we been doing, she might not let us stay in the house with them ladies no more."

"That's so," Virgil said. "Durn you. Hyer you done made me spend three dollars, and now you fixing to git us both throwed out."

"You do like I do," Fonzo said. "That's all you got to do. Dont say nothing."

Minnie let them in. The piano was going full blast. Miss Reba appeared in a door, with a tin cup in her hand. "Well, well," she said, "you boys been out mighty late tonight."

"Yessum," Fonzo said, prodding Virgil toward the stairs. "We been to prayer-meeting."

In bed, in the dark, they could still hear the piano.

"You made me spend three dollars," Virgil said.

"Aw, shut up," Fonzo said. "When I think I been here for two whole weeks almost . . ."

The next afternoon they came home through
236

the dusk, with the lights winking on, beginning to flare and gleam, and the women on their twinkling blonde legs meeting men and getting into automobiles and such.

"How about that three dollars now?" Fonzo said.

"I reckon we better not go over night," Virgil said. "It'll cost too much."

"That's right," Fonzo said. "Somebody might see us and tell her."

They waited two nights. "Now it'll be six dollars," Virgil said.

"Don't come, then," Fonzo said.

When they returned home Fonzo said: "Try to act like someding, this time. She near about caught us before on account of the way you acted."

"What if she does?" Virgil said in a sullen voice. "She caint eat us."

They stood outside the lattice, whispering.

"How you know she caint?" Fonzo said.

"She dont want to, then."

"How you know she dont want to?"

"Maybe she dont," Virgil said. Fonzo. opened the lattice door. "I caint eat that six dollars, noways," Virgil said. "Wisht I could."

Minnie let them in. She said: "Somebody huntin you all." They waited in the hall.

"We done caught now," Virgil said. "I told you about throwing that money away."

"Aw, shut up," Fonzo said.

A man emerged from a door, a big man with his hat cocked over one ear, his arm about a blonde woman in a red dress. "There's Cla'-ence," Virgil said.

In their room Clarence said: "How'd you get into this place?"

"Just found it," Virgil said. They told him about it. He sat on the bed, in his soiled hat, a cigar in his fingers.

"Where you been tonight?" he said. They didn't answer. They looked at him with blank, watchful faces. "Come on. I know. Where was it?" They told him.

"Cost me three dollars, too," Virgil said.

"I'll be durned if you aint the biggest fool this side of Jackson," Clarence said. "Come on here." They followed sheepishly. He led them from the house and for three or four blocks. They crossed a street of negro stores and the-atres and turned into a narrow, dark street and stopped at a house with red shades in the lighted windows. Clarence rang the bell. They could hear music inside, and shrill voices, and feet. They were admitted into a bare hallway where two shabby negro men argued with a drunk white man in greasy overalls. Through an open

238

door they saw a room filled with coffee-colored women in bright dresses, with ornate hair and golden smiles.

"Them's niggers," Virgil said.

" 'Course they're niggers," Clarence said, "But see this?" he waved a banknote in his cousin's face. "This stuff is color-blind."

XXII

On THE THIRD DAY OF HIS SEARCH, HORACE
found a domicile for the woman and child. It
was in the ramshackle house of an old half-
crazed white woman who was believed to manu-
facture spells for negroes. It was on the edge of
town, set in a tiny plot of ground choked and
massed with waist-high herbage in an unbroken
jungle across the front. At the back a path had
been trodden from the broken gate to the door.
All night a dim light burned in the crazy depths
of the house and at almost any hour of the
twenty-four a wagon or a buggy might be seen
tethered in the lane behind it and a negro entering or leaving the back door.

The house had been entered once by officers
searching for whisky. They found nothing save
a few dried bunches of weeds, and a collection of
dirty bottles containing liquid of which they
could say nothing surely save that it was not al-

coholic, while the old woman, held by two men, her lank grayish hair shaken before the glittering collapse of her face, screamed invective at them in her cracked voice. In a lean-to shed room containing a bed and a barrel of anonymous refuse and trash in which mice rattled all night long, the woman found a home.

"You'll be all right here," Horace said. "You can always get me by telephone, at—" giving her the name of a neighbor. "No: wait; tomorrow I'll have the telephone put back in. Then you can—"

"Yes," the woman said. "I reckon you better not be coming out here."

"Why? Do you think that would—that I'd care a damn what—"

"You have to live here."

"I'm damned if I do. I've already let too many women run my affairs for me as it is, and if these uxorious . . ." But he knew he was just talking. He knew that she knew it too, out of that feminine reserve of unflagging suspicion of all peoples' actions which seems at first to be mere affinity for evil but which is in reality practical wisdom.

"I guess I'll find you if there's any need," she said. "There's not anything else I could do."

"By God," Horace said, "dont you let them . . . Bitches," he said; "bitches."

241

The next day he had the telephone installed. He did not see his sister for a week; she had no way of learning that he had a phone, yet when, a week before the opening of Court, the telephone shrilled into the quiet where he sat reading one evening, he thought it was Narcissa until, across a remote blaring of victrola or radio music, a man's voice spoke in a guarded, tomb-like tone.

"This is Snopes," it said. "How're you, Judge?"

"What?" Horace said. "Who is it?"

"Senator Snopes, Cla'ence Snopes." The victrola blared, faint, far away; he could see the man, the soiled hat, the thick shoulders, leaning above the instrument—in a drugstore or a restaurant—whispering into it behind a soft, huge, ringed hand, the telephone toylike in the other.

"Oh," Horace said. "Yes? What is it?"

"I got a little piece of information that might interest you."

"Information that would interest me?"

"I reckon so. That would interest a couple of parties." Against Horace's ear the radio or the victrola performed a reedy arpeggio of saxophones. Obscene, facile, they seemed to be quarreling with one another like two dexterous monkeys in a cage. He could hear the gross breathing of the man at the other end of the wire.

242

"All right," he said. "What do you know that would interest me?"

"I'll let you judge that."

"All right. I'll be down town in the morning. You can find me somewhere." Then he said immediately: "Hello!" The man sounded as though he were breathing in Horace's ear: a placid, gross sound, suddenly portentous somehow. "Hello!" Horace said.

"It evidently dont interest you, then. I reckon I'll dicker with the other party and not trouble you no more. Goodbye."

"No; wait," Horace said. "Hello! Hello!"

"Yeuh?"

"I'll come down tonight. I'll be there in about fifteen—"

" 'Taint no need of that," Snopes said. "I got my car. I'll drive up there."

He walked down to the gate. There was a moon tonight. Within the black-and-silver tunnel of cedars fireflies drifted in fatuous pinpricks. The cedars were black and pointed on the sky like a paper silhouette; the sloping lawn had a faint sheen, a patina like silver. Somewhere a whippoorwill called, reiterant, tremulous, plaintful above the insects. Three cars passed. The fourth slowed and swung toward the gate. Horace stepped into the light. Behind the wheel Snopes loomed bulkily, giving the impression of

243

having been inserted into the car before the top was put on. He extended his hand.

"How're you tonight, Judge? Didn't know you was living in town again until I tried to call you out to Mrs Sartorises."

"Well, thanks," Horace said. He freed his hand. "What's this you've got hold of?"

Snopes creased himself across the wheel and peered out beneath the top, toward the house.

"We'll talk here," Horace said. "Save you having to turn around."

"It aint very private here," Snopes said. "But that's for you to say." Huge and thick he loomed, hunched, his featureless face moonlike itself in the refraction of the moon. Horace could feel Snopes watching him, with that sense of portent which had come over the wire; a quality calculating and cunning and pregnant. It seemed to him that he watched his mind flicking this way and that, striking always that vast, soft, inert bulk, as though it were caught in an avalanche of cottonseed-hulls.

"Let's go to the house," Horace said. Snopes opened the door. "Go on," Horace said, "I'll walk up." Snopes drove on. He was getting out of the car when Horace overtook him. "Well, what is it?" Horace said.

Again Snopes looked at the house. "Keeping batch, are you?" he said. Horace said nothing.

"Like I always say, every married man ought to have a little place of his own, where he can git off to himself without it being nobody's business what he does. 'Course a man owes something to his wife, but what they dont know caint hurt them, does it? Long's he does that, I caint see where she's got ere kick coming. Aint that what you say?"

"She's not here," Horace said, "if that's what you're hinting it. What did you want to see me about?"

Again he felt Snopes watching him, the unabashed stare calculating and completely unbelieving. "Well, I always say, caint nobody tend to a man's private business but himself. I aint blaming you. But when you know me better, you'll know I aint loose-mouthed. I been around. I been there. . . . Have a cigar?" His big hand flicked to his breast and offered two cigars.

"No, thanks."

Snopes lit a cigar, his face coming out of the match like a pie set on edge.

"What did you want to see me about?" Horace said.

Snopes puffed the cigar. "Couple days ago I come onto a piece of information which will be of value to you, if I aint mistook."

"Oh. Of value. What value?"

"I'll leave that to you. I got another party I could dicker with, but being as me and you was fellow-townsmen and all that."

Here and there Horace's mind flicked and darted. Snopes' family originated somewhere near Frenchman's Bend and still lived there. He knew of the devious means by which information passed from man to man of that illiterate race which populated that section of the county. But surely it cant be something he'd try to sell to the State, he thought. Even he is not that big a fool.

"You'd better tell me what it is, then," he said.

He could feel Snopes watching him. "You remember one day you got on the train at Oxford, where you'd been on some bus——"

"Yes," Horace said.

Snopes puffed the cigar to an even coal, carefully, at some length. He raised his hand and drew it across the back of his neck. "You recall speaking to me about a girl."

"Yes. Then what?"

"That's for you to say."

He could smell the honeysuckle as it bore up the silver slope, and he heard the whippoorwill, liquid, plaintful, reiterant. "You mean, you know where she is?" Snopes said nothing. "And that for a price you'll tell?" Snopes said nothing. Horace shut his hands and put them in his pock-

246

ets, shut against his flanks. "What makes you think that information will interest me?"

"That's for you to judge. I aint conducting no murder case. I wasn't down there at Oxford looking for her. Of course, if it dont, I'll dicker with the other party. I just give you the chance."

Horace turned toward the steps. He moved gingerly, like an old man. "Let's sit down," he said. Snopes followed and sat on the step. They sat in the moonlight. "You know where she is?"

"I seen her." Again he drew his hand across the back of his neck. "Yes, sir. If she aint— hasn't been there, you can git your money back. I caint say no fairer, can I?"

"And what's your price?" Horace said. Snopes puffed the cigar to a careful coal. "Go on," Horace said. "I'm not going to haggle." Snopes told him. "All right," Horace said. "I'll pay it." He drew his knees up and set his elbows on them and laid his hands to his face. "Where is— Wait. Are you a Baptist, by any chance?"

"My folks is. I'm putty liberal, myself. I aint hidebound in no sense, as you'll find when you know me better."

"All right," Horace said from behind his hands. "Where is she?"

"I'll trust you," Snopes said. "She's in a Memphis 'ho'-house."

XXIII

As Horace entered Miss Reba's gate and approached the lattice door, someone called his name from behind him. It was evening; the windows in the weathered, scaling wall were close pale squares. He paused and looked back. Around an adjacent corner Snopes' head peered, turkey like. He stepped into view. He looked up at the house, then both ways along the street. He came along the fence and entered the gate with a wary air

"Well, Judge," he said. "Boys will be boys, wont they?" He didn't offer to shake hands. Instead he bulked above Horace with that air somehow assured and alert at the same time, glancing over his shoulder at the street. "Like I say, it never done no man no harm to git out now and then and—"

"What is it now?" Horace said. "What do you want with me?"

248

"Now, now, Judge. I aint going to tell this at home. Git that idea clean out of your mind. If us boys started telling what we know, caint none of us git off a train at Jefferson again, hey?"

"You know as well as I do what I'm doing here. What do you want with me?"

"Sure; sure," Snopes said. "I know how a feller feels, married and all and not being sho where his wife is at." Between jerky glances over his shoulder he winked at Horace. "Make your mind easy. It's the same with me as if the grave knowed it. Only I hate to see a good—" Horace had gone on toward the door. "Judge," Snopes said in a penetrant undertone. Horace turned. "Dont stay."

"Dont stay?"

"See her and then leave. It's a sucker place. Place for farm-boys. Higher'n Monte Carlo. I'll wait out hyer and I'll show you a place where—" Horace went on and entered the lattice. Two hours later, as he sat talking to Miss Reba in her room while beyond the door feet and now and then voices came and went in the hall and on the stair, Minnie entered with a torn scrap of paper and brought it to Horace.

"What's that?" Miss Reba said.

"That big pie-face-ted man left it fer him," Minnie said. "He say fer you to come on down there."

249

"Did you let him in?" Miss Reba said.

"Nome. He never tried to git in."

"I guess not," Miss Reba said. She grunted. "Do you know him?" she said to Horace.

"Yes. I cant seem to help myself," Horace said. He opened the paper. Torn from a hand-bill, it bore an address in pencil in a neat, flowing hand.

"He turned up here about two weeks ago," Miss Reba said. "Come in looking for two boys and sat around the dining-room blowing his head off and feeling the girls' behinds, but if he ever spent a cent I don't know it. Did he ever give you an order, Minnie?"

"Nome," Minnie said.

"And couple of nights later he was here again. Didn't spend nuttin, didn't do nuttin but talk, and I says to him 'Look here, mister, folks what uses this waiting-room has got to get on the train now and then.' So next time he brought a half-pint of whisky with him. I don't mind that, from a good customer. But when a fellow like him comes here three times, pinching my girls and bringing one half-pint of whisky and order-ing four coca-colas . . . Just a cheap, vulgar man, honey. So I told Minnie not to let him in anymore, and here one afternoon I aint no more than laid down for a nap when—I never did find out what he done to Minnie to get in. I know he never give her nuttin. How did he do it, Minnie? He must a showed you something you never seen before. Didn't he?"

Minnie tossed her head. "He aint got nothing I wantin to see. I done seed too many now fer my own good." Minnie's husband had quit her. He didn't approve of Minnie's business. He was a cook in a restaurant and he took all the clothes and jewelry the white ladies had given Minnie and went off with a waitress in the restaurant.

"He kept on asking and hinting around about that girl," Miss Reba said, "and me telling him to go ask Popeye if he wanted to know right bad. Not telling him nuttin except to get out and stay out, see; so this day it's about two in the afternoon and I'm asleep and Minnie lets him in and he asks her who's here and she tells him aint nobody, and he goes on up stairs. And Minnie says about that time Popeye comes in. She says she dont know what to do. She's scared not to let him in, and she says she knows if she does and he spatters that big bastard all over the upstairs floor, she knows I'll fire her and her husband just quit her and all.

"So Popeye goes on upstairs on them cat feet of his and comes on your friend on his knees, peeping through the keyhole. Minnie says Popeye stood behind him for about a minute, with

251

his hat cocked over one eye. She says he took out a cigarette and struck a match on his thumbnail without no noise and lit it and then she says he reached over and held the match to the back of your friend's neck, and Minnie says she stood there halfway up the stairs and watched them: that fellow kneeling there with his face like a pie took out of the oven too soon and Popeye squirting smoke through his nose and kind of jerking his head at him. Then she come on down and in about ten seconds here he comes down the stairs with both hands on top of his head, going wump-wump-wump inside like one of these here big dray-horses, and he pawed at the door for about a minute, moaning to himself like the wind in a chimney Minnie says, until she opened the door and let him out. And that's the last time he's even rung this bell until tonight. . . . Let me see that." Horace gave her the paper. "That's a nigger whore-house," she said. "The lous— Minnie, tell him his friend aint here. Tell him I dont know where he went."

Minnie went out. Miss Reba said.

"I've had all sorts of men in my house, but I got to draw the line somewhere. I had lawyers, too. I had the biggest lawyer in Memphis back there in my dining-room, treating my girls. A millionaire. He weighed two hundred and eighty pounds and he had his own special bed made and sent down here. It's upstairs right this minute. But all in the way of my business, not theirs. I aint going to have none of my girls pestered by lawyers without good reason."

"And you dont consider this good reason? That a man is being tried for his life for something he didn't do? You may be guilty right now of harboring a fugitive from justice."

"Then let them come take him. I got nuttin to do with it. I had too many police in this house to be scared of them." She raised the tankard and drank and drew the back of her hand across her mouth. "I aint going to have nuttin to do with nuttin I dont know about. What Popeye done outside is his business. When he starts killing folks in my house, then I'll take a hand."

"Have you any children?" She looked at him. "I dont mean to pry into your affairs," he said. "I was just thinking about that woman. She'll be on the streets again, and God only knows what will become of that baby."

"Yes," Miss Reba said. "I'm supporting four, in a Arkansaw home now. Not mine, though." She lifted the tankard and looked into it, oscillating it gently. She set it down again. "It better not been born at all," she said. "None of them had." She rose and came toward him, moving heavily, and stood above him with her harsh breath. She put her hand on his head and tilted his face up. "You aint lying to me, are you?" she said, her eyes piercing and intent and sad. "No, you aint." She released him. "Wait here a minute. I'll see." She went out. He heard her speak to Minnie in the hall, then he heard her toil up the stairs.

He sat quietly as she had left him. The room contained a wooden bed, a painted screen, three over-stuffed chairs, a wall safe. The dressing-table was littered with toilet articles tied in pink satin bows. The mantel supported a wax lily beneath a glass bell; above it, draped in black, the photograph of a meek-looking man with an enormous moustache. On the walls hung a few lithographs of spurious Greek scenes, and one picture done in tatting. Horace rose and went to the door. Minnie sat in a chair in the dim hall.

"Minnie," he said, "I've got to have a drink. A big one."

He had just finished it when Minnie entered again. "She say fer you to come on up," she said.

He mounted the stairs. Miss Reba waited at the top. She led the way up the hall and opened a door into a dark room. "You'll have to talk to her in the dark," she said. "She wont have no light." Light from the hall fell through the door and across the bed. "This aint hers," Miss Reba said. "Wouldn't even see you in her room at all. I reckon you better humor her until you

254

find out what you want." They entered. The light fell across the bed, upon a motionless curving ridge of bedclothing, the general tone of the bed unbroken. She'll smother, Horace thought. "Honey," Miss Reba said. The ridge did not move. "Here he is, honey. Long as you're all covered up, let's have some light. Then we can close the door." She turned the light on.

"She'll smother," Horace said.

"She'll come out in a minute," Miss Reba said. "Go on. Tell her what you want. I better stay. But dont mind me. I couldn't a stayed in my business without learning to be deaf and dumb a long time before this. And if I'd ever a had any curiosity, I'd have worn it out long ago in this house. Here's a chair." She turned, but Horace anticipated her and drew up two chairs. He sat down beside the bed and, talking at the top of the unstirring ridge, he told her what he wanted.

"I just want to know what really happened. You wont commit yourself. I know that you didn't do it. I'll promise before you tell me a thing that you wont have to testify in Court unless they are going to hang him without it. I know how you feel. I wouldn't bother you if the man's life were not at stake."

The ridge did not move.

"They're going to hang him for something he never done," Miss Reba said. "And she wont have nuttin, nobody. And you with diamonds, and her with that poor little kid. You seen it, didn't you?"

The ridge did not move.

"I know how you feel," Horace said. "You can use a different name, wear clothes nobody will recognise you in, glasses."

"They aint going to catch Popeye, honey," Miss Reba said. "Smart as he is. You dont know his name, noway, and if you have to go and tell them in the court, I'll send him word after you leave and he'll go somewheres and send for you. You and him dont want to stay here in Memphis. The lawyer'll take care of you and you wont have to tell nuttin you—" The ridge moved. Temple flung the covers back and sat up. Her head was tousled, her face puffed, two spots of rouge on her cheekbones and her mouth painted into a savage cupid's bow. She stared for an instant at Horace with black antagonism, then she looked away.

"I want a drink," she said, pulling up the shoulder of her gown.

"Lie down," Miss Reba said. "You'll catch cold."

"I want another drink," Temple said.

"Lie down and cover up your nekkidness,

256

anyway," Miss Reba said, rising. "You already had three since supper."

Temple dragged the gown up again. She looked at Horace. "You give me a drink, then."

"Come on, honey," Miss Reba said, trying to push her down. "Lie down and get covered up and tell him about that business. I'll get you a drink in a minute."

"Let me alone," Temple said, writhing free. Miss Reba drew the covers about her shoulders. "Give me a cigarette, then. Have you got one?" she asked Horace.

"I'll get you one in a minute," Miss Reba said. "Will you do what he wants you to?"

"What?" Temple said. She looked at Horace with her black, belligerent stare.

"You needn't tell me where your—he—" Horace said.

"Dont think I'm afraid to tell," Temple said. "I'll tell it anywhere. Dont think I'm afraid. I want a drink."

"You tell him, and I'll get you one," Miss Reba said.

Sitting up in the bed, the covers about her shoulders, Temple told him of the night she had spent in the ruined house, from the time she entered the room and tried to wedge the door with the chair, until the woman came to the bed and led her out. That was the only part of the whole

257

experience which appeared to have left any impression on her at all: the night which she had spent in comparative inviolation. Now and then Horace would attempt to get her on ahead to the crime itself, but she would elude him and return to herself sitting on the bed, listening to the men on the porch, or lying in the dark while they entered the room and came to the bed and stood there above her.

"Yes; that," she would say. "It just happened. I dont know. I had been scared so long that I guess I had just gotten used to being. So I just sat there in those cottonseeds and watched him. I thought it was the rat at first. There were two of them there. One was in one corner looking at me and the other was in the other corner. I dont know what they lived on, because there wasn't anything there but corn-cobs and cottonseeds. Maybe they went to the house to eat. But there wasn't any in the house. I never did hear one in the house. I thought it might have been a rat when I first heard them, but you can feel people in a dark room: did you know that? You dont have to see them. You can feel them like you can in a car when they begin to look for a good place to stop—you know: park for a while." She went on like that, in one of those bright, chatty monologues which women can carry on when they realise that they have the center of the stage; suddenly Horace realised that she was recounting the experience with actual pride, a sort of naive and impersonal vanity, as though she were making it up, looking from him to Miss Reba with quick, darting glances like a dog driving two cattle along a lane.

"And so whenever I breathed I'd hear those shucks. I dont see how anybody ever sleeps on a bed like that. But maybe you get used to it. Or maybe they're tired at night. Because when I breathed I could hear them, even when I was just sitting on the bed. I didn't see how it could be just breathing, so I'd sit as still as I could, but I could still hear them. That's because breathing goes down. You think it goes up, but it doesn't. It goes down you, and I'd hear them getting drunk on the porch. I got to thinking I could see where their heads were leaning back against the wall and I'd say Now this one's drinking out of the jug. Now that one's drinking. Like the mashed-in place on the pillow after you got up, you know.

"That was when I got to thinking a funny thing. You know how you do when you're scared. I was looking at my legs and I'd try to make like I was a boy. I was thinking about if I just was a boy and then I tried to make myself into one by thinking. You know how you do things like that. Like when you know one problem in class and

259

when they came to that you look at him and think right hard, Call on me. Call on me. Call on me. I'd think about what they tell children, about kissing your elbow, and I tried to. I actually did. I was that scared, and I'd wonder if I could tell when it happened. I mean, before I looked, and I'd think I had and how I'd go out and show them—you know. I'd strike a match and say Look. See? Let me alone, now. And then I could go back to bed. I'd think how I could go to bed and go to sleep then, because I was sleepy. I was so sleepy I simply couldn't hardly hold my eyes open.

"So I'd hold my eyes tight shut and say Now I am. I am now. I'd look at my legs and I'd think about how much I had done for them. I'd think about how many dances I had taken them to—crazy, like that. Because I thought how much I'd done for them, and now they'd gotten me into this. So I'd think about praying to be changed into a boy and I would pray and then I'd sit right still and wait. Then I'd think maybe I couldn't tell it and I'd get ready to look. Then I'd think maybe it was too soon to look; that if I looked too soon I'd spoil it and then it wouldn't, sure enough. So I'd count. I said to count fifty at first, then I thought it as still too soon, and I'd say to count fifty more. Then I'd think if I didn't look at the right time, it would be too late.

"Then I thought about fastening myself up some way. There was a girl went abroad one summer that told me about a kind of iron belt in a museum a king or something used to lock the queen up in when he had to go away, and I thought if I just had that. That was why I got the raincoat and put it on. The canteen was hanging by it and I got it too and put it in the—"

"Canteen?" Horace said. "Why did you do that?"

"I dont know why I took it. I was just scared to leave it there, I guess. But I was thinking if I just had that French thing. I was thinking maybe it would have long sharp spikes on it and he wouldn't know it until too late and I'd jab it into him. I'd jab it all the way through him and I'd think about the blood running on me and how I'd say I guess that'll teach you! I guess you'll let me alone now! I'd say. I didn't know it was going to be just the other way . . . I want a drink."

"I'll get you one in a minute," Miss Reba said. " Go on and tell him."

"Oh, yes; this was something else funny I did." She told about lying in the darkness with Gowan snoring beside her, listening to the

261

shucks and hearing the darkness full of movement, feeling Popeye approaching. She could hear the blood in her veins, and the little muscles at the corners of her eyes cracking faintly wider and wider, and she could feel her nostrils going alternately cool and warm. Then he was standing over and she was saying Come on. Touch me. Touch me! You're a coward if you dont. Coward! Coward!

"I wanted to go to sleep, you see. And he just kept on standing there. I thought if he'd just go on and get it over with, I could go to sleep. So I'd say You're a coward if you dont! You're a coward if you dont! and I could feel my mouth getting fixed to scream, and that little hot ball inside you that screams. Then it touched me, that nasty little cold hand, fiddling around inside the coat where I was naked. It was like alive ice and my skin started jumping away from it like those little flying fish in front of a boat. It was like my skin knew which way it was going to go before it started moving, and my skin would keep on jerking just ahead of it like there wouldn't be anything there when the hand got there.

"Then it got down to where my insides begin, and I hadn't eaten since yesterday at dinner and my insides started bubbling and going on and the shucks began to make so much noise it was like laughing. I'd think they were laughing at me because all the time his hand was going inside the top of my knickers and I hadn't changed into a boy yet.

"That was the funny thing, because I wasn't breathing then. I hadn't breathed in a long time. So I thought I was dead. Then I did a funny thing. I could see myself in the coffin. I looked sweet—you know: all in white. I had on a veil like a bride, and I was crying because I was dead or looked sweet or something. No: it was because they had put shucks in the coffin. I was crying because they had put shucks in the coffin where I was dead, but all the time I could feel my nose going cold and hot and cold and hot, and I could see all the people sitting around the coffin, saying Dont she look sweet. Dont she look sweet.

"But I kept on saying Coward! Coward! Touch me, coward! I got mad, because he was so long doing it. I'd talk to him. I'd say Do you think I'm going to lie here all night, just waiting on you? I'd say. Let me tell you what I'll do, I'd say. And I'd lie there with the shucks laughing at me and me jerking away in front of his hand and I'd think what I'd say to him, I'd talk to him like the teacher does in school, and then I was a teacher in school and it was a little black thing like a nigger boy, kind of, and I was the teacher. Because I'd **say** How old am I? and

263

I'd say I'm forty-five years old. I had iron-gray hair and spectacles and I was all big up here like women get. I had on a gray tailored suit, and I never could wear gray. And I was telling it what I'd do, and it kind of drawing up and drawing up like it could already see the switch.

"Then I said That wont do. I ought to be a man. So I was an old man, with a long white beard, and then the little black man got littler and littler and I was saying Now. You see now. I'm a man now. Then I thought about being a man, and as soon as I thought it, it happened. It made a kind of plopping sound, like blowing a little rubber tube wrong-side outward. It felt cold, like the inside of your mouth when you hold it open. I could feel it, and I lay right still to keep from laughing about how surprised he was going to be. I could feel the jerking going on inside my knickers ahead of his hand and me lying there trying not to laugh about how surprised and mad he was going to be in about a minute. Then all of a sudden I went to sleep. I couldn't even stay awake until his hand got there. I just went to sleep. I couldn't even feel myself jerking in front of his hand, but I could hear the shucks. I didn't wake up until that woman came and took me down to the crib."

As he was leaving the house Miss Reba said: "I wish you'd get her down there and not let her

come back. I'd find her folks myself, if I knowed
how to go about it. But you know how . . .
She'll be dead, or in the asylum in a year, way
him and her go on up there in that room. There's
something funny about it that I aint found out
about yet. Maybe it's her. She wasn't born for
this kind of life. You have to be born for this
like you have to be born a butcher or a barber, I
guess. Wouldn't anybody be either of them just
for money or fun."

Better for her if she were dead tonight, Horace thought, walking on. For me, too. He
thought of her, Popeye, the woman, the child,
Goodwin, all put into a single chamber, bare,
lethal, immediate and profound: a single blot-
ting instant between the indignation and the surprise. And I too; thinking how that were the
only solution. Removed, cauterised out of the
old and tragic flank of the world. And I, too.
now that we're all isolated; thinking of a gentle
dark wind blowing in the long corridors of sleep:
of lying beneath a low cozy roof under the long
sound of the rain: the evil, the injustice, the
tears. In an alley-mouth two figures stood, face
to face, not touching; the man speaking in a low
tone unprintable epithet after epithet in a caressing whisper, the woman motionless before
him as though in a musing swoon of voluptuous
ecstasy. Perhaps it is upon the instant that we

265

realise, admit, that there is a logical pattern to evil, that we die, he thought, thinking of the expression he had once seen in the eyes of a dead child, and of other dead: the cooling indignation, the shocked despair fading, leaving two empty globes in which the motionless world lurked profoundly in miniature.

He did not even return to his hotel. He went to the station. He could get a train at midnight. He had a cup of coffee and wished immediately that he had not, for it lay in a hot ball on his stomach. Three hours later, when he got off at Jefferson, it was still there, unassimilated. He walked to town and crossed the deserted square. He thought of the other morning when he had crossed it. It was as though there had not been any elapsed time between: the same gesture of the lighted clock-face, the same vulture-like shadows in the doorways; it might be the same morning and he had merely crossed the square, about-faced and was returning; all between a dream filled with all the nightmare shapes it had taken him forty-three years to invent, concentrated in a hot, hard lump in his stomach. Suddenly he was walking fast, the coffee jolting like a hot, heavy rock inside him.

He walked quietly up the drive, beginning to smell the honeysuckle from the fence. The house was dark, still, as though it were marooned in space by the ebb of all time. The insects had fallen to a low monotonous pitch, everywhere, nowhere, spent, as though the sound were the chemical agony of a world left stark and dying above the tide-edge of the fluid in which it lived and breathed. The moon stood overhead, but without light; the earth lay beneath, without darkness. He opened the door and felt his way into the room and to the light. The voice of the night—insects, whatever it was—had followed him into the house; he knew suddenly that it was the friction of the earth on its axis, approaching that moment when it must decide to turn on or to remain forever still: a motionless ball in cooling space, across which a thick smell of honeysuckle writhed like cold smoke.

He found the light and turned it on. The photograph sat on the dresser. He took it up, holding it in his hands. Enclosed by the narrow imprint of the missing frame Little Belle's face dreamed with that quality of sweet chiaroscuro. Communicated to the cardboard by some quality of the light or perhaps by some infinitesimal movement of his hands, his own breathing, the face appeared to breathe in his palms in a shallow bath of highlight, beneath the slow, smoke-like tongues of invisible honeysuckle. Almost palpable enough to be seen, the scent filled the room and the small face seemed to swoon in a

267

voluptuous languor, blurring still more, fading, leaving upon his eye a soft and fading aftermath of invitation and voluptuous promise and secret affirmation like a scent itself.

Then he knew what that sensation in his stomach meant. He put the photograph down hurriedly and went to the bathroom. He opened the door running and fumbled at the light. But he had not time to find it and he gave over and plunged forward and struck the lavatory and leaned upon his braced arms while the shucks set up a terrific uproar beneath her thighs. Lying with her head lifted slightly, her chin depressed like a figure lifted down from a crucifix, she watched something black and furious go roaring out of her pale body. She was bound naked on her back on a flat car moving at speed through a black tunnel, the blackness streaming in rigid threads overhead, a roar of iron wheels in her ears. The car shot bodily from the tunnel in a long upward slant, the darkness overhead now shredded with parallel attenuations of living fire, toward a crescendo like a held breath, an interval in which she would swing faintly and lazily in nothingness filled with pale, myriad points of light. Far beneath her she could hear the faint, furious uproar of the shucks.

268

XXIV

THE FIRST TIME TEMPLE WENT TO THE head of the stairs Minnie's eyeballs rolled out of the dusky light beside Miss Reba's door. Leaning once more within her bolted door Temple heard Miss Reba toil up the stairs and knock. Temple leaned silently against the door while Miss Reba panted and wheezed beyond it with a mixture of blandishment and threat. She made no sound. After a while Miss Reba went back down the stairs.

Temple turned from the door and stood in the center of the room, beating her hands silently together, her eyes black in her livid face. She wore a street dress, a hat. She removed the hat and hurled it into a corner and went and flung herself face down upon the bed. The bed had not been made. The table beside it was littered with cigarette stubs, the adjacent floor strewn with ashes. The pillow slip on that side

26g

was spotted with brown holes. Often in the night she would wake to smell tobacco and to see the single ruby eye where Popeye's mouth would be.

It was midmorning. A thin bar of sunlight fell beneath the drawn shade of the south window, lying upon the sill and then upon the floor in a narrow band. The house was utterly quiet, with that quality as of spent breathing which it had in midmorning. Now and then a car passed in the street beneath.

Temple turned over on the bed. When she did so she saw one of Popeye's innumerable black suits lying across a chair. She lay looking at it for a while, then she rose and snatched the garments up and hurled them into the corner where the hat was. In another corner was a closet improvised by a print curtain. It contained dresses of all sorts and all new. She ripped them down in furious wads and flung them after the suit, and a row of hats from a shelf. Another of Popeye's suits hung there also. She flung it down. Behind it, hanging from a nail, was an automatic pistol in a holster of oiled silk. She took it down gingerly and removed the pistol and stood with it in her hand. After a moment she went to the bed and hid it beneath the pillow.

The dressing-table was cluttered with toilet-things—brushes and mirrors, also new; with flasks and jars of delicate and bizarre shapes, bearing French labels. One by one she gathered them up and hurled them into the corner in thuds and splintering crashes. Among them lay a platinum bag: a delicate webbing of metal upon the smug orange gleam of banknotes. This followed the other things into the corner and she returned to the bed and lay again on her face in a slow thickening of expensive scent.

At noon Minnie tapped at the door. "Here yo dinner." Temple didn't move. "I ghy leave it here by the door. You can git it when you wants it." Her feet went away. Temple did not move.

Slowly the bar of sunlight shifted across the floor; the western side of the window-frame was now in shadow. Temple sat up, her head turned aside as though she were listening, fingering with deft habitude at her hair. She rose quietly and went to the door and listened again. Then she opened it. The tray sat on the floor. She stepped over it and went to the stairs and peered over the rail. After a while she made Minnie out, sitting in a chair in the hall.

"Minnie," she said. Minnie's head jerked up; again her eyes rolled whitely. "Bring me a drink," Temple said. She returned to her room. She waited fifteen minutes. She banged the door

271

and was tramping furiously down the stairs when Minnie appeared in the hall.

"Yessum," Minnie said, "Miss Reba say— We ain't got no—" Miss Reba's door opened. Without looking up at Temple she spoke to Minnie. Minnie lifted her voice again. "Yessum; all right. I bring it up in just a minute."

"You'd better," Temple said. She returned and stood just inside the door until she heard Minnie mount the stairs. Temple opened the door, holding it just ajar.

"Aint you going to eat no dinner?" Minnie said, thrusting at the door with her knee. Temple held it to.

"Where is it?" she said.

"I aint straightened your room up this mawnin," Minnie said.

"Give it here," Temple said, reaching her hand through the crack. She took the glass from the tray.

"You better make that un last," Minnie said. "Miss Reba say you aint ghy git no more. . . . What you want to treat him this-a-way, fer? Way he spend his money on you, you ought to be ashamed. He a right pretty little man, even if he aint no John Gilbert, and way he spendin his money—" Temple shut the door and shot the bolt. She drank the gin and drew a chair up to the bed and lit a cigarette and sat down with

272

her feet on the bed. After a while she moved the chair to the window and lifted the shade a little so she could see the street beneath. She lit another cigarette.

At five oclock she saw Miss Reba emerge, in the black silk and flowered hat, and go down the street. She sprang up and dug the hat from the mass of clothes in the corner and put it on. At the door she turned and went back to the corner and exhumed the platinum purse and descended the stairs. Minnie was in the hall.

"I'll give you ten dollars," Temple said. "I wont be gone ten minutes."

"I caint do it, Miss Temple. Hit be worth my job if Miss Reba find it out, and my th'oat too, if Mist Poyeye do."

"I swear I'll be back in ten minutes. I swear I will. Twenty dollars." She put the bill in Minnie's hand.

"You better come back," Minnie said, opening the door. "If you aint back here in ten minutes, I aint going to be, neither."

Temple opened the lattice and peered out. The street was empty save for a taxi at the curb across the way, and a man in a cap standing in a door beyond it. She went down the street, walking swiftly. At the corner a cab overtook her, slowing, the driver looking at her interrogatively. She turned into the drug store at the corner and went back to the telephone booth. Then she returned to the house. As she turned the corner she met the man in the cap who had been leaning in the door. She entered the lattice. Minnie opened the door.

"Thank goodness," Minnie said. "When that cab over there started up, I got ready to pack up too. If you aint ghy say nothing about it, I git you a drink."

When Minnie fetched the gin Temple started to drink it. Her hand was trembling and there was a sort of elation in her face as she stood again just inside the door, listening, the glass in her hand. I'll need it later, she said. I'll need more than that. She covered the glass with a saucer and hid it carefully. Then she dug into the mass of garments in the corner and found a dancing-frock and shook it out and hung it back in the closet. She looked at the other things a moment, but she returned to the bed and lay down again. At once she rose and drew the chair up and sat down, her feet on the unmade bed. While daylight died slowly in the room she sat smoking cigarette after cigarette, listening to every sound on the stairs.

At half-past six Minnie brought her supper up. On the tray was another glass of gin. "Miss Reba sont this un," she said. "She say, how you feelin?"

"Tell her, all right," Temple said. "I'm going to have a bath and then go to bed, tell her."

When Minnie was gone Temple poured the two drinks into a tumbler and gloated over it, the glass shaking in her hands. She set it carefully away and covered it and ate her supper from the bed. When she finished she lit a cigarette. Her movements were jerky; she smoked swiftly, moving about the room. She stood for a moment at the window, the shade lifted aside, then she dropped it and turned into the room again, spying herself in the mirror. She turned before it, studying herself, puffing at the cigarette.

She snapped it behind her, toward the fireplace, and went to the mirror and combed her hair. She ripped the curtain aside and took the dress down and laid it on the bed and returned and drew out a drawer in the dresser and took a garment out. She paused with the garment in her hand, then she replaced it and closed the drawer and caught up the frock swiftly and hung it back in the closet. A moment later she found herself walking up and down the room, another cigarette burning in her hand, without any recollection of having lit it. She flung it away and went to the table and looked at her watch and propped it against the pack of cigarettes so she could see it from the bed, and lay down. When she did so she felt the pistol through the pillow. She slipped it out and looked at it, then she slid it under her flank and lay motionless, her legs straight, her hands behind her head, her eyes focussing into black pinheads at every sound on the stairs.

At nine she rose. She picked up the pistol again; after a moment she thrust it beneath the mattress and undressed and in a spurious Chinese robe splotched with gold dragons and jade and scarlet flowers she left the room. When she returned her hair curled damply about her face. She went to the washstand and took up the tumbler, holding it in her hands, but she set it down again.

She dressed, retrieving the bottles and jars from the corner. Her motions before the glass were furious yet painstaking. She went to the washstand and took up the glass, but again she paused and went to the corner and got her coat and put it on and put the platinum bag in the pocket and leaned once more to the mirror. Then she went and took up the glass and gulped the gin and left the room, walking swiftly.

A single light burned in the hall. It was empty. She could hear voices in Miss Reba's room, but the lower hall was deserted. She descended swiftly and silently and gained the door. She believed that it would be at the door that they would stop her and she thought of the pistol with acute regret, almost pausing, knowing that she would use it without any compunction whatever, with a kind of pleasure. She sprang to the door and pawed at the bolt, her head turned over her shoulder.

It opened. She sprang out and out the lattice door and ran down the walk and out the gate. As she did so a car, moving slowly along the curb, stopped opposite her. Popeye sat at the wheel. Without any apparent movement from him the door swung open. He made no movement, spoke no word. He just sat there, the straw hat slanted a little aside.

"I wont!" Temple said. "I wont!"

He made no movement, no sound. She came to the car.

"I wont, I tell you!" Then she cried wildly: "You're scared of him! You're scared to!"

"I'm giving him his chance," he said. "Will you go back in that house, or will you get in this car?"

"You're scared to!"

"I'm giving him his chance," he said, in his cold soft voice. "Come on. Make up your mind."

She leaned forward, putting her hand on his arm. "Popeye," she said; "daddy." His arm felt frail, no larger than a child's, dead and hard and light as a stick.

"I dont care which you do," he said. "But do it. Come on."

She leaned toward him, her hand on his arm. Then she got into the car. "You wont do it. You're afraid to. He's a better man than you are."

He reached across and shut the door. "Where?" he said. "Grotto?"

"He's a better man than you are!" Temple said shrilly. "You're not even a man! He knows it. Who does know it if he dont?" The car was in motion. She began to shriek at him. "You, a man, a bold bad man, when you cant even— When you had to bring a real man in to— And you hanging over the bed, moaning and slobbering like a— You couldn't fool me but once, could you? No wonder I bled and bluh—" his hand came over her mouth, hard, his nails going into her flesh. With the other hand he drove the car at reckless speed. When they passed beneath lights she could see him watching her as she struggled, tugging at his hand, whipping her head this way and that.

She ceased struggling, but she continued to twist her head from side to side, tugging at his hand. One finger, ringed with a thick ring, held her lips apart, his finger-tips digging into her cheek. With the other hand he whipped the car

278

in and out of traffic, bearing down upon other cars until they slewed aside with brakes squealing, shooting recklessly across intersections. Once a policeman shouted at them, but he did not even look around.

Temple began to whimper, moaning behind his hand, drooling upon his fingers. The ring was like a dentist's instrument; she could not close her lips to regurgitate. When he removed it she could feel the imprint of his fingers cold on her jaw. She lifted her hand to it.

"You hurt my mouth," she whimpered. They were approaching the outskirts of the city, the speedometer at fifty miles. His hat slanted above his delicate hooked profile. She nursed her jaw. The houses gave way to broad, dark subdivisions out of which realtors' signs loomed abrupt and ghostly, with a quality of forlorn assurance. Between them low, far lights hung in the cool empty darkness blowing with fireflies. She began to cry quietly, feeling the cooling double drink of gin inside her. "You hurt my mouth," she said in a voice small and faint with self-pity. She nursed her jaw with experimental fingers, pressing harder and harder until she found a twinge. "You'll be sorry for this," she said in a muffled voice. "When I tell Red. Dont you wish you were Red? Dont you? Dont you wish you could do what he can do? Dont you wish he was the one watching us instead of you?"

They turned into the Grotto, passing along a closely curtained wall from which a sultry burst of music came. She sprang out while he was locking the car and ran on up the steps. "I gave you your chance," she said. "You brought me here. I didn't ask you to come."

She went to the washroom. In the mirror she examined her face. "Shucks," she said, "it didn't leave a mark, even"; drawing the flesh this way and that. "Little runt," she said, peering at her reflection. She added a phrase, glibly obscene, with a detached parrotlike effect. She painted her mouth again. Another woman entered. They examined one another's clothes with brief, covert, cold, embracing glances.

Popeye was standing at the door to the dance-hall, a cigarette in his fingers.

"I gave you your chance," Temple said. "You didn't have to come."

"I dont take chances," he said.

"You took one," Temple said. "Are you sorry? Huh?"

"Go on," he said, his hand on her back. She was in the act of stepping over the sill when she turned and looked at him, their eyes almost on a level; then her hand flicked toward his armpit. He caught her wrist; the other hand flicked toward him. He caught that one too in his soft, cold hand. They looked eye to eye, her mouth open and the rouge spots darkening slowly on her face.

"I gave you your chance back there in town," he said. "You took it."

Behind her the music beat, sultry, evocative; filled with movement of feet, the voluptuous hysteria of muscles warming the scent of flesh, of the blood. "Oh, God; oh, God," she said, her lips scarce moving. "I'll go. I'll go back."

"You took it," he said. "Go on."

In his grasp her hands made tentative plucking motions at his coat just out of reach of her finger-tips. Slowly he was turning her toward the door, her head reverted. "You just dare!" she cried. "You just—" His hand closed upon the back of her neck, his fingers like steel, yet cold and light as aluminum. She could hear the vertebrae grating faintly together, and his voice, cold and still.

"Will you?"

She nodded her head. Then they were dancing. She could still feel his hand at her neck. Across his shoulder she looked swiftly about the room, her gaze flicking from face to face among the dancers. Beyond a low arch, in another room, a group stood about the crap-table. She leaned this way and that, trying to see the faces of the group.

Then she saw the four men. They were sitting at a table near the door. One of them was chewing gum; the whole lower part of his face seemed to be cropped with teeth of an unbelievable whiteness and size. When she saw them she swung Popeye around with his back to them, working the two of them toward the door again. Once more her harried gaze flew from face to face in the crowd.

When she looked again two of the men had risen. They approached. She dragged Popeye into their path, still keeping his back turned to them. The men paused and essayed to go around her; again she backed Popeye into their path. She was trying to say something to him, but her mouth felt cold. It was like trying to pick up a pin with the fingers numb. Suddenly she felt herself lifted bodily aside, Popeye's small arms light and rigid as aluminum. She stumbled back against the wall and watched the two men leave the room. "I'll go back," she said. "I'll go back." She began to laugh shrilly.

"Shut it," Popeye said. "Are you going to shut it?"

"Get me a drink," she said. She felt his hand; her legs felt cold too, as if they were not hers. They were sitting at a table. Two tables away the man was still chewing, his elbows on the table. The fourth man sat on his spine, smoking, his coat buttoned across his chest.

She watched hands: a brown one in a white sleeve, a soiled white one beneath a dirty cuff, setting bottles on the table. She had a glass in her hand. She drank, gulping; with the glass in her hand she saw Red standing in the door, in a gray suit and a spotted bow tie. He looked like a college boy, and he looked about the room until he saw her. He looked at the back of Popeye's head, then at her as she sat with the glass in her hand. The two men at the other table had not moved. She could see the faint, steady movement of the one's ears as he chewed. The music started.

She held Popeye's back toward Red. He was still watching her, almost a head taller than any body else. "Come on," she said in Popeye's ear. "If you're going to dance, dance."

She had another drink. They danced again. Red had disappeared. When the music ceased she had another drink. It did no good. It merely lay hot and hard inside her. "Come on," she said, "dont quit." But he wouldn't get up, and she stood over him, her muscles flinching and jerking with exhaustion and terror. She began to jeer at him. "Call yourself a man, a bold, bad man, and let a girl dance you off your feet."

Then her face drained, became small and haggard and sincere; she spoke like a child, with sober despair. "Popeye." He sat with his hands on the table, finicking with a cigarette, the second glass with its melting ice before him. She put her hand on his shoulder. "Daddy," she said. Moving to shield them from the room, her hand stole toward his armpit, touching the butt of the flat pistol. It lay rigid in the light, dead vise of his arm and side. "Give it to me," she whispered. "Daddy. Daddy." She leaned her thigh against his shoulder, caressing his arm with her flank. "Give it to me, daddy," she whispered. Suddenly her hand began to steal down his body in a swift, covert movement; then it snapped away in a movement of revulsion. "I forgot," she whispered; "I didn't mean . . . I didn't . . ."

One of the men at the other table hissed once through his teeth. "Sit down," Popeye said. She sat down. She filled her glass, watching her hands perform the action. Then she was watching the corner of the gray coat. He's got a broken button, she thought stupidly. Popeye had not moved.

"Dance this?" Red said.

His head was bent but he was not looking at her. He was turned a little, facing the two men at the other table. Still Popeye did not move.

He shredded delicately the end of the cigarette, pinching the tobacco off. Then he put it into his mouth.

"I'm not dancing," Temple said through her cold lips.

"Not?" Red said. He said, in a level tone, without moving: "How's the boy?"

"Fine," Popeye said. Temple watched him scrape a match, saw the flame distorted through glass. "You've had enough," Popeye said. His hand took the glass from her lips. She watched him empty it into the ice bowl. The music started again. She sat looking quietly about the room. A voice began to buzz faintly at her hearing, then Popeye was gripping her wrist, shaking it, and she found that her mouth was open and that she must have been making a noise of some sort with it. "Shut it, now," he said. "You can have one more." He poured the drink into the glass.

"I haven't felt it at all," she said. He gave her the glass. She drank. When she set the glass down she realised that she was drunk. She believed that she had been drunk for some time. She thought that perhaps she had passed out and that it had already happened. She could hear herself saying I hope it has. I hope it has. Then she believed it had and she was overcome by a sense of bereavement and of physical desire. She thought, It will never be again, and she sat in a floating swoon of agonised sorrow and erotic longing, thinking of Red's body, watching her hand holding the empty bottle over the glass.

"You've drunk it all," Popeye said. "Get up, now. Dance it off." They danced again. She moved stiffly and languidly, her eyes open but unseeing; her body following the music without hearing the tune for a time. Then she became aware that the orchestra was playing the same tune as when Red was asking her to dance. If that were so, then it couldn't have happened yet. She felt a wild surge of relief. It was not too late: Red was still alive; she felt long shuddering waves of physical desire going over her, draining the color from her mouth, drawing her eyeballs back into her skull in a shuddering swoon.

They were at the crap-table. She could hear herself shouting to the dice. She was rolling them, winning; the counters were piling up in front of her as Popeye drew them in, coaching her, correcting her in his soft, querulous voice. He stood beside her, shorter than she.

He had the cup himself. She stood beside him cunningly, feeling the desire going over her in wave after wave, involved with the music and with the smell of her own flesh. She became
286

quiet. By infinitesimal inches she moved aside until someone slipped into her place. Then she was walking swiftly and carefully across the floor toward the door, the dancers, the music swirling slowly about her in a bright myriad wave. The table where the two men had sat was empty, but she did not even glance at it. She entered the corridor. A waiter met her.

"Room," she said. "Hurry."

The room contained a table and four chairs. The waiter turned on the light and stood in the door. She jerked her hand at him; he went out. She leaned against the table on her braced arms, watching the door, until Red entered.

He came toward her. She did not move. Her eyes began to grow darker and darker, lifting into her skull above a half moon of white, without focus, with the blank rigidity of a statue's eyes. She began to say Ah-ah-ah-ah in an expiring voice, her body arching slowly backward as though faced by an exquisite torture. When he touched her she sprang like a bow, hurling herself upon him, her mouth gaped and ugly like that of a dying fish as she writhed her loins against him.

He dragged his face free by main strength. With her hips grinding against him, her mouth gaping in straining protrusion, bloodless, she began to speak. "Let's hurry. Anywhere. I've

287

quit him. I told him so. It's not my fault. Is it
my fault? You dont need your hat and I dont
either. He came here to kill you but I said I
gave him his chance. It wasn't my fault. And
now it'll just be us. Without him there watching. Come on. What're you waiting for?" She
strained her mouth toward him, dragging his
head down, making a whimpering moan. He
held his face free. "I told him I was. I said if
you bring me here. I gave you your chance I
said. And now he's got them there to bump you
off. But you're not afraid. Are you?"

"Did you know that when you telephoned
me?" he said.

"What? He said I wasn't to see you again.
He said he'd kill you. But he had me followed
when I telephoned. I saw him. But you're not
afraid. He's not even a man, but you are. You're
a man. You're a man." She began to grind
against him, dragging at his head, murmuring
to him in parrotlike underworld epithet, the
saliva running pale over her bloodless lips.
"Are you afraid?"

"Of that dopey bastard?" Lifting her bodily
he turned so that he faced the door, and slipped
his right hand free. She did not seem to be
aware that he had moved.

"Please. Please. Please. Please. Dont make
me wait. I'm burning up."
288

"All right. You go on back. You wait till I give you the sign. Will you go on back?"

"I cant wait. You've got to. I'm on fire, I tell you." She clung to him. Together they blundered across the room toward the door, he holding her clear of his right side; she in a voluptuous swoon, unaware that they were moving, straining at him as though she were trying to touch him with all of her body-surface at once. He freed himself and thrust her into the passage.

"Go on," he said. "I'll be there in a minute."

"You wont be long? I'm on fire. I'm dying, I tell you."

"No. Not long. Go on, now."

The music was playing. She moved up the corridor, staggering a little. She thought that she was leaning against the wall, when she found that she was dancing again; then that she was dancing with two men at once; then she found that she was not dancing but that she was moving toward the door between the man with the chewing gum and the one with the buttoned coat. She tried to stop, but they had her under the arms; she opened her mouth to scream, taking one last despairing look about the swirling room.

"Yell," the man with the buttoned coat said. "Just try it once."

Red was at the crap-table. She saw his head turned, the cup in his lifted hand. With it he made her a short, cheery salute. He watched her disappear through the door, between the two men. Then he looked briefly about the room. His face was bold and calm, but there were two white lines at the base of his nostrils and his forehead was damp. He rattled the cup and threw the dice steadily.

"Eleven," the dealer said.

"Let it lay," Red said. "I'll pass a million times tonight."

They helped Temple into the car. The man in the buttoned coat took the wheel. Where the drive joined the lane that led to the highroad a long touring car was parked. When they passed it Temple saw, leaning to a cupped match, Popeye's delicate hooked profile beneath the slanted hat as he lit the cigarette. The match flipped outward like a dying star in miniature, sucked with the profile into darkness by the rush of their passing.

XXV

THE TABLES HAD BEEN MOVED TO ONE END of the dance floor. On each one was a black table-cloth. The curtains were still drawn; a thick, salmon-colored light fell through them. Just beneath the orchestra platform the coffin sat. It was an expensive one: black, with silver fittings, the trestles hidden by a mass of flowers. In wreaths and crosses and other shapes of ceremonial mortality, the mass appeared to break in a symbolical wave over the bier and on upon the platform and the piano, the scent of them thickly oppressive.

The proprietor of the place moved about among the tables, speaking to the arrivals as they entered and found seats. The negro waiters, in black shirts beneath their starched jackets, were already moving in and out with glasses and bottles of ginger ale. They moved with swaggering and decorous repression; already the scene was vivid, with a hushed, macabre air a little febrile.

The archway to the dice-room was draped in black. A black pall lay upon the crap-table, upon which the overflow of floral shapes was beginning to accumulate. People entered steadily, the men in dark suits of decorous restraint, others in the light, bright shades of spring, increasing the atmosphere of macabre paradox. The women—the younger ones—wore bright colors also, in hats and scarves; the older ones in sober gray and black and navy blue, and glittering with diamonds: matronly figures resembling housewives on a Sunday afternoon excursion.

The room began to hum with shrill, hushed talk. The waiters moved here and there with high, precarious trays, their white jackets and black shirts resembling photograph negatives. The proprietor went from table to table with his bald head, a huge diamond in his black cravat, followed by the bouncer, a thick, musclebound, bullet-headed man who appeared to be on the point of bursting out of his dinner-jacket through the rear, like a cocoon.

In a private dining-room, on a table draped in black, sat a huge bowl of punch floating with ice and sliced fruit. Beside it leaned a fat man in a shapeless greenish suit, from the sleeves of which dirty cuffs fell upon hands rimmed with

292

black nails. The soiled collar was wilted about his neck in limp folds, knotted by a greasy black tie with an imitation ruby stud. His face gleamed with moisture and he adjured the throng about the bowl in a harsh voice:

"Come on, folks. It's on Gene. It dont cost you nothing. Step up and drink. There wasn't never a better boy walked than him." They drank and fell back, replaced by others with extended cups. From time to time a waiter entered with ice and fruit and dumped them into the bowl; from a suit case under the table Gene drew fresh bottles and decanted them into the bowl; then, proprietorial, adjurant, sweating, he resumed his harsh monologue, mopping his face on his sleeve. "Come on, folks. It's all on Gene. I aint nothing but a bootlegger, but he never had a better friend than me. Step up and drink, folks. There's more where that come from."

From the dance hall came a strain of music. The people entered and found seats. On the platform was the orchestra from a downtown hotel, in dinner coats. The proprietor and a second man were conferring with the leader.

"Let them play jazz," the second man said. "Never nobody liked dancing no better than Red."

"No, no," the proprietor said. "Time Gene

gets them all ginned up on free whisky, they'll start dancing. It'll look bad."

"How about the Blue Danube?" the leader said.

"No, no; don't play no blues, I tell you," the proprietor said. "There's a dead man in that bier."

"That's not blues," the leader said.

"What is it?" the second man said.

"A waltz. Strauss."

"A wop?" the second man said. "Like hell. Red was an American. You may not be, but he was. Dont you know anything American? Play I Cant Give You Anything but Love. He always liked that."

"And get them all to dancing?" the proprietor said. He glanced back at the tables, where the women were beginning to talk a little shrilly. "You better start off with Nearer, My God, To Thee," he said, "and sober them up some. I told Gene it was risky about that punch, starting it so soon. My suggestion was to wait until we started back to town. But I might have knowed somebody'd have to turn it into a carnival. Better start off solemn and keep it up until I give you the sign."

"Red wouldn't like it solemn," the second man said. "And you know it."

"Let him go somewheres else, then," the pro-

prietor said. "I just done this as an accommodation. I aint running no funeral parlor."

The orchestra played Nearer, My God, To
Thee. The audience grew quiet. A woman
in a red dress came in the door unsteadily.
"Whoopee," she said, "so long, Red. He'll be
in hell before I could even reach Little Rock."

"Shhhhhhhh!" voices said. She fell into a
seat. Gene came to the door and stood there until the music stopped.

"Come on, folks," he shouted, jerking his
arms in a fat, sweeping gesture, "come and get
it. It's on Gene. I don't want a dry throat or
eye in this place in ten minutes." Those at the
rear moved toward the door. The proprietor
sprang to his feet and jerked his hand at the
orchestra. The cornetist rose and played In
That Haven of Rest in solo, but the crowd at
the back of the room continued to dwindle
through the door where Gene stood waving his
arm. Two middle-aged women were weeping
quietly beneath flowered hats.

They surged and clamored about the diminishing bowl. From the dance hall came the rich
blare of the cornet. Two soiled young men
worked their way toward the table, shouting
"Gangway. Gangway" monotonously, carrying
suit cases. They opened them and set bottles on
the table, while Gene, frankly weeping now,

295

opened them and decanted them into the bowl. "Come up, folks. I couldn't a loved him no better if he'd a been my own son," he shouted hoarsely, dragging his sleeve across his face.

A waiter edged up to the table with a bowl of ice and fruit and went to put them into the punch bowl. "What the hell you doing?" Gene said, "putting that slop in there? Get to hell away from here."

"Ra-a-a-a-y-y-y-y!" they shouted, clashing their cups, drowning all save the pantomime as Gene knocked the bowl of fruit from the waiter's hand and fell again to dumping raw liquor into the bowl, sploshing it into and upon the extended hands and cups. The two youths opened bottles furiously.

As though swept there upon a brassy blare of music the proprietor appeared in the door, his face harried, waving his arms. "Come on, folks," he shouted, "let's finish the musical program. It's costing us money."

"Hell with it," they shouted.

"Costing who money?"

"Who cares?"

"Costing who money?"

"Who begrudges it? I'll pay it. By God, I'll buy him two funerals."

"Folks! Folks!" the proprietor shouted. "Don't you realise there's a bier in that room?"

"Costing who money?"

"Beer?" Gene said. "Beer?" he said in a broken voice. "Is anybody here trying to insult me by—"

"He begrudges Red the money."

"Who does?"

"Joe does, the cheap son of a bitch."

"Is somebody here trying to insult me—"

"Let's move the funeral, then. This is not the only place in town."

"Let's move Joe."

"Put the son of a bitch in a coffin. Let's have two funerals."

"Beer? Beer? Is somebody—"

"Put the son of a bitch in a coffin. See how he likes it."

"Put the son of a bitch in a coffin," the woman in red shrieked. They rushed toward the door, where the proprietor stood waving his hands above his head, his voice shrieking out of the uproar before he turned and fled.

In the main room a male quartet engaged from a vaudeville house was singing. They were singing mother songs in close harmony; they sang Sonny Boy. The weeping was general among the older women. Waiters were now carrying cups of punch in to them and they sat holding the cups in their fat, ringed hands, crying.

The orchestra played again. The woman in red staggered into the room. "Come on, Joe," she shouted, "open the game. Get that damn stiff out of here and open the game." A man tried to hold her; she turned upon him with a burst of filthy language and went on to the shrouded crap table and hurled a wreath to the floor. The proprietor rushed toward her, followed by the bouncer. The proprietor grasped the woman as she lifted another floral piece. The man who had tried to hold her intervened, the woman cursing shrilly and striking at both of them impartially with the wreath. The bouncer caught the man's arm; he whirled and struck at the bouncer, who knocked him halfway across the room. Three more men entered. The fourth rose from the floor and all four of them rushed at the bouncer.

He felled the first and whirled and sprang with unbelievable celerity, into the main room. The orchestra was playing. It was immediately drowned in a sudden pandemonium of chairs and screams. The bouncer whirled again and met the rush of the four men. They mingled; a second man flew out and skittered along the floor on his back; the bouncer sprang free. Then he whirled and rushed them and in a whirling plunge they bore down upon the bier and crashed into it. The orchestra had ceased and

298

were now climbing onto their chairs, with their instruments. The floral offerings flew; the coffin teetered. "Catch it!" a voice shouted. They sprang forward, but the coffin crashed heavily to the floor, coming open. The corpse tumbled slowly and sedately out and came to rest with its face in the center of a wreath.

"Play something!" the proprietor bawled, waving his arms; "play! Play!"

When they raised the corpse the wreath came too, attached to him by a hidden end of a wire driven into his cheek. He had worn a cap which, tumbling off, exposed a small blue hole in the center of his forehead. It had been neatly plugged with wax and was painted, but the wax had been jarred out and lost. They couldn't find it, but by unfastening the snap in the peak, they could draw the cap down to his eyes.

As the cortège neared the downtown section more cars joined it. The hearse was followed by six Packard touring cars with the tops back, driven by liveried chauffeurs and filled with flowers. They looked exactly alike and were of the type rented by the hour by the better class agencies. Next came a nondescript line of taxis, roadsters, sedans, which increased as the procession moved slowly through the restricted district where faces peered from beneath lowered shades, toward the main artery that led back out of town, toward the cemetery.

On the avenue the hearse increased its speed, the procession stretching out at swift intervals. Presently the private cars and the cabs began to drop out. At each intersection they would turn this way or that, until at last only the hearse and the six Packards were left, each carrying no occupant save the liveried driver. The street was broad and now infrequent, with a white line down the center that diminished on ahead into the smooth asphalt emptiness. Soon the hearse was making forty miles an hour and then forty-five and then fifty.

One of the cabs drew up at Miss Reba's door. She got out, followed by a thin woman in sober, severe clothes and gold nose-glasses, and a short plump woman in a plumed hat, her face hidden by a hankerchief, and a small bullet-headed boy of five or six. The woman with the handkerchief continued to sob in snuffy gasps as they went up the walk and entered the lattice. Beyond the house door the dogs set up a falsetto uproar. When Minnie opened the door they surged about Miss Reba's feet. She kicked them aside. Again they assailed her with snapping eagerness; again she flung them back against the wall in muted thuds.

"Come in, come in," she said, her hand to her

breast. Once inside the house the woman with the handkerchief began to weep aloud.

"Didn't he look sweet?" she wailed. "Didn't he look sweet!"

"Now, now," Miss Reba said, leading the way to her room, "come in and have some beer. You'll feel better. Minnie!" They entered the room with the decorated dresser, the safe, the screen, the draped portrait. "Sit down, sit down," she panted, shoving the chairs forward. She lowered herself into one and stooped terrifically toward her feet.

"Uncle Bud, honey," the weeping woman said, dabbing at her eyes, "come and unlace Miss Reba's shoes."

The boy knelt and removed Miss Reba's shoes. "And if you'll just reach me them house slippers under the bed there, honey," Miss Reba said. The boy fetched the slippers. Minnie entered, followed by the dogs. They rushed at Miss Reba and began to worry the shoes she had just removed.

"Scat!" the boy said, striking at one of them with his hand. The dog's head snapped around, its teeth clicking, its half-hidden eyes bright and malevolent. The boy recoiled. "You bite me, you thon bitch," he said.

"Uncle Bud!" the fat woman said, her round face, rigid in fatty folds and streaked with tears, turned upon the boy in shocked surprise, the plumes nodding precariously above it. Uncle Bud's head was quite round, his nose bridged with freckles like splotches of huge summer rain on a sidewalk. The other woman sat primly erect, in gold nose-glasses on a gold chain and neat iron-gray hair. She looked like a school-teacher. "The very idea!" the fat woman said. "How in the world he can learn such words on an Arkansaw farm, I dont know."

"They'll learn meanness anywhere," Miss Reba said. Minnie leaned down a tray bearing three frosted tankards. Uncle Bud watched with round cornflower eyes as they took one each. The fat woman began to cry again.

"He looked so sweet!" she wailed.

"We all got to suffer it," Miss Reba said. "Well, may it be a long day," lifting her tankard. They drank, bowing formally to one another. The fat woman dried her eyes; the two guests wiped their lips with prim decorum. The thin one coughed delicately aside, behind her hand.

"Such good beer," she said.

"Aint it?" the fat one said. "I always say it's the greatest pleasure I have to call on Miss Reba."

They began to talk politely, in decorous half-completed sentences, with little gasps of agreement. The boy had moved aimlessly to the window, peering beneath the lifted shade.

"How long's he going to be with you, Miss Myrtle?" Miss Reba said.

"Just till Sat'dy," the fat woman said. "Then he'll go back home. It makes a right nice little change for him, with me for a week or two. And I enjoy having him."

"Children are such a comfort to a body," the thin one said.

"Yes," Miss Myrtle said. "Is them two nice young fellows still with you, Miss Reba?"

"Yes," Miss Reba said. "I think I got to get shut of them, though. I aint specially tender-hearted, but after all it aint no use in helping young folks to learn this world's meanness until they have to. I already had to stop the girls running around the house without no clothes on, and they dont like it."

They drank again, decorously, handling the tankards delicately, save Miss Reba who grasped hers as though it were a weapon, her other hand lost in her breast. She set her tankard down empty. "I get so dry, seems like," she said. "Wont you ladies have another?" They murmured, ceremoniously. "Minnie!" Miss Reba shouted.

Minnie came and filled the tankards again. "Reely, I'm right ashamed," Miss Myrtle said.

303

"But Miss Reba has such good beer. And then we've all had a kind of upsetting afternoon."

"I'm just surprised it wasn't upset no more," Miss Reba said. "Giving away all that free liquor like Gene done."

"It must have cost a good piece of jack," the thin woman said.

"I believe you," Miss Reba said. "And who got anything out of it? Tell me that. Except the privilege of having his place hell-full of folks not spending a cent." She had set her tankard on the table beside her chair. Suddenly she turned her head sharply and looked at it. Uncle Bud was now behind her chair, leaning against the table. "You aint been into my beer, have you, boy?" she said.

"You, Uncle Bud," Miss Myrtle said. "Aint you ashamed? I declare, it's getting so I dont dare take him nowhere. I never see such a boy for snitching beer in my life. You come out here and play, now. Come on."

"Yessum," Uncle Bud said. He moved, in no particular direction. Miss Reba drank and set the tankard back on the table and rose.

"Since we all been kind of tore up," she said, "maybe I can prevail on you ladies to have a little sup of gin?"

"No; reely," Miss Myrtle said.

"Miss Reba's the perfect hostess," the thin

one said. "How many times you heard me say that, Miss Myrtle?"

"I wouldn't undertake to say, dearie," Miss Myrtle said.

Miss Reba vanished behind the screen.

"Did you ever see it so warm for June, Miss Lorraine?" Miss Myrtle said.

"I never did," the thin woman said. Miss Myrtle's face began to crinkle again. Setting her tankard down she began to fumble for her handkerchief.

"It just comes over me like this," she said, "and them singing that Sonny Boy and all. He looked so sweet," she wailed.

"Now, now," Miss Lorraine said. "Drink a little beer. You'll feel better. Miss Myrtle's took again," she said, raising her voice.

"I got too tender a heart," Miss Myrtle said. She snuffled behind the handkerchief, groping for her tankard. She groped for a moment, then it touched her hand. She looked quickly up. "You, Uncle Bud!" she said. "Didn't I tell you to come out from behind there and play? Would you believe it? The other afternoon when we left here I was so mortified I didn't know what to do. I was ashamed to be seen on the street with a drunk boy like you."

Miss Reba emerged from behind the screen with three glasses of gin. "This'll put some heart into us," she said. "We're setting here like three old sick cats." They bowed formally and drank, patting their lips. Then they began to talk. They were all talking at once, again in half-completed sentences, but without pauses for agreement or affirmation.

"It's us girls," Miss Myrtle said. "Men just cant seem to take us and leave us for what we are. They make us what we are, then they expect us to be different. Expect us not to never look at another man, while they come and go as they please."

"A woman that wants to fool with more than one man at a time is a fool," Miss Reba said. "They're all trouble, and why do you want to double your trouble? And the woman that cant stay true to a good man when she gets him, a free-hearted spender that never give her a hour's uneasiness or a hard word . . ." looking at them, her eyes began to fill with a sad, unutterable expression, of baffled and patient despair.

"Now, now," Miss Myrtle said. She leaned forward and patted Miss Reba's huge hand. Miss Lorraine made a faint clucking sound with her tongue. "You'll get yourself started."

"He was such a good man," Miss Reba said. "We was like two doves. For eleven years we was like two doves."

306

"Now, dearie; now, dearie," Miss Myrtle said.

"It's when it comes over me like this," Miss Reba said. "Seeing that boy laying there under them flowers."

"He never had no more than Mr Binford had," Miss Myrtle said. "Now, now. Drink a little beer."

Miss Reba brushed her sleeve across her eyes. She drank some beer.

"He ought to known better than to take a chance with Popeye's girl," Miss Lorraine said.

"Men dont never learn better than that, dearie," Miss Myrtle said. "Where you reckon they went, Miss Reba?"

"I dont know and I dont care," Miss Reba said. "And how soon they catch him and burn him for killing that boy, I dont care neither. I dont care none."

"He goes all the way to Pensacola every summer to see his mother," Miss Myrtle said. "A man that'll do that cant be all bad."

"I dont know how bad you like them, then," Miss Reba said. "Me trying to run a respectable house, that's been running a shooting-gallery for twenty years, and him trying to turn it into a peep-show."

"It's us poor girls," Miss Myrtle said, "causes all the trouble and gets all the suffering."

"I heard two years ago he wasn't no good that way," Miss Lorraine said.

"I knew it all the time," Miss Reba said. "A young man spending his money like water on girls and not never going to bed with one. It's against nature. All the girls thought it was because he had a little woman out in town somewhere, but I says mark my words, there's something funny about him. There's a funny business somewhere."

"He was a free spender, all right," Miss Lorraine said.

"The clothes and jewelry that girl bought, it was a shame," Miss Reba said. "There was a Chinee robe she paid a hundred dollars for—imported, it was—and perfume at ten dollars an ounce; next morning when I went up there, they was all wadded in the corner and the perfume and rouge busted all over them like a cyclone. That's what she'd do when she got mad at him, when he'd beat her. After he shut her up and wouldn't let her leave the house. Having the front of my house watched like it was a . . ." She raised the tankard from the table to her lips. Then she halted it, blinking. "Where's my—"

"Uncle Bud!" Miss Myrtle said. She grasped the boy by the arm and snatched him out from behind Miss Reba's chair and shook him, his
308

round head bobbing on his shoulders with an expression of equable idiocy. "Aint you ashamed? Aint you *ashamed?* Why cant you stay out of these ladies' beer? I'm a good mind to take that dollar back and make you buy Miss Reba a can of beer, I am for a fact. Now, you go over there by that window and stay there, you hear?"

"Nonsense," Miss Reba said. "There wasn't much left. You ladies are about ready too, aint you? Minnie!"

Miss Lorraine touched her mouth with her handkerchief. Behind her glasses her eyes rolled aside in a veiled, secret look. She laid the other hand to her flat spinster's breast.

"We forgot about your heart, honey," Miss Myrtle said. "Dont you reckon you better take gin this time?"

"Reely, I—" Miss Lorraine said.

"Yes; do," Miss Reba said. She rose heavily and fetched three more glasses of gin from be-hind the screen. Minnie entered and refilled the tankards. They drank, patting their lips.

"That's what was going on, was it?" Miss Lorraine said.

"First I knowed was when Minnie told me there was something funny going on," Miss Reba said. "How he wasn't here hardly at all, gone about every other night, and that when he

309

was here, there wasn't no signs at all the next morning when she cleaned up. She'd hear them quarrelling, and she said it was her wanting to get out and he wouldn't let her. With all them clothes he was buying her, mind, he didn't want her to leave the house, and she'd get mad and lock the door and wouldn't even let him in."

"Maybe he went off and got fixed up with one of these glands, these monkey glands, and it quit on him," Miss Myrtle said.

"Then one morning he come in with Red and took him up there. They stayed about an hour and left, and Popeye didn't show up again until next morning. Then him and Red come back and stayed up there about an hour. When they left, Minnie come and told me what was going on, so next day I waited for them. I called him in here and I says 'Look here, you son of a buh—' " She ceased. For an instant the three of them sat motionless, a little forward. Then slowly their heads turned and they looked at the boy leaning against the table.

"Uncle Bud, honey," Miss Myrtle said, "dont you want to go and play in the yard with Reba and Mr Binford?"

"Yessum," the boy said. He went toward the door. They watched him until the door closed upon him. Miss Lorraine drew her chair up; they leaned together.

310

"And that's what they was doing?" Miss Myrtle said.

"I says 'I been running a house for twenty years, but this is the first time I ever had anything like this going on in it. If you want to turn a stud in to your girl' I says 'go somewhere else to do it. I aint going to have my house turned into no French joint.'"

"The son of a bitch," Miss Lorraine said.

"He'd ought to've had sense enough to got a old ugly man," Miss Myrtle said. "Tempting us poor girls like that."

"Men always expects us to resist temptation," Miss Lorraine said. She was sitting upright like a school-teacher. "The lousy son of a bitch."

"Except what they offers themselves," Miss Reba said. "Then watch them. . . . Every morning for four days that was going on, then they didn't come back. For a week Popeye didn't show up at all, and that girl wild as a young mare. I thought he was out of town on business maybe, until Minnie told me he wasn't and that he give her five dollars a day not to let that girl out of the house nor use the telephone. And me trying to get word to him to come and take her out of my house because I didn't want nuttin like that going on in it. Yes, sir, Minnie said the two of them would be nekkid as two snakes, and Popeye hanging over the foot of the bed without

even his hat took off, making a kind of whinnying
sound."

"Maybe he was cheering for them," Miss
Lorraine said. "The lousy son of a bitch."

Feet came up the hall; they could hear
Minnie's voice lifted in adjuration. The door
opened. She entered, holding Uncle Bud erect
by one hand. Limp-kneed he dangled, his face
fixed in an expression of glassy idiocy. "Miss
Reba," Minnie said, "this boy done broke in
the icebox and drunk a whole bottle of beer.
You, boy!" she said, shaking him, "stan up!"
Limply he dangled, his face rigid in a slobbering grin. Then upon it came an expression of
concern, consternation; Minnie swung him
sharply away from her as he began to vomit.

XXVI

WHEN THE SUN ROSE, HORACE HAD NOT
been to bed nor even undressed. He was just
finishing a letter to his wife, addressed to her
at her father's in Kentucky, asking for a divorce.
He sat at the table, looking down at the single
page written neatly and illegibly over, feeling
quiet and empty for the first time since he had
found Popeye watching him across the spring
four weeks ago. While he was sitting there he
began to smell coffee from somewhere. "I'll
finish this business and then I'll go to Europe. I
am sick. I am too old for this. I was born too
old for it, and so I am sick to death for quiet."

He shaved and made coffee and drank a cup
and ate some bread. When he passed the hotel,
the bus which met the morning train was at the
curb, with the drummers getting into it. Clarence
Snopes was one of them, carrying a tan suit case.

"Going down to Jackson for a couple of days
on a little business," he said. "Too bad I missed

313

you last night. I come on back in a car. I reckon you was settled for the night, maybe?" He looked down at Horace, vast, pasty, his intention unmistakable. "I could have took you to a place most folks dont know about. Where a man can do just whatever he is big enough to do. But there'll be another time, since I done got to know you better." He lowered his voice a little, moving a little aside. "Dont you be uneasy. I aint a talker. When I'm here, in Jefferson, I'm one fellow; what I am up town with a bunch of good sports aint nobody's business but mine and theirn. Aint that right?"

Later in the morning, from a distance he saw his sister on the street ahead of him turn and disappear into a door. He tried to find her by looking into all the stores within the radius of where she must have turned, and asking the clerks. She was in none of them. The only place he did not investigate was a stairway that mounted between two stores, to a corridor of offices on the first floor, one of which was that of the District Attorney, Eustace Graham.

Graham had a club foot, which had elected him to the office he now held. He worked his way into and through the State University; as a youth the town remembered him as driving wagons and trucks for grocery stores. During his first year at the University he made a name for himself by his industry. He waited on table in the commons and he had the government contract for carrying the mail to and from the local postoffice at the arrival of each train, hobbling along with the sack over his shoulder: a pleasant, open-faced young man with a word for everyone and a certain alert rapacity about the eyes. During his second year he let his mail contract lapse and he resigned from his job in the commons; he also had a new suit. People were glad that he had saved through his industry to where he could give all his time to his studies. He was in the law school then, and the law professors groomed him like a race-horse. He graduated well, though without distinction. "Because he was handicapped at the start," the professors said. "If he had had the same start that the others had . . . He will go far," they said.

It was not until he had left school that they learned that he had been playing poker for three years in the office of a livery stable, behind drawn shades. When, two years out of school, he got elected to the State legislature, they began to tell an anecdote of his school days.

It was in the poker game in the livery stable office. The bet came to Graham. He looked across the table at the owner of the stable, who was his only remaining opponent.

"How much have you got there, Mr Harris?" he said.

"Forty-two dollars, Eustace," the proprietor said. Eustace shoved some chips into the pot. "How much is that?" the proprietor said.

"Forty-two dollars, Mr Harris."

"Hmmm," the proprietor said. He examined his hand. "How many cards did you draw, Eustace?"

"Three, Mr Harris."

"Hmmm. Who dealt the cards, Eustace?"

"I did, Mr Harris."

"I pass, Eustace."

He had been District Attorney but a short time, yet already he had let it be known that he would announce for Congress on his record of convictions, so when he found himself facing Narcissa across the desk in his dingy office, his expression was like that when he had put the forty-two dollars into the pot.

"I only wish it were your brother," he said. "I hate to see a brother-in-arms, you might say, with a bad case." She was watching him with a blank, enveloping look. "After all, we've got to protect society, even when it does seem that society does not need protection."

"Are you sure he cant win?" she said.

"Well, the first principle of law is, God alone

3·6

knows what the jury will do. Of course, you cant expect—"

"But you dont think he will."

"Naturally, I—"

"You have good reason to think he cant. I suppose you know things about it that he doesn't."

He looked at her briefly. Then he picked up a pen from his desk and began to scrape at the point with a paper cutter. "This is purely confidential. I am violating my oath of office. I wont have to tell you that. But it may save you worry to know that he hasn't a chance in the world. I know what the disappointment will be to him, but that cant be helped. We happen to know that the man is guilty. So if there's any way you know of to get your brother out of the case, I'd advise you to do it. A losing lawyer is like a losing anything else, ballplayer or merchant or doctor: his business is to—"

"So the quicker he loses, the better it would be, wouldn't it?" she said. "If they hung the man and got it over with." His hands became perfectly still. He did not look up. She said, her tone cold and level: "I have reasons for wanting Horace out of this case. The sooner the better. Three nights ago that Snopes, the one in the legislature, telephoned out home, trying to

317

find him. The next day he went to Memphis. I
dont know what for. You'll have to find that
out yourself. I just want Horace out of this
business as soon as possible."

She rose and moved toward the door. He
hobbled over to open it; again she put that
cold, still, unfathomable gaze upon him as
though he were a dog or a cow and she waited
for it to get out of her path. Then she was gone.
He closed the door and struck a clumsy clog-
step, snapping his fingers just as the door opened
again; he snapped his hands toward his tie and
looked at her in the door, holding it open.

"What day do you think it will be over
with?" she said.

"Why, I cuh— Court opens the twentieth,"
he said. "It will be the first case. Say . . . Two
days. Or three at the most, with your kind as-
sistance. And I need not assure you that this
will be held in strictest confidence between
us. . . ." He moved toward her, but her blank
calculating gaze was like a wall, surrounding
him.

"That will be the twenty-fourth." Then she
was looking at him again. "Thank you," she
said, and closed the door.

That night she wrote Belle that Horace
would be home on the twenty-fourth. She telephoned Horace and asked for Belle's address.
318

"Why?" Horace said.

"I'm going to write her a letter," she said, her voice tranquil, without threat. Dammit, Horace thought, holding the dead wire in his hand, How can I be expected to combat people who will not even employ subterfuge. But soon he forgot it, forgot that she had called. He did not see her again before the trial opened.

Two days before it opened Snopes emerged from a dentist's office and stood at the curb, spitting. He took a gold-wrapped cigar from his pocket and removed the foil and put the cigar gingerly between his teeth. He had a black eye, and the bridge of his nose was bound in soiled adhesive tape. "Got hit by a car in Jackson," he told them in the barber-shop. "But dont think I never made the bastard pay," he said, showing a sheaf of yellow bills. He put them into a notecase and stowed it away. "I'm an American," he said. "I dont brag about it, because I was born one. And I been a decent Baptist all my life, too. Oh, I aint no preacher and I aint no old maid; I been around with the boys now and then, but I reckon I aint no worse than lots of folks that pretends to sing loud in church. But the lowest, cheapest thing on this earth aint a nigger: it's a jew. We need laws against them. Drastic laws. When a durn lowlife jew can come to a free country like this and just because he's got a law degree, it's time to put a stop to things. A jew is the lowest thing on this creation. And the lowest kind of jew is a jew lawyer. And the lowest kind of jew lawyer is a Memphis jew lawyer. When a jew lawyer can hold up an American, a white man, and not give him but ten dollars for something that two Americans, Americans, southron gentlemen; a judge living in the capital of the State of Mississippi and a lawyer that's going to be as big a man as his pa some day, and a judge too; when they give him ten times as much for the same thing than the lowlife jew, we need a law. I been a liberal spender all my life; whatever I had has always been my friends' too. But when a durn, stinking, lowlife jew will refuse to pay an American one tenth of what another American, and a judge at that—"

"Why did you sell it to him, then?" the barber said.

"What?" Snopes said. The barber was looking at him.

"What was you trying to sell to that car when it run over you?" the barber said.

"Have a cigar," Snopes said.

XXVII

THE TRIAL WAS SET FOR THE TWENTIETH OF June. A week after his Memphis visit, Horace telephoned Miss Reba. "Just to know if she's still there," he said. "So I can reach her if I need to."

"She's here," Miss Reba said. "But this reaching. I dont like it. I dont want no cops around here unless they are on my business."

"It'll be only a bailiff," Horace said. "Someone to hand a paper into her own hand."

"Let the postman do it, then," Miss Reba said. "He comes here anyway. In a uniform too. He dont look no worse in it than a full-blowed cop, neither. Let him do it."

"I wont bother you," Horace said. "I wont make you any trouble."

"I know you aint," Miss Reba said. Her voice was thin, harsh, over the wire. "I aint going to let you. Minnie's done took a crying spell tonight, over that bastard that left her, and me and Miss Myrtle was sitting here, and we got started crying too. Me and Minnie and Miss Myrtle. We drunk up a whole new bottle of gin. I cant afford that. So dont you be sending no jay cops up here with no letters for nobody. You telephone me and I'll turn them both out on the street and you can have them arrested there."

On the night of the nineteenth he telephoned her again. He had some trouble in getting in touch with her.

"They're gone," she said. "Both of them. Dont you read no papers?"

"What papers?" Horace said. "Hello. Hello!"

"They aint here no more, I said," Miss Reba said. "I dont know nuttin about them and I dont want to know nuttin except who's going to pay me a week's room rent on—"

"But cant you find where she went to? I may need her."

"I dont know nuttin and I dont want to know nuttin," Miss Reba said, He heard the receiver click. Yet the disconnection was not made at once. He heard the receiver thud onto the table where the telephone sat, and he could hear Miss Reba shouting for Minnie: "Minnie. Minnie!" Then some hand lifted the receiver and set it onto the hook; the wire clicked in his ear. After

322

a while a detached Delsarte-ish voice said: "Pine Bluff dizzent . . . Enkyew!"

The trial opened the next day. On the table lay the sparse objects which the District Attorney was offering: the bullet from Tommy's skull, a stoneware jug containing corn whisky.

"I will call Mrs Goodwin to the stand," Horace said. He did not look back. He could feel Goodwin's eyes on his back as he helped the woman into the chair. She was sworn, the child lying on her lap. She repeated the story as she had told it to him on the day after the child was ill. Twice Goodwin tried to interrupt and was silenced by the Court. Horace would not look at him.

The woman finished her story. She sat erect in the chair, in her neat, worn gray dress and hat with the darned veil, the purple ornament on her shoulder. The child lay on her lap, its eyes closed in that drugged immobility. For a while her hand hovered about its face, performing those needless maternal actions as though unawares.

Horace went and sat down. Then only did he look at Goodwin. But the other sat quietly now, his arms folded and his head bent a little, but Horace could see that his nostrils were waxy white with rage against his dark face. He

323

leaned toward him and whispered, but Goodwin did not move.

The District Attorney now faced the woman.

"Mrs Goodwin," he said, "what was the date of your marriage to Mr Goodwin?"

"I object!" Horace said, on his feet.

"Can the prosecution show how this question is relevant?" the Court said.

"I waive, your Honor," the District Attorney said, glancing at the jury.

When court adjourned for the day Goodwin said bitterly: "Well, you've said you would kill me someday, but I didn't think you meant it. I didn't think that you———"

"Dont be a fool," Horace said. "Dont you see your case is won? That they are reduced to trying to impugn the character of your witness?" But when they left the jail he found the woman still watching him from some deep reserve of foreboding. "You mustn't worry at all, I tell you. You may know more about making whisky or love than I do, but I know more about criminal procedure than you, remember."

"You dont think I made a mistake?"

"I know you didn't. Dont you see how that explodes their case? The best they can hope for now is a hung jury. And the chances of that are not one in fifty. I tell you, he'll walk out of that jail tomorrow a free man.

324

"Then I guess it's time to think about paying you."

"Yes," Horace said, "all right. I'll come out tonight."

"Tonight?"

"Yes. He may call you back to the stand tomorrow. We'd better prepare for it, anyway."

At eight oclock he entered the mad woman's yard. A single light burned in the crazy depths of the house, like a firefly caught in a brier patch, but the woman did not appear when he called. He went to the door and knocked. A shrill voice shouted something; he waited a moment. He was about to knock again when he heard the voice again, shrill and wild and faint, as though from a distance, like a reedy pipe buried by an avalanche. He circled the house in the rank, waist-high weeds. The kitchen door was open. The lamp was there, dim in a smutty chimney, filling the room—a jumble of looming shapes rank with old foul female flesh—not with light but with shadow. White eyeballs rolled in a high, tight bullet head in brown gleams above a torn singlet strapped into overalls. Beyond the negro the mad woman turned in an open cupboard, brushing her lank hair back with her forearm.

"Your bitch has gone to jail," she said. "Go on with her."

"Jail?" Horace said.

"That's what I said. Where the good folks live. When you get a husband, keep him in jail where he cant bother you." She turned to the negro, a small flask in her hand. "Come on, dearie. Give me a dollar for it. You got plenty money."

Horace returned to town, to the jail. They admitted him. He mounted the stairs; the jailer locked a door behind him.

The woman admitted him to the cell. The child lay on the cot. Goodwin sat beside it, his arms crossed, his legs extended in the attitude of a man in the last stage of physical exhaustion.

"Why are you sitting there, in front of that slit?" Horace said. "Why not get into the corner, and we'll put the mattress over you."

"You come to see it done, did you?" Goodwin said. "Well, that's no more than right. It's your job. You promised I wouldn't hang, didn't you?"

"You've got an hour yet," Horace said. "The Memphis train doesn't get here until eight-thirty. He's surely got better sense than to come here in that canary-colored car." He turned to the woman. "But you. I thought better of you. I know that he and I are fools, but I expected better of you."

"You're doing her a favor," Goodwin said.

"She might have hung on with me until she was too old to hustle a good man. If you'll just promise to get the kid a newspaper grift when he's old enough to make change, I'll be easy in my mind."

The woman had returned to the cot. She lifted the child onto her lap. Horace went to her. He said: "You come on, now. Nothing's going to happen. He'll be all right here. He knows it. You've got to go home and get some sleep, because you'll both be leaving here tomorrow. Come, now."

"I reckon I better stay," she said.

"Damn it, dont you know that putting yourself in the position for disaster is the surest way in the world to bring it about? Hasn't your own experience shown you that? Lee knows it. Lee, make her stop this."

"Go on, Ruby," Goodwin said. "Go home and go to bed."

"I reckon I better stay," she said.

Horace stood over them. The woman mused above the child, her face bent and her whole body motionless. Goodwin leaned back against the wall, his brown wrists folded into the faded sleeves of his shirt. "You're a man now," Horace said. "Aren't you? I wish that jury could see you now, locked up in a concrete cell, scaring women and children with fifth grade ghost stories. They'd know you never had the guts to kill anybody."

"You better go on and go to bed yourself," Goodwin said. "We could sleep here, if there wasn't so much noise going on."

"No; that's too sensible for us to do," Horace said. He left the cell. The jailer unlocked the door for him and he quitted the building. In ten minutes he returned, with a parcel. Goodwin had not moved. The woman watched him open the package. It contained a bottle of milk, a box of candy, a box of cigars. He gave Goodwin one of the cigars and took one himself. "You brought his bottle, didn't you?"

The woman produced the bottle from a bundle beneath the cot. "It's got some in it," she said. She filled it from the bottle. Horace lit his and Goodwin's cigars. When he looked again the bottle was gone.

"Not time to feed him yet?" he said.

"I'm warming it," the woman said.

"Oh," Horace said. He tilted the chair against the wall, across the cell from the cot.

"Here's room on the bed," the woman said. "It's softer. Some."

"Not enough to change, though," Horace said.

328

"Look here," Goodwin said, "you go on home. No use in you doing this."

"We've got a little work to do," Horace said. "That lawyer'll call her again in the morning. That's his only chance: to invalidate her testimony someway. You might try to get some sleep while we go over it."

"All right," Goodwin said.

Horace began to drill the woman, tramping back and forth upon the narrow floor. Goodwin finished his cigar and sat motionless again, his arms folded and his head bent. The clock above the square struck nine and then ten. The child whimpered, stirred. The woman stopped and changed it and took the bottle from beneath her flank and fed it. Then she leaned forward carefully and looked into Goodwin's face. "He's asleep," she whispered.

"Shall we lay him down?" Horace whispered.

"No. Let him stay there." Moving quietly she laid the child on the cot and moved herself to the other end of it. Horace carried the chair over beside her. They spoke in whispers.

The clock struck eleven. Still Horace drilled her, going over and over the imaginary scene. At last he said: "I think that's all. Can you remember it, now? If he should ask you anything you cant answer in the exact words you've learned tonight, just say nothing for a moment. I'll attend to the rest. Can you remember, now?"

"Yes," she whispered. He reached across and took the box of candy from the cot and opened it, the glazed paper crackling faintly. She took a piece. Goodwin had not moved. She looked at him, then at the narrow slit of window.

"Stop that," Horace whispered. "He couldn't reach him through that window with a hat-pin, let alone a bullet. Dont you know that?"

"Yes," she said. She held the bon-bon in her hand. She was not looking at him. "I know what you're thinking," she whispered.

"What?"

"When you got to the house and I wasn't there. I know what you're thinking." Horace watched her, her averted face. "You said tonight was the time to start paying you."

For a while longer he looked at her. "Ah," he said. "O tempora! O mores! O hell! Can you stupid mammals never believe that any man, every man— You thought that was what I was coming for? You thought that if I had intended to, I'd have waited this long?"

She looked at him briefly. "It wouldn't have done you any good if you hadn't waited."

"What? Oh. Well. But you would have to-night?"

"I thought that was what—"

330

"You would now, then?" She looked around at Goodwin. He was snoring a little. "Oh, I dont mean right this minute," he whispered. "But you'll pay on demand."

"I thought that was what you meant. I told you we didn't have— If that aint enough pay, I don't know that I blame you."

"It's not that. You know it's not that. But cant you see that perhaps a man might do something just because he knew it was right, necessary to the harmony of things that it be done?"

The woman turned the bon-bon slowly in her hand. "I thought you were mad about him."

"Lee?"

"No. Him." She touched the child. "Because I'd have to bring him with us."

"You mean, with him at the foot of the bed, maybe? perhaps you holding him by the leg all the time, so he wouldn't fall off?"

She looked at him, her eyes grave and blank and contemplative. Outside the clock struck twelve.

"Good God," he whispered. "What kind of men have you known?"

"I got him out of jail once that way. Out of Leavenworth, too. When they knew he was guilty."

"You did?" Horace said. "Here. Take another piece. That one's about worn out." She

331

looked down at her chocolate-stained fingers and the shapeless bon-bon. She dropped it behind the cot. Horace extended his handkerchief.

"It'll soil it," she said. "Wait." She wiped her fingers on the child's discarded garment and sat again, her hands clasped in her lap. Goodwin was snoring regularly. "When he went to the Philippines he left me in San Francisco. I got a job and I lived in a hall room, cooking over a gas-jet, because I told him I would. I didn't know how long he'd be gone, but I promised him I would and he knew I would. When he killed that other soldier over that nigger woman, I didn't even know it. I didn't get a letter from him for five months. It was just when I happened to see an old newspaper I was spreading on a closet shelf in the place where I worked that I saw the regiment was coming home, and when I looked at the calender it was that day. I'd been good all that time. I'd had good chances; every day I had them with the men coming in the restaurant.

"They wouldn't let me off to go and meet the ship, so I had to quit. Then they wouldn't let me see him, wouldn't even let me on the ship. I stood there while they came marching off it, watching for him and asking the ones that passed if they knew where he was and them kidding me if I had a date that night, telling me they never heard of him or that he was dead or he had run off to Japan with the colonel's wife. I tried to get on the ship again, but they wouldn't let me. So that night I dressed up and went to the cabarets until I found one of them and let him pick me up, and he told me. It was like I had died. I sat there with the music playing and all, and that drunk soldier pawing at me, and me wondering why I didn't let go, go on with him, get drunk and never sober up again and me thinking And this is the sort of animal I wasted a year over. I guess that was why I didn't.

"Anyway, I didn't. I went back to my room and the next day I started looking for him. I kept on, with them telling me lies and trying to make me, until I found he was in Leavenworth. I didn't have enough money for a ticket, so I had to get another job. It took two months to get enough money. Then I went to Leavenworth. I got another job as waitress, in Childs', nightshifts, so I could see Lee every other Sunday afternoon. We decided to get a lawyer. We didn't know that a lawyer couldn't do anything for a federal prisoner. The lawyer didn't tell me, and I hadn't told Lee how I was getting the lawyer. He thought I had saved some money. I lived with the lawyer two months before I found it out.

"Then the war came and they let Lee out and sent him to France. I went to New York and got a job in a munitions plant. I stayed straight

333

too, with the cities full of soldiers with money to spend, and even the little ratty girls wearing silk. But I stayed straight. Then he came home. I was at the ship to meet him. He got off under arrest and they sent him back to Leavenworth for killing that soldier three years ago. Then I got a lawyer to get a Congressman to get him out. I gave him all the money I had saved too. So when Lee got out, we had nothing. He said we'd get married, but we couldn't afford it. And when I told him about the lawyer, he beat me."

Again she dropped a shapeless piece of candy behind the cot and wiped her hands on the garment. She chose another piece from the box and ate it. Chewing, she looked at Horace, turning upon him a blank, musing gaze for an unhurried moment. Through the slotted window the darkness came chill and dead.

Goodwin ceased snoring. He stirred and sat up.

"What time is it?" he said.

"What?" Horace said. He looked at his watch. "Half-past two."

"He must have had a puncture," Goodwin said.

Toward dawn Horace himself slept, sitting in the chair. When he waked a narrow rosy pencil of sunlight fell level through the window. Goodwin and the woman were talking quietly on the cot. Goodwin looked at him bleakly.

"Morning," he said.

"I hope you slept off that nightmare of yours," Horace said.

"If I did, it's the last one I'll have. They say you dont dream there."

"You've certainly done enough not to miss it," Horace said. "I suppose you'll believe us, after this."

"Believe, hell," Goodwin said, who had sat so quiet, so contained, with his saturnine face, negligent in his overalls and blue shirt; "do you think for one minute that man is going to let me walk out of that door and up the street and into that courthouse, after yesterday? What sort of men have you lived with all your life? In a nursery? I wouldn't do that, myself."

"If he does, he has sprung his own trap," Horace said.

"What good will that do me? Let me tell—"

"Lee," the woman said.

—"you something: the next time you want to play dice with a man's neck—"

"Lee," she said. She was stroking her hand slowly on his head, back and forth. She began to smooth his hair into a part, patting his collarless shirt smooth. Horace watched them.

"Would you like to stay here today?" he said quietly. "I can fix it."

"No," Goodwin said. "I'm sick of it. I'm going to get it over with. Just tell that goddamned deputy not to walk too close to me. You and her better go and eat breakfast."

"I'm not hungry," the woman said.

"You go on like I told you," Goodwin said. "Lee."

"Come," Horace said. "You can come back afterward."

Outside, in the fresh morning, he began to breathe deeply. "Fill your lungs," he said. "A night in that place would give anyone the jim-jams. The idea of three grown people . . . My Lord, sometimes I believe that we are all children, except children themselves. But today will be the last. By noon he'll walk out of there a free man: do you realise that?"

They walked on in the fresh sunlight, beneath the high, soft sky. High against the blue fat little clouds blew up from the south-west, and the cool steady breeze shivered and twinkled in the locusts where the blooms had long since fallen.

"I dont know how you'll get paid," she said.

"Forget it. I've been paid. You wont understand it, but my soul has served an apprenticeship that has lasted for forty-three years. Forty-three years. Half again as long as you have lived. So you see that folly, as well as poverty, cares for its own."

"And you know that he—that—"

"Stop it, now. We dreamed that away, too. God is foolish at times, but at least He's a gentleman. Dont you know that?"

"I always thought of Him as a man," the woman said.

The bell was already ringing when Horace crossed the square toward the courthouse. Already the square was filled with wagons and cars and the overalls and khaki thronged slowly beneath the gothic entrance of the building. Overhead the clock was striking nine as he mounted the stairs.

The broad double doors at the head of the cramped stair were open. From beyond them came a steady preliminary stir of people settling themselves. Above the seat-backs Horace could see their heads—bald heads, gray heads, shaggy heads and heads trimmed to recent feather-edge above sun-baked necks, oiled heads above urban collars and here and there a sunbonnet or a flowered hat.

The hum of their voices and movements came back upon the steady draft which blew through the door. The air entered the open windows and blew over the heads and back to Horace in

337

the door, laden with smells of tobacco and stale sweat and the earth and with that unmistakable odor of courtrooms; that musty odor of spent lusts and greeds and bickerings and bitterness, and withal a certain clumsy stability in lieu of anything better. The windows gave upon balconies close under the arched porticoes. The breeze drew through them, bearing the chirp and coo of sparrows and pigeons that nested in the eaves, and now and then the sound of a motor horn from the square below, rising out of and sinking back into a hollow rumble of feet in the corridor below and on the stairs.

The Bench was empty. At one side, at the long table, he could see Goodwin's black head and gaunt brown face, and the woman's gray hat. At the other end of the table sat a man picking his teeth. His skull was capped closely by tightly-curled black hair thinning upon a bald spot. He had a long, pale nose. He wore a tan palm beach suit; upon the table near him lay a smart leather brief-case and a straw hat with a red-and-tan band, and he gazed lazily out a window above the ranked heads, picking his teeth. Horace stopped just within the door. "It's a lawyer," he said. "A Jew lawyer from Memphis." Then he was looking at the backs of the heads about the table, where the witnesses and such would

338

be. "I know what I'll find before I find it," he said. "She will have on a black hat."

He walked up the aisle. From beyond the balcony window where the sound of the bell seemed to be and where beneath the eaves the guttural pigeons crooned, the voice of the bailiff came:

"The honorable Circuit Court of Yoknapatawpha county is now open according to law. . . ."

Temple had on a black hat. The clerk called her name twice before she moved and took the stand. After a while Horace realised that he was being spoken to, a little testily, by the Court.

"Is this your witness, Mr Benbow?"

"It is, your Honor."

"You wish her sworn and recorded?"

"I do, your Honor."

Beyond the window, beneath the unhurried pigeons, the bailiff's voice still droned, reiterant, importunate, and detached, though the sound of the bell had ceased.

XXVIII

THE DISTRICT ATTORNEY FACED THE JURY. "I offer as evidence this object which was found at the scene of the crime." He held in his hand a corn-cob. It appeared to have been dipped in dark brownish paint. "The reason this was not offered sooner is that its bearing on the case was not made clear until the testimony of the defendant's wife which I have just caused to be read aloud to you gentlemen from the record.

"You have just heard the testimony of the chemist and the gynecologist—who is, as you gentlemen know, an authority on the most sacred affairs of that most sacred thing in life: womanhood—who says that this is no longer a matter for the hangman, but for a bonfire of gasoline—"

"I object!" Horace said: "The prosecution is attempting to sway—"

"Sustained," the Court said. "Strike out the

340

phrase beginning 'who says that,' mister clerk. You may instruct the jury to disregard it, Mr. Benbow. Keep to the matter in hand, Mr District Attorney."

The District Attorney bowed. He turned to the witness stand, where Temple sat. From beneath her black hat her hair escaped in tight red curls like clots of resin. The hat bore a rhinestone ornament. Upon her black satin lap lay a platinum bag. Her pale tan coat was open upon a shoulder knot of purple. Her hands lay motionless, palm-up on her lap. Her long blonde legs slanted, lax-ankled, her two motionless slippers with their glittering buckles lay on their sides as though empty. Above the ranked intent faces white and pallid as the floating bellies of dead fish, she sat in an attitude at once detached and cringing, her gaze fixed on something at the back of the room. Her face was quite pale, the two spots of rouge like paper discs pasted on her cheek bones, her mouth painted into a savage and perfect bow, also like something both symbolical and cryptic cut carefully from purple paper and pasted there.

The District Attorney stood before her.

"What is your name?" She did not answer. She moved her head slightly, as though he had obstructed her view, gazing at something in the back of the room. "What is your name?" he repeated, moving also, into the line of her vision again. Her mouth moved. "Louder," he said. "Speak out. No one will hurt you. Let these good men, these fathers and husbands, hear what you have to say and right your wrong for you."

The Court glanced at Horace, his eyebrows raised. But Horace made no move. He sat with his head bent a little, his hands clutched in his lap.

"Temple Drake," Temple said.

"Your age?"

"Eighteen."

"Where is your home?"

"Memphis," she said in a scarce distinguishable voice.

"Speak a little louder. These men will not hurt you. They are here to right the wrong you have suffered. Where did you live before you went to Memphis?"

"In Jackson."

"Have you relations there?"

"Yes."

"Come. Tell these good men—"

"My father."

"Your mother is dead?"

"Yes."

"Have you any sisters?"

"No."

"You are your father's only daughter?"

Again the Court looked at Horace; again he made no move.

"Yes."

"Where have you been living since May twelfth of this year?" Her head moved faintly, as though she would see beyond him. He moved into her line of vision, holding her eyes. She stared at him again, giving her parrotlike answers.

"Did your father know you were there?"

"No."

"Where did he think you were?"

"He thought I was in school."

"You were in hiding, then, because something had happened to you and you dared not—"

"I object!" Horace said. "The question is lead—"

"Sustained," the Court said. "I have been on the point of warning you for some time, Mr Attorney, but defendant would not take exception, for some reason."

The District Attorney bowed toward the Bench. He turned to the witness and held her eyes again.

"Where were you on Sunday morning, May twelfth?"

"I was in the crib."

The room sighed, its collective breath hissing in the musty silence. Some newcomers entered,

343

but they stopped at the rear of the room in a clump and stood there. Temple's head had moved again. The District Attorney caught her gaze and held it. He half turned and pointed at Goodwin.

"Did you ever see that man before?" She gazed at the District Attorney, her face quite rigid, empty. From a short distance her eyes, the two spots of rouge and her mouth, were like five meaningless objects in a small heart-shaped dish. "Look where I am pointing."

"Yes."

"Where did you see him?"

"In the crib."

"What were you doing in the crib?"

"I was hiding."

"Who were you hiding from?"

"From him."

"That man there? Look where I am pointing."

"Yes."

"But he found you."

"Yes."

"Was anyone else there?"

"Tommy was. He said——"

"Was he inside the crib or outside?"

"He was outside by the door. He was watching. He said he wouldn't let——"

344

"Just a minute. Did you ask him not to let anyone in?"

"Yes."

"And he locked the door on the outside?"

"Yes."

"But Goodwin came in."

"Yes."

"Did he have anything in his hand?"

"He had the pistol."

"Did Tommy try to stop him?"

"Yes. He said he—"

"Wait. What did he do to Tommy?"

She gazed at him.

"He had the pistol in his hand. What did he do then?"

"He shot him." The District Attorney stepped aside. At once the girl's gaze went to the back of the room and became fixed there. The District Attorney returned, stepped into her line of vision. She moved her head; he caught her gaze and held it and lifted the stained corncob before her eyes. The room sighed, a long hissing breath.

"Did you ever see this before?"

"Yes."

The District Attorney turned away. "Your honor and gentlemen, you have listened to this horrible, this unbelievable, story which this young girl has told; you have seen the evidence and heard the doctor's testimony: I shall no longer subject this ruined, defenseless child to the agony of—" he ceased; the heads turned as one and watched a man come stalking up the aisle toward the Bench. He walked steadily, paced and followed by a slow gaping of the small white faces, a slow hissing of collars. He had neat white hair and a clipped moustache like a bar of hammered silver against his dark skin. His eyes were pouched a little. A small paunch was buttoned snugly into his immaculate linen suit. He carried a panama hat in one hand and a slender black stick in the other. He walked steadily up the aisle in a slow expulsion of silence like a prolonged sigh, looking to neither side. He passed the witness stand without a glance at the witness, who still gazed at something in the back of the room, walking right through her line of vision like a runner crossing a tape, and stopped before the bar above which the Court had half-risen, his arms on the desk.

"Your Honor," the old man said, "is the Court done with this witness?"

"Yes, sir, Judge," the Court said; "yes, sir. Defendant, do you waive—"

The old man turned slowly, erect above the held breaths, the little white faces, and looked down at the six people at the counsel table. Behind him the witness had not moved. She sat in her attitude of childish immobility, gazing like a drugged person above the faces, toward the rear of the room. The old man turned to her and extended his hand. She did not move. The room expelled its breath, sucked it quickly in and held it again. The old man touched her arm. She turned her head toward him, her eyes blank and all pupil above the three savage spots of rouge. She put her hand in his and rose, the platinum bag slipping from her lap to the floor with a thin clash, gazing again at the back of the room. With the toe of his small gleaming shoe the old man flipped the bag into the corner where the jury-box joined the Bench, where a spittoon sat, and steadied the girl down from the dais. The room breathed again as they moved on down the aisle.

Half way down the aisle the girl stopped again, slender in her smart open coat, her blank face rigid, then she moved on, her hand in the old man's. They returned down the aisle, the old man erect beside her, looking to neither side, paced by that slow whisper of collars. Again the girl stopped. She began to cringe back, her body arching slowly, her arm tautening in the old man's grasp. He bent toward her, speaking; she moved again, in that shrinking and rapt abasement. Four younger men were standing stiffly erect near the exit. They stood like soldiers, staring straight ahead until the old man and the girl reached them. Then they moved and surrounded the other two, and in a close body, the girl hidden among them, they moved toward the door. Here they stopped again; the girl could be seen shrunk against the wall just inside the door, her body arched again. She appeared to be clinging there, then the five bodies hid her again and again in a close body the group passed through the door and disappeared. The room breathed: a buzzing sound like a wind getting up. It moved forward with a slow increasing rush, on above the long table where the prisoner and the woman with the child and Horace and the District Attorney and the Memphis lawyer sat, and across the jury and against the Bench in a long sigh. The Memphis lawyer was sitting on his spine, gazing dreamily out the window. The child made a fretful sound, whimpering.

"Hush," the woman said. "Shhhhhhhh."

XXIX

THE JURY WAS OUT EIGHT MINUTES. WHEN Horace left the courthouse it was getting toward dusk. The tethered wagons were taking out, some of them to face twelve and sixteen miles of country road. Narcissa was waiting for him in the car. He emerged among the overalls, slowly; he got into the car stiffly, like an old man, with a drawn face. "Do you want to go home?" Narcissa said.

"Yes," Horace said.

"I mean, to the house, or out home?"

"Yes," Horace said.

She was driving the car. The engine was running. She looked at him, in a new dark dress with a severe white collar, a dark hat.

"Which one?"

"Home," he said. "I dont care. Just home."

They passed the jail. Standing along the fence were the loafers, the countrymen, the blackguard boys and youths who had followed Goodwin and the deputy from the courthouse. Beside the gate the woman stood, in the gray hat with the veil, carrying the child in her arms. "Standing where he can see it through the window," Horace said. "I smell ham, too. Maybe he'll be eating ham before we get home." Then he began to cry, sitting in the car beside his sister. She drove steadily, not fast. Soon they had left the town and the stout rows of young cotton swung at either hand in parallel and diminishing retrograde. There was still a little snow of locust blooms on the mounting drive. "It does last," Horace said. "Spring does. You'd almost think there was some purpose to it."

He stayed to supper. He ate a lot. "I'll go and see about your room," his sister said, quite gently.

"All right," Horace said. "It's nice of you." She went out. Miss Jenny's wheel chair sat on a platform slotted for the wheels. "It's nice of her," Horace said. "I think I'll go outside and smoke my pipe."

"Since when have you quit smoking it in here?" Miss Jenny said.

"Yes," Horace said. "It was nice of her." He walked across the porch. "I intended to stop here," Horace said. He watched himself cross
350

the porch and then tread the diffident snow of
the last locusts; he turned out of the iron gates,
onto the gravel. After about a mile a car slowed
and offered him a ride. "I'm just walking before
supper," he said; "I'll turn back soon." After
another mile he could see the lights of town. It
was a faint glare, low and close. It got stronger
as he approached. Before he reached town he
began to hear the sound, the voices. Then he
saw the people, a shifting mass filling the street,
and the bleak, shallow yard above which the
square and slotted bulk of the jail loomed. In
the yard, beneath the barred window, a man in
his shirt sleeves faced the crowd, hoarse, gesticu-
lant. The barred window was empty.

Horace went on toward the square. The sheriff was among the drummers before the hotel,
standing along the curb. He was a fat man, with
a broad, dull face which belied the expression
of concern about his eyes. "They wont do anything," he said. "There is too much talk. Noise.
And too early. When a mob means business, it
dont take that much time and talk. And it dont
go about its business where every man can
see it."

The crowd stayed in the street until late. It
was quite orderly, though. It was as though
most of them had come to see, to look at the
jail and the barred window, or to listen to the

man in shirt sleeves. After a while he talked himself out. Then they began to move away, back to the square and some of them homeward, until there was left only a small group beneath the arc light at the entrance to the square, among whom were two temporary deputies, and the night marshal in a broad pale hat, a flash light, a time clock and a pistol. "Git on home now," he said. "Show's over. You boys done had your fun. Git on home to bed, now."

The drummers sat a little while longer along the curb before the hotel, Horace among them; the south-bound train ran at one oclock. "They're going to let him get away with it, are they?" a drummer said. "With that corn cob? What kind of folks have you got here? What does it take to make you folks mad?"

"He wouldn't a never got to trial, in my town," a second said.

"To jail, even," a third said. "Who was she?"

"College girl. Good looker. Didn't you see her?"

"I saw her. She was some baby. Jeez. I wouldn't have used no cob."

Then the square was quiet. The clock struck eleven; the drummers went in and the negro porter came and turned the chairs back into the
352

wall. "You waiting for the train?" he said to Horace.

"Yes. Have you got a report on it yet?"

"It's on time. But that's two hours yet. You could lay down in the Sample Room, if you want."

"Can I?" Horace said.

"I'll show you," the negro said. The Sample Room was where the drummers showed their wares. It contained a sofa. Horace turned off the light and lay down on the sofa. He could see the trees about the courthouse, and one wing of the building rising above the quiet and empty square. But people were not asleep. He could feel the wakefulness, the people awake about the town. "I could not have gone to sleep, anyway," he said to himself.

He heard the clock strike twelve. Then—it might have been thirty minutes or maybe longer than that—he heard someone pass under the window, running. The runner's feet sounded louder than a horse, echoing across the empty square, the peaceful hours given to sleeping. It was not a sound Horace heard now; it was something in the air which the sound of the running feet died into.

When he went down the corridor toward the stairs he did not know he was running until he

353

heard beyond a door a voice say, "Fire! it's a . . ." Then he had passed it. "I scared him," Horace said. "He's just from Saint Louis, maybe, and he's not used to this." He ran out of the hotel, onto the street. Ahead of him the proprietor had just run, ludicrous; a broad man with his trousers clutched before him and his braces dangling beneath his nightshirt, a tousled fringe of hair standing wildly about his bald head; three other men passed the hotel running. They appeared to come from nowhere, to emerge in midstride out of nothingness, fully dressed in the middle of the street, running.

"It is a fire," Horace said. He could see the glare; against it the jail loomed in stark and savage silhouette.

"It's in that vacant lot," the proprietor said, clutching his trousers. "I cant go because there aint anybody on the desk. . ."

Horace ran. Ahead of him he saw other figures running, turning into the alley beside the jail; then he heard the sound of the fire; the furious sound of gasoline. He turned into the alley. He could see the blaze, in the center of a vacant lot where on market days wagons were tethered. Against the flames black figures showed, antic; he could hear panting shouts; through a fleeting gap he saw a man turn and run, a mass of flames, still carrying a five-gallon coal oil can which exploded with a rocket-like glare while he carried it, running.

He ran into the throng, into the circle which had formed about a blazing mass in the middle of the lot. From one side of the circle came the screams of the man about whom the coal oil can had exploded, but from the central mass of fire there came no sound at all. It was now indistinguishable, the flames whirling in long and thunderous plumes from a white-hot mass out of which there defined themselves faintly the ends of a few posts and planks. Horace ran among them; they were holding him, but he did not know it; they were talking, but he could not hear the voices.

"It's his lawyer."

"Here's the man that defended him. That tried to get him clear."

"Put him in, too. There's enough left to burn a lawyer."

"Do to the lawyer what we did to him. What he did to her. Only we never used a cob. We made him wish we had used a cob."

Horace couldn't hear them. He couldn't hear the man who had got burned screaming. He couldn't hear the fire, though it still swirled upward unabated, as though it were living upon itself, and soundless: a voice of fury like in a dream, roaring silently out of a peaceful void.

XXX

THE TRAINS AT KINSTON WERE MET BY AN old man who drove a seven passenger car. He was thin, with gray eyes and a gray moustache with waxed ends. In the old days, before the town boomed suddenly into a lumber town, he was a planter, a landholder, son of one of the first settlers. He lost his property through greed and gullibility, and he began to drive a hack back and forth between town and the trains, with his waxed moustache, in a top hat and a worn Prince Albert coat, telling the drummers how he used to lead Kinston society; now he drove it.

After the horse era passed, he bought a car, still meeting the trains. He still wore his waxed moustache, though the top hat was replaced by a cap, the frock coat by a suit of gray striped with red made by Jews in the New York tenement district. "Here you are," he said, when

Horace descended from the train. "Put your bag into the car," he said. He got in himself. Horace got into the front seat beside him. "You are one train late," he said.

"Late?" Horace said.

"She got in this morning. I took her home. Your wife."

"Oh," Horace said. "She's home?"

The other started the car and backed and turned. It was a good, powerful car, moving easily. "When did you expect her? . . ." They went on. "I see where they burned that fellow over at Jefferson. I guess you saw it."

"Yes," Horace said. "Yes. I heard about it."

"Served him right," the driver said. "We got to protect our girls. Might need them ourselves."

They turned, following a street. There was a corner, beneath an arc light. "I'll get out here," Horace said.

"I'll take you on to the door," the driver said.

"I'll get out here," Horace said. "Save you having to turn."

"Suit yourself," the driver said. "You're paying for it, anyway."

Horace got out and lifted out his suit case; the driver did not offer to touch it. The car went on. Horace picked up the suit case, the one which had stayed in the closet at his sister's home for ten years and which he had brought into town with him on the morning when she had asked him the name of the District Attorney.

His house was new, on a fairish piece of lawn, the trees, the poplars and maples which he had set out, still new. Before he reached the house, he saw the rose colored shade at his wife's windows. He entered the house from the back and came to her door and looked into the room. She was reading in bed, a broad magazine with a colored back. The lamp had a rose colored shade. On the table sat an open box of chocolates.

"I came back," Horace said.

She looked at him across the magazine.

"Did you lock the back door?" she said.

"Yes, I knew she would be," Horace said. "Have you tonight . . ."

"Have I what?"

"Little Belle. Did you telephone . . ."

"What for? She's at that house party. Why shouldn't she be? Why should she have to disrupt her plans, refuse an invitation?"

"Yes," Horace said. "I knew she would be. Did you . . ."

"I talked to her night before last. Go lock the back door."

"Yes," Horace said. "She's all right. Of course she is. I'll just . . ." The telephone sat on a table in the dark hall. The number was on a rural line; it took some time. Horace sat beside the telephone. He had left the door at the end of the hall open. Through it the light airs of the summer night drew, vague, disturbing. "Night is hard on old people," he said quietly, holding the receiver. "Summer nights are hard on them. Something should be done about it. A law."

From her room Belle called his name, in the voice of a reclining person. "I called her night before last. Why must you bother her?"

"I know," Horace said. "I wont be long at it."

He held the receiver, looking at the door through which the vague, troubling wind came. He began to say something out of a book he had read: "Less oft is peace. Less oft is peace," he said.

The wire answered. "Hello! Hello! Belle?" Horace said.

"Yes?" her voice came back thin and faint. "What is it? Is anything wrong?"

"No, no," Horace said. "I just wanted to tell you hello and good-night."

"Tell what? What is it? Who is speaking?" Horace held the receiver, sitting in the dark hall.

"It's me, Horace. Horace. I just wanted to—"

Over the thin wire there came a scuffling sound; he could hear Little Belle breathe. Then a voice said, a masculine voice: "Hello, Horace; I want you to meet a—"

"Hush!" Little Belle's voice said, thin and faint; again Horace heard them scuffling; a breathless interval. "Stop it!" Little Belle's voice said. "It's Horace! I live with him!" Horace held the receiver to his ear. Little Belle's voice was breathless, controlled, cool, discreet, detached. "Hello. Horace. Is Mamma all right?"

"Yes. We're all right. I just wanted to tell you . . ."

"Oh. Good-night."

"Good-night. Are you having a good time?"

"Yes. Yes. I'll write tomorrow. Didn't Mamma get my letter today?"

"I dont know. I just—"

"Maybe I forgot to mail it. I wont forget tomorrow, though. I'll write tomorrow. Was that all you wanted?"

"Yes. Just wanted to tell you . . ."

He put the receiver back; he heard the wire die. The light from his wife's room fell across the hall. "Lock the back door," she said.

XXXI

WHILE ON HIS WAY TO PENSACOLA TO VISIT his mother, Popeye was arrested in Birmingham for the murder of a policeman in a small Alabama town on June 17 of that year. He was arrested in August. It was on the night of June 17 that Temple had passed him sitting in the parked car beside the road house on the night when Red had been killed.

Each summer Popeye went to see his mother. She thought he was a night clerk in a Memphis hotel.

His mother was the daughter of a boarding house keeper. His father had been a professional strike-breaker hired by the street railway company to break a strike in 1900. His mother at that time was working in a department store downtown. For three nights she rode home on the car beside the motorman's seat on which Popeye's father rode. One night the strike-breaker got off at her corner with her and walked to her home.

"Wont you get fired?" she said.

"By who?" the strike-breaker said. They walked along together. He was well-dressed. "Them others would take me that quick. They know it, too."

"Who would take you?"

"The strikers. I dont care a damn who is running the car, see. I'll ride with one as soon as another. Sooner, if I could make this route every night at this time."

She walked beside him. "You dont mean that," she said.

"Sure I do." He took her arm.

"I guess you'd just as soon be married to one as another, the same way."

"Who told you that?" he said. "Have them bastards been talking about me?"

A month later she told them that they would have to be married.

"How do you mean, have to?" he said.

"I dont dare to tell them. I would have to go away. I dont dare."

"Well, dont get upset. I'd just as lief. I have to pass here every night anyway."

They were married. He would pass the corner at night. He would ring the foot-bell. Some-

362

cimes he would come home. He would give her
money. Her mother liked him; he would come
roaring into the house at dinner time on Sunday, calling the other clients, even the old ones,
by their first names. Then one day he didn't
come back; he didn't ring the foot-bell when
the trolley passed. The strike was over by then.
She had a Christmas card from him; a picture,
with a bell and an embossed wreath in gilt, from
a Georgia town. It said: "The boys trying to
fix it up here. But these folks awful slow. Will
maybe move on until we strike a good town ha
ha." The word, strike, was underscored.

Three weeks after her marriage, she had be-
gun to ail. She was pregnant then. She did not
go to a doctor, because an old negro woman
told her what was wrong. Popeye was born on
the Christmas day on which the card was re-
ceived. At first they thought he was blind. Then
they found that he was not blind, though he did
not learn to walk and talk until he was about
four years old. In the mean time, the second
husband of her mother, an undersized, snuffy
man with a mild, rich moustache, who pottered
about the house—he fixed all the broken steps
and leaky drains and such—left home one afternoon with a check signed in blank to pay a
twelve dollar butcher's bill. He never came

back. He drew from the bank his wife's fourteen hundred dollar savings account, and disappeared.

The daughter was still working down town, while her mother tended the child. One afternoon one of the clients returned and found his room on fire. He put it out; a week later he found a smudge in his waste-basket. The grandmother was tending the child. She carried it about with her. One evening she was not in sight. The whole household turned out. A neighbor turned in a fire alarm and the firemen found the grandmother in the attic, stamping out a fire in a handful of excelsior in the center of the floor, the child asleep in a discarded mattress nearby.

"Them bastards are trying to get him," the old woman said. "They set the house on fire." The next day, all the clients left.

The young woman quit her job. She stayed at home all the time. "You ought to get out and get some air," the grandmother said.

"I get enough air," the daughter said.

"You could go out and buy the groceries," the mother said. "You could buy them cheaper."

"We get them cheap enough."

She would watch all the fires; she would not have a match in the house. She kept a few hidden behind a brick in the outside wall. Popeye was three years old then. He looked about one, though he could eat pretty well. A doctor had told his mother to feed him eggs cooked in olive oil. One afternoon the grocer's boy, entering the area-way on a bicycle, skidded and fell. Something leaked from the package. "It aint eggs," the boy said. "See?" It was a bottle of olive oil. "You ought to buy that oil in cans, anyway," the boy said. "He cant tell no difference in it. I'll bring you another one. And you want to have that gate fixed. Do you want I should break my neck on it?"

He had not returned by six oclock. It was summer. There was no fire, not a match in the house. "I'll be back in five minutes," the daughter said.

She left the house. The grandmother watched her disappear. Then she wrapped the child up in a light blanket and left the house. The street was a side street, just off a main street where there were markets, where the rich people in limousines stopped on the way home to shop. When she reached the corner, a car was just drawing in to the curb. A woman got out and entered a store, leaving a negro driver behind the wheel. She went to the car.

"I want a half a dollar," she said.

The negro looked at her. "A which?"

"A half a dollar. The boy busted the bottle."

365

"Oh," the negro said. He reached in his pocket. "How am I going to keep it straight, with you collecting out here? Did she send you for the money out here?"

"I want a half a dollar. He busted the bottle."

"I reckon I better go in, then," the negro said. "Seem like to me you folks would see that folks got what they buy, folks that been trading here long as we is."

"It's a half a dollar," the woman said. He gave her a half dollar and entered the store. The woman watched him. Then she laid the child on the seat of the car, and followed the negro. It was a self-serve place, where the customers moved slowly along a railing in single file. The negro was next to the white woman who had left the car. The grandmother watched the woman pass back to the negro a loose handful of bottles of sauce and catsup. "That'll be a dollar and a quarter," she said. The negro gave her the money. She took it and passed them and crossed the room. There was a bottle of imported Italian olive oil, with a price tag. "I got twenty-eight cents more," she said. She moved on, watching the price tags, until she found one that said twenty-eight cents. It was seven bars of bath soap. With the two parcels she left the store. There was a policeman at the corner. "I'm out of matches," she said.

The policeman dug into his pocket. "Why didn't you buy some while you were there?" he said.

"I just forgot it. You know how it is, shopping with a child."

"Where is the child?" the policeman said.

"I traded it in," the woman said.

"You ought to be in vaudeville," the policeman said. "How many matches do you want? I aint got but one or two."

"Just one," the woman said. "I never do light a fire with but one."

"You ought to be in vaudeville," the policeman said. "You'd bring down the house."

"I am," the woman said. "I bring down the house."

"What house?" He looked at her. "The poor house?"

"I'll bring it down," the woman said. "You watch the papers tomorrow. I hope they get my name right."

"What's your name? Calvin Coolidge?"

"No, sir. That's my boy."

"Oh. That's why you had so much trouble shopping, is it? You ought to be in vaudeville. . . . Will two matches be enough?"

They had had three alarms from that address, so they didn't hurry. The first to arrive was the daughter. The door was locked, and when the firemen came and chopped it down, the house was already gutted. The grandmother was leaning out an upstairs window through which the smoke already curled. "Them bastards," she said. "They thought they would get him. But I told them I would show them. I told them so."

The mother thought that Popeye had perished also. They held her, shrieking, while the shouting face of the grandmother vanished into the smoke, and the shell of the house caved in; that was where the woman and the policeman carrying the child, found her: a young woman with a wild face, her mouth open, looking at the child with a vague air, scouring her loose hair slowly upward from her temples with both hands. She never wholly recovered. What with the hard work and the lack of fresh air, diversion, and the disease, the legacy which her brief husband had left her, she was not in any condition to stand shock, and there were times when she still believed that the child had perished, even though she held it in her arms crooning above it.

Popeye might well have been dead. He had no hair at all until he was five years old, by which time he was already a kind of day pupil at an institution: an undersized, weak child with a stomach so delicate that the slightest deviation from a strict regimen fixed for him by the doctor would throw him into convulsions. "Alcohol would kill him like strychnine," the doctor said. "And he will never be a man, properly speaking. With care, he will live some time longer. But he will never be any older than he is now." He was talking to the woman who had found Popeye in her car that day when his grandmother burned the house down and at whose instigation Popeye was under the doctor's care. She would fetch him to her home in afternoons and for holidays, where he would play by himself. She decided to have a children's party for him. She told him about it, bought him a new suit. When the afternoon of the party came and the guests began to arrive, Popeye could not be found. Finally a servant found a bathroom door locked. They called the child, but got no answer. They sent for a locksmith, but in the meantime the woman, frightened, had the door broken in with an axe. The bathroom was empty. The window was open. It gave onto a lower roof, from which a drain-pipe descended to the ground. But Popeye was gone. On the floor lay a wicker cage in which two lovebirds lived; beside it lay the birds themselves, and the bloody scissors with which he had cut them up alive.

Three months later, at the instigation of a neighbor of his mother, Popeye was arrested and sent to a home for incorrigible children. He had cut up a half-grown kitten the same way.

His mother was an invalid. The woman who had tried to befriend the child supported her, letting her do needlework and such. After Popeye was out—he was let out after five years, his behavior having been impeccable, as being cured —he would write to her two or three times a year, from Mobile and then New Orleans and then Memphis. Each summer he would return home to see her, prosperous, quiet, thin, black, and uncommunicative in his narrow black suits. He told her that his business was being night clerk in hotels; that, following his profession, he would move from town to town, as a doctor or a lawyer might.

While he was on his way home that summer they arrested him for killing a man in one town and at an hour when he was in another town killing somebody else—that man who made money and had nothing he could do with it, spend it for, since he knew that alcohol would kill him like poison, who had no friends and had never known a woman and knew he could never

—and he said, "For Christ's sake," looking about the cell in the jail of the town where the policeman had been killed, his free hand (the other was handcuffed to the officer who had brought him from Birmingham) finicking a cigarette from his coat.

"Let him send for his lawyer," they said, "and get that off his chest. You want to wire?"

"Nah," he said, his cold, soft eyes touching briefly the cot, the high small window, the grated door through which the light fell. They removed the handcuff; Popeye's hand appeared to flick a small flame out of thin air. He lit the cigarette and snapped the match toward the door. "What do I want with a lawyer? I never was in— What's the name of this dump?"

They told him. "You forgot, have you?"

"He wont forget it no more," another said.

"Except he'll remember his lawyer's name by morning," the first said.

They left him smoking on the cot. He heard doors clash. Now and then he heard voices from the other cells; somewhere down the corridor a negro was singing. Popeye lay on the cot, his feet crossed in small, gleaming black shoes. "For Christ's sake," he said.

The next morning the judge asked him if he wanted a lawyer.

"What for?" he said. "I told them last night I

never was here before in my life. I dont like your town well enough to bring a stranger here for nothing."

The judge and the bailiff conferred aside.

"You'd better get your lawyer," the judge said.

"All right," Popeye said. He turned and spoke generally into the room: "Any of you ginneys want a one-day job?"

The judge rapped on the table. Popeye turned back, his tight shoulders lifted in a faint shrug, his hand moving toward the pocket where he carried his cigarettes. The judge appointed him counsel, a young man just out of law school.

"And I wont bother about being sprung," Popeye said. "Get it over with all at once."

"You wouldn't get any bail from me, anyway," the judge told him.

"Yeuh?" Popeye said. "All right, Jack," he told his lawyer, "get going. I'm due in Pensacola right now."

"Take the prisoner back to jail," the judge said.

His lawyer had an ugly, eager, earnest face. He rattled on with a kind of gaunt enthusiasm while Popeye lay on the cot, smoking, his hat over his eyes, motionless as a basking snake save for the periodical movement of the hand that held the cigarette. At last he said: "Here. I aint the judge. Tell him all this."

"But I've got—"

"Sure. Tell it to them. I dont know nothing about it. I wasn't even there. Get out and walk it off."

The trial lasted one day. While a fellow policeman, a cigar-clerk, a telephone girl testified, while his own lawyer rebutted in a gaunt mixture of uncouth enthusiasm and earnest ill-judgment, Popeye lounged in his chair, looking out the window above the jury's heads. Now and then he yawned; his hand moved to the pocket where his cigarettes lay, then refrained and rested idle against the black cloth of his suit, in the waxy lifelessness of shape and size like the hand of a doll.

The jury was out eight minutes. They stood and looked at him and said he was guilty. Motionless, his position unchanged, he looked back at them in a slow silence for several moments. "Well, for Christ's sake," he said.

The judge rapped sharply with his gavel; the officer touched his arm.

"I'll appeal," the lawyer babbled, plunging along beside him. "I'll fight them through every court—"

"Sure," Popeye said, lying on the cot and light-

373

ing a cigarette; "but not in here. Beat it, now. Go take a pill."

The District Attorney was already making his plans for the appeal. "It was too easy," he said. "He took it— Did you see how he took it? like he might be listening to a song he was too lazy to either like or dislike, and the Court telling him on what day they were going to break his neck. Probably got a Memphis lawyer already there outside the supreme court door now, wait-ing for a wire. I know them. It's them thugs like that that have made justice a laughing-stock, until even when we get a conviction, everybody knows it wont hold."

Popeye sent for the turnkey and gave him a hundred dollar bill. He wanted a shaving-kit and cigarettes. "Keep the change and let me know when it's smoked up," he said.

"I reckon you wont be smoking with me much longer," the turnkey said. "You'll get a good lawyer, this time."

"Dont forget that lotion," Popeye said. "Ed Pinaud." He called it "Py-nawd."

It had ben a gray summer, a little cool. Little daylight ever reached the cell, and a light burned in the corridor all the time, falling into the cell in a broad pale mosaic, reaching the cot where his feet lay. The turnkey gave him a chair. He used it for a table; upon it the dollar watch lay,

374

and a carton of cigarettes and a cracked soup bowl of stubs, and he lay on the cot, smoking and contemplating his feet while day after day passed. The gleam of his shoes grew duller, and his clothes needed pressing, because he lay in them all the time, since it was cool in the stone cell.

One day the turnkey said: "There's folks here says that deppity invited killing. He done two-three mean things folks knows about." Popeye smoked, his hat over his face. The turnkey said: "They might not sent your telegram. You want me to send another one for you?" Leaning against the grating he could see Popeye's feet, his thin, black legs motionless, merging into the delicate bulk of his prone body and the hat slanted across his averted face, the cigarette in one small hand. His feet were in shadow, in the shadow of the turnkey's body where it blotted out the grating. After a while the turnkey went away quietly.

When he had six days left the turnkey offered to bring him magazines, a deck of cards.

"What for?" Popeye said. For the first time he looked at the turnkey, his head lifted, in his smooth, pallid face his eyes round and soft as those prehensile tips on a child's toy arrows. Then he lay back again. After that each morning the turnkey thrust a rolled newspaper

375

through the door. They fell to the floor and lay
there, accumulating, unrolling and flattening
slowly of their own weight in diurnal progres-
sion.

When he had three days left a Memphis lawyer arrived. Unbidden, he rushed up to the cell.
All that morning the turnkey heard his voice
raised in pleading and anger and expostulation;
by noon he was hoarse, his voice not much louder
than a whisper.

"Are you just going to lie here and let—"

"I'm all right," Popeye said. "I didn't send
for you. Keep your nose out."

"Do you want to hang? Is that it? Are you
trying to commit suicide? Are you so tired of
dragging down jack that . . . You, the smart-
est—"

"I told you once. I've got enough on you."

"You, to have it hung on you by a small-time
j.p.! When I go back to Memphis and tell them,
they won't believe it."

"Don't tell them, then." He lay for a time
while the lawyer looked at him in baffled and
raging unbelief. "Them durn hicks," Popeye
said. "Jesus Christ . . . Beat it, now," he said.
"I told you. I'm all right."

On the night before, a minister came in.

"Will you let me pray with you?" he said.

376

"Sure," Popeye said; "go ahead. Dont mind me."

The minister knelt beside the cot where Popeye lay smoking. After a while the minister heard him rise and cross the floor, then return to the cot. When he rose Popeye was lying on the cot, smoking. The minister looked behind him, where he had heard Popeye moving and saw twelve marks at spaced intervals along the base of the wall, as though marked there with burned matches. Two of the spaces were filled with cigarette stubs laid in neat rows. In the third space were two stubs. Before he departed he watched Popeye rise and go there and crush out two more stubs and lay them carefully beside the others.

Just after five oclock the minister returned. All the spaces were filled save the twelfth one. It was three quarters complete. Popeye was lying on the cot. "Ready to go?" he said.

"Not yet," the minister said. "Try to pray," he said. "Try."

"Sure," Popeye said; "go ahead." The minister knelt again. He heard Popeye rise once and cross the floor and then return.

At five-thirty the turnkey came. "I brought—" he said. He held his closed fist dumbly through the grating. "Here's your change from that hundred you never— I brought . . . It's forty-eight dollars," he said. "Wait; I'll count it again; I dont know exactly, but I can give you a list— them tickets . . ."

"Keep it," Popeye said, without moving. "Buy yourself a hoop."

They came for him at six. The minister went with him, his hand under Popeye's elbow, and he stood beneath the scaffold praying, while they adjusted the rope, dragging it over Popeye's sleek, oiled head, breaking his hair loose. His hands were tied, so he began to jerk his head, flipping his hair back each time it fell forward again, while the minister prayed, the others motionless at their posts with bowed heads.

Popeye began to jerk his neck forward in little jerks. "Psssst!" he said, the sound cutting sharp into the drone of the minister's voice; "pssssst!" The sheriff looked at him; he quit jerking his neck and stood rigid, as though he had an egg balanced on his head. "Fix my hair, Jack," he said.

"Sure," the sheriff said. "I'll fix it for you"; springing the trap.

It had been a gray day, a gray summer, a gray year. On the street old men wore overcoats, and in the Luxembourg Gardens as Temple and her father passed the women sat knitting in shawls
378

and even the men playing croquet played in coats and capes, and in the sad gloom of the chestnut trees the dry click of balls, the random shouts of children, had that quality of autumn, gallant and evanescent and forlorn. From beyond the circle with its spurious Greek balustrade, clotted with movement, filled with a gray light of the same color and texture as the water which the fountain played into the pool, came a steady crash of music. They went on, passed the pool where the children and an old man in a shabby brown overcoat sailed toy boats, and entered the trees again and found seats. Immediately an old woman came with decrepit promptitude and collected four sous.

In the pavilion a band in the horizon blue of the army played Massenet and Scriabine, and Berlioz like a thin coating of tortured Tschaikovsky on a slice of stale bread, while the twilight dissolved in wet gleams from the branches, onto the pavilion and the sombre toadstools of umbrellas. Rich and resonant the brasses crashed and died in the thick green twilight, rolling over them in rich sad waves. Temple yawned behind her hand, then she took out a compact and opened it upon a face in miniature sullen and discontented and sad. Beside her her father sat, his hands crossed on the head of his stick, the rigid bar of his moustache beaded with

379

moisture like frosted silver. She closed the compact and from beneath her smart new hat she seemed to follow with her eyes the waves of music, to dissolve into the dying brasses, across the pool and the opposite semicircle of trees where at sombre intervals the dead tranquil queens in stained marble mused, and on into the sky lying prone and vanquished in the embrace of the season of rain and death.

MISCELLANEOUS

MODERN LIBRARY GIANTS

A series of full-sized library editions of books that formerly
were available only in cumbersome and expensive sets.
THE MODERN LIBRARY GIANTS REPRESENT A
SELECTION OF THE WORLD'S GREATEST BOOKS

These volumes contain from 600 to 1,400 pages each

DA